Praise for *UNUSUAL SUSPECTS*

"This warmly loving and personal homage to all the suspicious characters herein assembled will keep you turning pages long after you planned to turn out the light. . . . His chapter on evolving a play from a single idea to a richly entertaining, Edgar Award-winning thriller is easily worth the price of admission."

Rupert Holmes, Edgar- and Tony Award-winning playwright and composer

"Filled with gems: fascinating stories about people you knew you were interested in (Dashiell Hammett), people you didn't (Lucille Fletcher), people you thought you already knew (Stephen Sondheim) – and Joe himself. Anyone who enjoys crime in literature and on the stage will love this book."

SJ Rozan, Bestselling author of *Paper Son*

"Chock-full of fascinating information and facts, all of it effortlessly delivered, the kind of book one will want to read again and again. . . . Scrupulously researched biographical data that has the reader sit up and say *aha!* . . . Tremendously entertaining and informative."

Jonathan Santlofer, Nero Award-winning author of *The Death Artist*

"Joseph Goodrich is an alchemist. Beware: This book will cost you. It will make you want to buy every novel, play, and video mentioned and spend all your time in the world of these unusual suspects."

Tom Straw, Bestselling *New York Times* author

UNUSUAL SUSPECTS

By JOSEPH GOODRICH

UNUSUAL SUSPECTS: Selected Non-Fiction

BLOOD RELATIONS:
The Selected Letters of Ellery Queen 1947-1950

SOUTH OF SUNSET: Nine Plays

from Perfect Crime Books

UNUSUAL SUSPECTS

Selected Non-Fiction

JOSEPH GOODRICH

Foreword by Martin Edwards

Perfect Crime Books

Email: Crime@PerfectCrimeBooks.com
Perfect Crime Books™ is a registered Trademark.

Printed in the United States of America.

Some of the contents appeared first appeared in *Mystery Scene* magazine, *Ellery Queen's Mystery Magazine,* and other publications. A list appears on pages 179- 180.

Cover art: Kevin Egeland
Note: Artistic license converted normal author photos into mug shots.

Excerpts from papers of Manfred B. Lee, Derek Marlowe and others are used with permission of the copyright owners, who reserve all rights.

Library of Congress Cataloguing-in-Publication Data
Goodrich, Joseph
Unusual Suspects: Selected Non-Fiction

ISBN: 978-1-935797-83-8

First Edition: July 2020

UNUSUAL
SUSPECTS

For
William Link and Margery Nelson:
A Grand Master and A Force of Nature

CONTENTS

ELLERY QUEEN, MASTER DETECTIVE

REQUIEM FOR A DANDY

FOREWORD

Unusual Suspects is a delightful potpourri of writings about an eclectic range of topics linked, in assorted ways, to the crime genre. Joseph Goodrich's subjects include famous names — Dashiell Hammett and Stephen Sondheim among others — and, pleasingly, those who are much less well-known. Derek Marlowe, for instance, is a writer of whom I've been aware since learning about *A Dandy in Aspic* from Julian Symons's *Bloody Murder*, but I've never actually read him. Joseph's extended study of his life and work makes me want to repair that omission as soon as possible.

This section of the book illustrates the strengths of *Unusual Suspects*. The essays are always well-informed and skillfully composed, but what counts most for me is their enthusiasm — a vital ingredient in a book of this kind. Joseph had a slight personal connection to Marlowe, but it's the sheer zest with which he tells the man's story that is so appealing. There have been innumerable writers like Marlowe who began brilliantly, only for their literary careers to falter. Joseph gives us a clear idea of what went wrong after the publication of *A Dandy in Aspic*, but also of what went right. And his non-judgmental style is captured in a memorable, surely tongue-in-cheek quote from Michael Wells: "I don't know what you'd call a heavy drinker, but [Marlowe] got through at least half a bottle of whisky a day."

Aspects of Ellery Queen's work are explored in depth, and that's as it should be, given that Joseph was responsible for *Blood Relations*, a gripping account through correspondence of the love-hate relationship of the cousins who collaborated together as Queen. *Blood Relations* affords fascinating insight into the creative process, and as a creator himself, Joseph's interest in how different writers approach that process is evident throughout this book.

He offers an illustration of his own approach in "Pushing the 'Panic' Button, Or: How Plays Get Written," explaining how an initial premise evolved into a play which (although the essay does not mention this) won an Edgar from the Mystery Writers of America in 2008. He captures his credo perfectly, with wit as well as insight, when he says, "I came to see that there is nothing wrong with entertaining an audience. Now, this may sound like a strange confession from a playwright . . ."

Unusual Suspects benefits from a quirky unpredictability and from being a mine of intriguing nuggets of information. I hadn't, for instance, been aware that Nicholas Meyer wrote a screenplay featuring Robert Van Gulik's Judge Dee after graduating from college. Or that Lieutenant Columbo made his debut as long ago as 1960 in *The Chevy Mystery Show*. And I was pleased to find a book that discussed such interesting writers as Elizabeth Daly, Lucille Fletcher, Amnon Kabatchnik — as well as a bookstore owner, Dilys Winn.

Whether you dip into *Unusual Suspects* or read it from cover to cover in a sitting (as I did, such was my delight in the contents), you'll find plenty here to entertain as well as inform you. Enjoy.

MARTIN EDWARDS

Martin Edwards is the latest recipient of the CWA Diamond Dagger, the highest honour in UK crime writing. He is the author of nineteen novels, most recently Mortmain Hall and Gallows Court. He has received the Edgar, Agatha, H.R.F. Keating and Poirot awards, two Macavity awards, the CWA Margery Allingham Short Story Prize, the CWA Short Story Dagger, and the CWA Dagger in the Library. He has twice been nominated for CWA Gold Daggers and once for the Historical Dagger; he has also been shortlisted for the Theakston's Prize for best crime novel of the year for The Coffin Trail. He is consultant to the British Library's Crime Classics series, a former chair of the Crime Writers' Association, and current President of the Detection Club. His works include the Harry Devlin series and the Lake District Mysteries, nine non-fiction books, and seventy short stories. He has edited over forty anthologies. His website is www.martinedwardsbooks.com.

INTRODUCTION

The essays in this collection are the product of passions: for a book, for a play, for a movie, for a piece of music. Some of these passions are of long-standing, like Ellery Queen and Lucille Fletcher. Others are of more recent vintage. The men and women profiled here have done marvelous things on the page or the stage or the screen; my goal was to elucidate and celebrate their achievements.

I've included several pieces that detail aspects of my life in the theater. These deal with matters of voice and craft, and I hope they provide some insight into the habits and processes of a working playwright.

A shadow figure lurks behind many of the ostensible subjects. That figure is me. I'm taken aback by how much of my own experience and past migrated into these pages. It couldn't be helped. These writers–unusual suspects, every one of them–have become a part of my life, almost as close as blood kin. I am profoundly grateful to them all.

JOSEPH GOODRICH

Nicholas Meyer and Ashley Weaver: Bringing the Past to Glorious Life.

Frederick Irving Anderson, Elizabeth Daly, and Gordon McAlpine: Literary Magicians.

Barry Gifford (L)
and
David Goodis:
Noir Sensibility
Incarnate.

THE LINE-UP

Dashiell Hammett

Dashiell Hammett: BEYOND THURSDAY

Hard-boiled icon Dashiell Hammett has been dead for over a half-century, but the man and his work fascinate readers to this day. In 2013 he was the subject of two novels: Sam Toperoff's *Lillian and Dash* and Gordon McAlpine's *Hammett Unwritten*. Sally Cline's biography, *Dashiell Hammett: Man of Mystery*, was published early in 2014. This trio of books is proof of the ongoing interest in the creator of *The Maltese Falcon*. They also illustrate the problems one faces in writing about the famously enigmatic Pinkerton-operative-turned-scribe.

Of the trinity of great private eye novelists–Hammett, Raymond Chandler, Ross Macdonald–Hammett is the most inscrutable. Chandler wore his heart on his Harris Tweed sleeve, and his letters overflow with his passions and prejudices. Hammett's letters reveal relatively little. Macdonald utilized the emotionally volatile material of his life and turned it into fiction. Beyond a certain point, Hammett was unable to write at all. His inner life can only be guessed at, and he remains a mystery with no solution, a lock without a key.

This is why Cline decided to write a biography. "I was drawn to Hammett partly because he was essentially a mysterious man," she says. "No one seemed to know who he was or what impelled or drove him, or what his long silence from writing was about."

Why Hammett stopped writing at the height of his career, publishing no fiction for the last 27 years of his life, remains the grand unanswered question. Hammett's creative silence was mirrored by his taciturn, stoical personality. "I can stand anything I've got to stand," Ned Beaumont says in *The Glass Key*. Hammett lived by those words. From tuberculosis as a young man to the Blacklist and a stint in federal prison for contempt of court in his later years, he suffered mutely, neither complaining nor explaining.

That penchant for silence was evident from his childhood, which brings to mind the title of one of Thomas Mann's short stories: "Disorder and Early Sorrow." Cline ably sketches the writer's less-than-promising origins. Hammett's father was a hard-drinking, abusive ne'er-do-well. His mother was kind but sickly. The family shuttled from rural Maryland to Philadelphia and Baltimore, finding economic and emotional stability nowhere. Hammett had little formal education. Incapable of or uninterested in holding a job for any length of time, he was headed down his father's unhappy path when he chanced upon an advertisement in a Baltimore newspaper. The ad promised adventure and excitement. Hammett answered it, and soon began working for Pinkerton's National Detective Agency. He'd stumbled into something he could do — and do well. Cline observes: "It was a silent, secretive occupation that matched his personality."

Hammett's stint with Pinkerton's lasted until tuberculosis made the rough-and-tumble life of an operative too much to bear. He turned to writing as a way of supplementing his veteran's pension. He not only made a living; almost singlehandedly, he invented the straight-talking, street-smart private eye. The debt owed to Hammett is incalculable. Paraphrasing Dostoyevsky's remark about Gogol, Ross Macdonald once stated: "We all came out from under Hammett's black mask." (*Black Mask* was, of course, the pulp magazine that featured the works of Hammett, Chandler, Erle Stanley Gardner and many other hardboiled writers.)

Writing brought Hammett fame, money, and work in Hollywood –where he met Lillian Hellman. He launched Hellman's playwriting career by supplying her with the story that served as the basis of *The Children's Hour*. A fearsome taskmaster, he drove her through draft after draft until she had a play worthy of production. Hammett served as consultant and editor for almost all of Hellman's plays. She in turn sheltered Hammett when disease and poverty overtook him near the end of his life.

Cline neither demonizes nor canonizes Hellman. "I never thought of her as a villain," she says, "merely as a controversial, sad, smart woman, an excellent playwright and a fascinating, unreliable memoirist." A note Hellman made shortly before Hammett's death speaks volumes about the highly ambivalent nature of their long-lasting relationship. The dying man, Cline writes, "still fretted about *Tulip*," a fragment of an unfinished novel. Hellman wrote: "Said he couldn't work, had never liked writers who didn't know what they were doing, and now he didn't know what he was doing . . . I am so torn with pity and love and hate and so bored by the struggle."

Research for the book took Cline across the country and to almost two-dozen libraries, archives and research centers. She includes several small discoveries she made along the way. In one of her memoirs, Hellman states that

Hammett wrote a crucial monologue for her play *The Autumn Garden*. This monologue–a rueful summation of a life "frittered away"–is often considered to be Hammett's view of himself, and this passage figures in many biographies as a key to his character. Cline's research indicates that Hellman wrote the speech. Attributing the monologue to Hammett is, according to Cline, an example of Hellman's "generosity" to an older writer and friend.

Cline captures the sad arc of Hammett's life: from rags to riches, and back to rags again. She adroitly points out the many contradictions he embodied. He was a sick man who wrote about tough guys; a ladies' man who preferred the company of men; a Marxist with extravagant tastes; a country boy who spent years in the jungle of cities.

Less convincing when it comes to analyzing Hammett's writing and its place in and effect upon the mystery genre, Cline emphasizes "the arbitrary nature of truth" in Hammett's work. The books are filled with liars, and Hammett's heroes are morally ambiguous. But Hammett is no post-modern author, playing with signs and symbols in a world of interchangeable realities. In an essay featured on the HiLobrow website, novelist Gordon Dahlquist notes that Hammett and Chandler were "19th century men in their hearts, tracking its slow-motion death into the first half of the 20th." Their work reflects the spiritual, economic and literary deflation that followed the First World War.

Cline posits no specific reasons for Hammett's writer's block, but surely what she describes as "his alcoholism, his tuberculosis, and his determination to avoid self-exploration" contributed to his inability to complete a new novel. Sam Toperoff and Gordon McAlpine address this issue, among others, in their fictional portrayals of Hammett. Their books can be added to a shelf that includes Joe Gores's *Hammett*, Laurie R. King's *Locked Rooms*, Ace Atkins's *Devil's Garden*, and several titles by William F. Nolan.

Toperoff's book is a well written if episodic recreation of Hammett's 30-year relationship with Hellman. In the author's words, it's "a novel of conjecture." Toperoff argues that biographies give us the "who, what, when and where" of a life, but leave out the "why." His novel is an attempt to use the devices of fiction to provide motivation and explanation for actions and events that seemingly lacked those elements in reality. The results are hit-and-miss. A bit of acute psychological insight turns up next to a scene that awkwardly wanders the margin between fact and fancy. Powerful in parts, the book is ultimately unsatisfying as biography or fiction.

McAlpine's *Hammett Unwritten* is a happy success. The book is credited to "Owen Fitzstephen"–a variant on the name of the novelist/villain of *The Dain Curse* — with notes and an afterword by McAlpine. It's a marvelously inventive reworking of *The Maltese Falcon*. Years after his time as a Pinkerton operative, Hammett gives away a souvenir of his last case: a hunk of stone that resembles a black bird. It seems that he also gave away his ability to write. Decades pass by in one futile attempt to write after another. Then, near the end of his life, Hammett makes one last attempt to get the black bird back.

Hammett Unwritten is an engaging, highly imaginative book about artistic sterility. One of the best novels of 2013, it's a loving and witty nod to a master. Like Cline and Toperoff, McAlpine leads us back to Hammett's novels and short stories, the true source of his posthumous reputation.

Screenwriter/producer Nunnally Johnson was once asked why he thought Hammett led such a profligate life, throwing away his time and money on self-destructive drinking binges and ladies of the evening. Johnson's answer: "His behavior could be accounted for only by the assumption that he had no expectation of being alive much beyond Thursday."

Hammett lived beyond Thursday. He outlasted his talent and the good fortune it brought him. He died of cancer in 1961. The Continental Op, Sam Spade, Ned Beaumont, Nick and Nora Charles are immortal.

Elizabeth Daly: EAST SIDE STORIES

In 2009 I spent a great deal of time at Columbia University's Butler Library. Month after glorious month, I transcribed the correspondence between Frederic Dannay and Manfred B. Lee, the creators of Ellery Queen.

During my lunch break I'd often step into a bookstore just across the street from the University's wrought-iron gates. The store had a well-stocked mystery section, where a used paperback caught my eye. Its cover intrigued me.

A room contains a chair, a desk with a lamp, the pages of a manuscript and a typewriter. Through an open window we see the orderly green of a garden maze. Late afternoon sun illumines room and maze alike. The room is empty, but in the maze one mysterious figure spies upon another.

The look was vintage, the feeling unsettling. This was catnip to me. Especially that typewriter—I'm crazy about typewriters.

I left the bookstore with Elizabeth Daly's *Nothing Can Rescue Me*, and started reading it on the subway home. To my delight, I found that I hadn't merely bought a nicely designed book.

I'd discovered the world of Henry Gamadge.

Henry Gamadge, bibliophile sleuth, is Daly's hero. Daly published sixteen novels featuring Gamadge between 1940 and 1951. Most of them take place in a long-vanished Manhattan. It's a genteel and civilized locale, one in which visitors place calling cards on silver salvers, bridge is played, dinner is something to dress for, and family brownstones house floor-to-ceiling libraries.

Maggie Topkis, publisher of Felony & Mayhem Press, believes this appealing milieu is why Daly keeps finding new readers. "The series depicts New

York at its most gorgeously glamorous," Topkis says. "The future was beckoning just enough to make social mobility an actual possibility for many people. The past was a sufficiently solid presence to create, for Gamadge and his pals, a sense of Anglo-style elegance and culture. It's a world in which the Chrysler Building and collections of 18th-century manuscripts exist in close proximity. If part of Sayers's appeal is the love affair between readers and Peter Wimsey, for the Gamadge books, the love affair is between readers and New York."

Not all runs smoothly in this well-heeled universe. The passage of time engenders shocking changes in manners and morals. (Gamadge's Aunt Florence looks askance at young ladies who wear slacks, so she won't allow them to be worn at her country retreat.) The upheavals of World War II further erode the economic and cultural verities this world is based on. Privilege is a source of envy for those who want everything and have nothing. Envy can lead to murder.

That's where Henry Gamadge steps in. A tall, tweedy, unassuming figure in his mid-30s with blunt features and green eyes, he's the investigator of choice when Easy Street falls upon hard times. He can be trusted with the facts about the family scandal, the disturbing incident at the summerhouse, the spinster daughter who's disappeared. If anyone can quietly and efficiently solve the case and keep the press away, it's Henry.

Given Gamadge's expertise in rare books and old documents, he frequently finds himself embroiled in crimes involving literary matters. A manuscript is altered to sinister purpose in *Nothing Can Rescue Me*. A dead playwright's papers figure in *The Book of the Lion*. A missing collection of Byron's poetry is returned under strange circumstances in *The Murder in Volume 2*. Many of Gamadge's exploits are literary mysteries in every sense of the word.

Ouija boards, cultists of one stripe or another, ghosts and weird occurrences also come under Gamadge's cool scrutiny. Reason prevails, and the supernatural is shown to be the work of all-too-human criminals.

Like her hero, Daly's origins were in upper class New York. Born in 1878, Daly was the product of a prosperous and well-placed family. Her father, Joseph Francis Daly, was a Justice in the Supreme Court of New York. Her uncle was the playwright and man-of-the-theater Augustin Daly. Educated at Bryn Mawr and Columbia University, Daly epitomized staid, old-money Manhattan.

One senses in Daly a conflict between the respectable and the raffish; she didn't publish her first mystery until she was in her early sixties. Daly might have taken a while to get started, but made up for lost time with a steady stream of Gamadge mysteries.

Daly has a sharp eye for the lives of the well to do — the pre-dinner highball, the lightweight summer suit and Panama hat, the airless interior of a city residence closed up for the summer, the elaborate codes of behavior appropriate for "our kind."

She knows the foibles of the rich. In *Nothing Can Rescue Me*, Gamadge's lawyer friend Bob Macloud reports that he's been dismissed by some wealthy clients. When Gamadge asks why, Macloud tells him: "For sending in a bill, I suppose. They have a failing they share with some other rich persons — they think paupers ought to work for them for love."

World War II may be shaking things up but, for Gamadge and his contemporaries, society retains its familiar shape. A genial paternalism holds sway. Servants are never suspects; their only purpose is to do their jobs and not get in the way. Gamadge is looked after by Theodore, who is described as "an old colored servant." Although Theodore is portrayed with a modicum of dignity, Gamadge's world is overwhelmingly white.

Mystery critic Lenore Glen Offord claims that the distinguishing feature of Daly's work is its charm. Offord is exactly right. We love to spend time with Gamadge and his circle. Character is Daly's strong point, and we relish all those who live in that house in the east sixties: Harold Bantz, Gamadge's curious assistant, who never eats sitting down; the beautiful Clara, whom Gamadge marries once he's cleared her of a murder charge; Martin, the old yellow cat; Clara's chow dog; and — later in the series — a son to carry on the Gamadge name.

Often compared to Agatha Christie, Daly was Dame Agatha's favorite mystery writer. These doyennes of death share certain qualities: intelligence, civility, and an understated knowledge of the evil that men (and women) do.

Maggie Topkis speculates on the roots of Christie's fondness for Daly's books. "The other great writers of the day, Sayers and Allingham and so on — their male protagonists are *so* strong, they eat up so much air. Christie had rotten luck with men. In particular, she had married a dashing, air-eating one, and he made her miserable. So I wonder if a series in which the male protagonist is *not* wildly dashing, is instead calm and pleasant and not given to flights of delirious verbiage, might appeal to Christie."

In 1961 Daly was awarded a special Edgar Award for being "the grande dame of women mystery writers." She died in 1967 at the age of 88.

In the early 1980s Bantam reissued a number of Gamadges with eye-catching and evocative covers by Dennis Ziemienski. I snapped up every Bantam in that bookstore near Columbia and read them on my way to and from the Butler Library.

Over the last several years Felony & Mayhem Press has reprinted all of Daly's titles. Anyone who appreciates good writing, plenty of atmosphere, and a winning cast of characters will enjoy the Gamadge books.

The Felony & Mayhem covers — fetching combinations of vintage photographs, classic fonts and a limited color scheme — are pretty darn nice, too.

Nicholas Meyer: AN APPRECIATION

Nicholas Meyer's work as a novelist, screenwriter and director is a testament to the power of popular art to entertain, illuminate and — on occasion — affect the course of history. He's taken audiences from Victorian England (*The Seven-Per-Cent Solution*) to the 23rd century (*Star Trek II, IV* and *VI*) to the end of the world as we know it (*The Day After*). A firm believer in story and character, he upholds these virtues in an industry that prides itself on spectacle and stereotype.

Meyer's own story began in New York City on Christmas Eve, 1945. The son of psychiatrist/author Bernard C. Meyer and concert pianist Elly Kassman, he was raised in comfort on the Upper East Side. Meyer was one of those children who are motivated by interest and not by discipline. School was a trial and a chore. Jules Verne, Alexandre Dumas, *Classics Illustrated* comic books and late-night movies provided his true education.

After graduating from the University of Iowa, he worked as a publicist for Paramount Pictures, then moved to Los Angeles in the early 1970s to pursue a career as a screenwriter. Early efforts included the TV movies *Judge Dee and The Monastery Murders* (1974) and *The Night That Panicked America* (1975, co-written with Anthony Wilson). *Dee* was an adaptation of one of Robert Van Gulik's mysteries about a real-life Tang dynasty circuit court judge. *Night* was a re-telling of the havoc created by Orson Welles's 1938 *War of the Worlds* radio broadcast. Both scripts reveal Meyer's penchant for stories set in the past that involve historic characters — a proclivity that would bring him his first major success.

The Writers Guild of America went on strike in 1973. As Meyer writes in his memoir *The View From the Bridge*, he finally had the opportunity to start

14

"banging away at my long-gestating notion of a Doyle pastiche" in which Sherlock Holmes met, matched wits with, and finally collaborated with Dr. Sigmund Freud. Freud cures Holmes's cocaine addiction; in return, Holmes's methodology sets Freud on the analytic path that will lead to psychoanalysis.

Not content to merely put Holmes and Watson through their paces, Meyer reexamined the very basis of their world. Far from being "the Napoleon of Crime," Professor Moriarty is a victim of Holmes's cocaine-induced paranoia. He's also the reason for the kinks in Holmes's psychology: the great detective's misogyny as well as his single-minded crusade against crime stem from Moriarty's traumatic role in Holmes's childhood.

Published in 1974, *The Seven-Per-Cent Solution* delighted readers, topped the bestseller lists, and launched a thousand Holmes pastiches. Two years later it was made into a splashy, big-budget movie with Nicol Williamson as Holmes and Alan Arkin as Freud. Meyer's screenplay garnered an Academy Award nomination.

Two sequels followed. *The West End Horror* (1976) is set in Victorian London's theatre world and peopled with such luminaries as Oscar Wilde, Bram Stoker, Gilbert and Sullivan, and G.B. Shaw. A copy of *Romeo and Juliet* provides a dying clue to a secret that could destroy England, if not the Continent itself. *Horror* is a better-constructed book than *Solution*, which divides into two enjoyable halves — Holmes's cure and the case that followed. *Horror*'s story is all of a piece.

The Canary Trainer (1993) takes place during the period of Holmes's peregrinations through Europe after his "death" at Reichenbach Falls. Employed in the orchestra of the Paris Opera as a violinist, Holmes must grapple with the ghost-like figure who haunts the building's vast and gloomy underground. Meyer's third Holmesian adventure builds to an explosive ending, thanks to dynamite belonging to the builders of the Paris Metro.

Negotiations with the Conan Doyle estate for the use of the Holmes and Watson characters dragged on for so long that Meyer wrote another book while waiting for *Solution* to be cleared for publication.

Meyer has called *Target Practice* (1974) a Ross Macdonald pastiche, as its first-person narration owes something to Lew Archer's wearily sympathetic tone. More importantly, Meyer shares with Macdonald a sense of how private torment and public events are intertwined. For Macdonald's characters, the public event was often World War II. For the characters in *Target Practice*, it's Viet Nam.

Sergeant Harold Rollins III, accused of collaborating with the enemy while being held in a North Korean P.O.W. camp, has committed suicide. His sister Shelly suspects he may not have killed himself and wants him posthumously cleared of the charges. She hires private detective Mark Brill to investigate. Brill is a middle-aged widower, an ex-cop and ex-military man who uses his job as a screen between himself and the rest of the world. The case takes him from Los Angeles to the East Coast and the Midwest before a skein of incest and murder is untangled and another death occurs. *Target Practice* was deservedly nominated for a Best First Novel Edgar. (It lost to Gregory Mcdonald's *Fletch*.)

Time After Time (1979) marked Meyer's debut as a film director. He also wrote the screenplay, based on a novel by University of Iowa classmate Karl Alexander. In the film H.G. Wells doesn't just write about a time machine — he's invented one. It's stolen by a doctor acquaintance who is secretly Jack the Ripper. Jack finds himself in 20th century San Francisco. Wells follows the Ripper to the city by the bay and attempts to drag him back to the 19th century where, as Wells puts it, "you will face the consequences of your acts." Jack doesn't want to leave; the chaos and violence of the modern world suit him. "I belong here, completely and utterly," he says to Wells. "I'm home." *Time After Time* is a gem of a film, witty, moving, and sometimes terrifying.

As a director, Meyer's biggest challenge — and proudest accomplishment — was the TV movie *The Day After* (1983). What if the unthinkable happened and a nuclear weapon was dropped on an American city? Ed Hume's script followed a handful of characters in Lawrence, Kansas before and after a nuclear strike. The devastation is immense. The suffering is too much to bear. In the words of William Butler Yeats, all is "changed, changed utterly."

Filming *The Day After* was a massive undertaking. ABC was skittish about the project and tried to soften the portrayal of nuclear destruction. The finished product was attacked by conservative pundits and apologists like Henry Kissinger and William F. Buckley. It's estimated that over 100 million people watched *The Day After* when it was broadcast the evening of November 20, 1983. President Ronald Reagan saw the film before its ABC showing. His belief that a nuclear war could be won was changed by *The Day After*. Reagan claimed the movie contributed to his signing of the Intermediate-Range Nuclear Forces Treaty in 1987.

Meyer is perhaps best known as the man who saved *Star Trek* — and killed Spock in the process. For the lowdown on his involvement as a writer and/or director on three of the original-cast films, read *The View From the Bridge: Memories of Star Trek and a Life in Hollywood* (2009). The Trek devotee will not be disappointed. *Bridge* is as thoughtful and outspoken as its author. Meyer is as quick to tell you about his flaws and failures as he is of his successes. *Bridge*'s only flaw is that it isn't longer.

Meyer's novel *Confessions of a Homing Pigeon* (1981) isn't a mystery, though it deals with the biggest mysteries of all: love and loss, life and death. When young George Bernini's trapeze artist parents die in a circus accident, he's sent to post-war Paris to live with his Uncle Fritz, an eccentric composer/pianist. Their adventures together are wild and winning but come to an abrupt end when Fritz loses custody of the child to an aunt in Chicago. George is dropped into the heart of Eisenhower's America. A most unhappy fish out of water, he dreams of nothing but returning to France. But how is he going to do it?

It's clear that *Confessions* draws on the circumstances of Meyer's life. A checkered school career, the power of art to soothe and save, the death of a loved one from cancer are part of Meyer's experience — and that of others.

I'm one of those others. When I first saw *Confessions* on the new arrivals shelf in a small-town library, I took it home. It's my favorite of Meyer's books. A copy of it rests on the desk beside me, all these many homes later.

A new Sherlock Holmes pastiche was published in the autumn of 2019. *The Adventure of the Peculiar Protocols* partakes of the verve and originality that distinguish its predecessors.

1905 London: Mycroft Holmes asks his younger brother Sherlock to investigate the origins of "The Protocols of the Learned Elders of Zion," a document which appears to reveal a secret Jewish plot for world domination. Is this troublesome document real or a forgery? In their search for the answer, Holmes and Dr. Watson travel from Edwardian England to the Tsar's Russia.

A hallmark of Meyer's work is the mingling of historical and fictional characters. *Protocols* is no exception. In the course of their investigation our stalwarts cross paths with such real-life figures as noted playwright and Zionist Israel Zangwill; Chaim Weizmann, a professor of chemistry at the University of Manchester who later became the first President of Israel; and, most importantly, the American Socialist leader William English Walling and his wife, the novelist Anna Strunsky Walling, recently returned from a year in Russia. Mrs. Walling serves as Holmes and Watson's guide to that vast and troubled country.

Watson depicts the effects of a pogrom in Kishinev in his journal: "On those dusty, dried-mud streets, one could not help observing the vacant lots where homes once stood, their owners fled or dead. The charred ruins were gone, but square patches of ground remained ominously black." Meyer offers a trenchant critique of Anti-Semitism and the ways in which such pernicious beliefs take root in the public imagination.

Protocols is an effective thriller, rich in atmosphere and period detail, as well as a wise, affectionate, and sometimes deeply melancholy portrait of Holmes and his world. It's a masterful concoction that Sherlockian devotees will savor.

Nicholas Meyer is alive and well and working in Los Angeles. I can't wait to see what he does next.

Frederick Irving Anderson: INFALLIBLE

In another life, in another city, I once worked in an American Express mailroom, collating documents pertaining to other people's money. It was a simple, tedious job that required little more than knowledge of the alphabet and the ability to count to ten. If you'd mastered those skills and showed up on time, you were assured of plentiful (if not particularly profitable) work. It wasn't a bad gig for a writer.

While I sorted and assembled, I listened to audiobooks — a *lot* of audiobooks. Novels, short stories, biographies, history, old radio shows, anything that would help me through the workday. I gravitated toward mysteries and revisited old favorites like *The Valley of Fear, The Confidential Agent,* and *Red Harvest.* And I made some new discoveries.

One very pleasant surprise was part of an audio collection titled *More of the Greatest Mysteries of All Time.* The venerable Otto Penzler had chosen the stories, classics by such authors as Vincent Starrett, Ruth Rendell, and Harlan Ellison, whose work I knew and admired. But Frederick Irving Anderson? Who was he? The name was vaguely familiar. I'd never read him, I knew that much. I also know that "The Infallible Godahl" captivated me from its first sentence to its last.

I've always had a taste for New York City history, and I relished the vision of pre-World-War-I era Gotham that Anderson's stories offer. Fans of Jack Finney's *Time and Again* and Caleb Carr's *The Alienist* will revel in Anderson's settings: private clubs and well-appointed drawing rooms peopled by society lionesses, explorers of exotic climes, and choleric plutocrats brandishing horsewhips.

In other ways, Anderson's Manhattan is not so different from mine. It's a city in transition, dynamic and tumultuous. Construction is booming; the Grand Central Terminal is being built in "The Infallible Godahl." Science and technology are transforming the social and economic landscape. Respectable citizens and pocket-picking thieves share the bustling streets. Then as now, New York City was a place to make money — or steal it.

Anderson's protagonist is the highly successful author Oliver Armiston, who owes his fame and fortune to his wildly popular tales about a master criminal named Godahl. He's never been caught, this Godahl, or even suspected of a crime; he's a super-villain after the Moriarty fashion, though he's a far more dashing figure. It's no mistake that such a resourceful, clever and powerful character bears a name that begins with the letters G, O, and D. There's something distinctly God-like about Godahl.

Armiston's confidence borders on the God-like, as well, but he's in for a rude awakening; a possible subtitle for the story could be "Or, The Author's Nightmare." The blade of his ingenuity is turned against him, and Armiston learns a hard lesson concerning the cost of egotism.

Those with a taste for metafiction will be intrigued by the way art and life intermingle in "The Infallible Godahl." Modernist ideas of narrative were beginning to infiltrate the world of popular fiction. Joyce's *Dubliners* was published the same year — 1914 — as the collected Godahl stories. Innovation and experiment were in the air, whether one wrote for *The Saturday Evening Post* or *The Little Review*.

According to *The Saint James Guide to Crime and Mystery Writers*, Frederick Irving Anderson was born in Aurora, Illinois in 1877 and died in 1947. A former journalist who'd worked for newspapers in Illinois and New York, Anderson turned to freelance writing in 1910. Although many of his stories were published in the slick magazines of the era, he's relatively unknown today. *The Saint James Guide* claims that

> Anderson was probably the only detective story writer to capture successfully the pre-Titanic syndrome of ultra-sophistication mingled with vulgarity, refinement with crude greed, hedonism with a zest for cultural color. He brought a certain Stevensonian glamour and fairytale quality into even police routine.

Anderson wrote five other stories featuring that dapper rogue Godahl — too few, for this fan, but we're lucky to have them. For Godahl is not only infallible . . . he's irresistible.

Barry Gifford: YOU WANT IT DARKER

Long before the poets of the pulps were canonized, the work of such masters as David Goodis, Cornell Woolrich, and Horace McCoy was almost impossible to find. Noir-hungry collectors haunted used bookstores and rummage sales, hoping that a coveted title might turn up. It came down to speed and the luck of the draw — get there first and buy it now, because it might not be there when you come back.

In 1977 Barry Gifford — a young novelist, poet, and noir devotee — met Don Ellis, founder of the Creative Arts Book Company in Berkeley, CA. The two joined forces to form the Black Lizard imprint. Their goal was to bring obscure, neglected, or forgotten works back into circulation. The result was a flood of books by such writers as Helen Nielsen, Charles Willeford, and Jim Thompson.

Black Lizard's advocacy for Thompson created a groundswell of interest in his rough-hewn tales of lowlifes and losers which led to several film adaptations, including *The Grifters* and the criminally underrated *After Dark, My Sweet* (both released in 1990), as well as a number of biographies and critical studies. Gifford and Black Lizard initiated the process that brought attention, respect, and academic legitimacy not only to Thompson but to classic noir fiction in general.

Co-written with Lawrence Lee, *Jack's Book: An Oral History of Jack Kerouac* and *Saroyan: A Biography* further demonstrated Gifford's interest in what Kerouac called "the unspeakable visions of the individual." Kerouac's mad journey through post-war America and the freewheeling young William Saroyan's iconoclastic vigor marked them as outsiders. Gifford has always been fascinated with misfits and opium eaters and spinners of dark and lonely tales. His own work is filled with them; and so is his life.

Born in Chicago in 1946, Gifford grew up in a decidedly raffish milieu. He's described his father, Rudolph Winston, as a "racketeer." Winston hung out with small-time Chicago gangsters like "Suitcase Solly" Banks and Willie "The Hero" Nero. Winston ran a liquor store, but his real occupation was never clear to the young Gifford. Once, in the lobby of the Waldorf Astoria Hotel, he turned to Dummy Fish, one of his father's colleagues. "'Does my dad have a job?' 'Sure he does,' he said. 'Of course. Your dad has to work, just like everybody else.' 'What is it?' Dummy wiped the sweat from his face with a white-and-blue checked handkerchief. 'He talks to people,' Dummy told me. 'Your dad is a great talker.'"

If Winston's income was dubious, what he called home was another source of confusion. "We supposedly lived in Chicago but my dad had places in Miami, New York, and Acapulco. We traveled, mostly without my mother, who stayed at home in Chicago and went to church a lot." Winston's travels ended early; he died of natural causes in 1958 at the age of 47. Gifford was 12 at the time. The already-mysterious Rudy Winston became — as Gifford titled his memoir of the man — *the phantom father*.

Gifford spent a lot of time in hotels. "I was born in a hotel," he told the *Los Angeles Times* in 1981, "lived in hotels all through my early life. And so my mother and my father would be gone at night. I would stay up all night watching movies on TV . . . From a very early age — five, six, seven years old — I was just watching movies, and I think that's how I developed my sense of narrative."

The Devil Thumbs a Ride (1988) and *Out of the Past: Adventures in Film Noir* (2001) are the result of years of late-night television watching. They're a fan's notes, brief, impressionistic accounts of four decades of noir and neo-noir film-making. More precisely, the essays are a compendium of moments, images, bits of dialogue that encapsulate the genre's mood and philosophy. *Mystery Scene* co-founder Ed Gorman prompted Gifford to write the pieces, and they first appeared in its pages.

Of *Mildred Pierce*, Gifford writes: "When Joan [Crawford] comes off as the good girl you know you've got wild horses loose in the drawing room and forget about the furniture."

Gilda: ". . . one of a kind, a masterpiece as gripping if not as clean and well-proportioned as *Sunset Boulevard*; or as purposefully noir, as say, *Touch of Evil*. We see Rita [Hayworth] at her very best in this; she does her strip number, 'Put the Blame on Mame,' and gets to twirl her red hair and flaunt her magnificent frame without interruption. Not even the plot gets in the way."

The Asphalt Jungle: "The charm of the film is its relentless domino action, the clack of one piece falling against the next until the entire row collapses."

Shoot the Piano Player: "One of the most touching and beautiful scenes in movie history is when Marie is shot and rolls over and over down a snowy hill. . . . That roll down the hill is utterly sensual; the beautiful girl dead in Charlie's arms with snow in her hair. The thugs are buffoons, yes, stupid, stepping on the innocent flower. Nobody gets left alone, ever."

Gifford wasn't only a movie fan. He was an early and enthusiastic reader, with a particular interest in the kind of fiction you hide from your mother. This interest led to a defining moment for the teenaged writer-to-be.

In the summer of 1959, Gifford and a friend sought relief from the fearsome humidity of a Florida summer. They found it in the dark coolness of the River Grove Drugstore, where they sat at the soda fountain, drank Dr Pepper, "and read passages to each other from such immortal sleazeball paperback classics as *Sin Doll* by Orrie Hitt and *Four Boys, A Girl and a Gun* by Willard Weiner."

One day he "plucked from the rack a faded-blue Gold Medal novel by an unheralded and little known writer named Jim Thompson entitled *The Killer Inside Me*." Thompson's tale of a psychotic small town sheriff who took the law into his own hands hit Gifford hard. He knew he'd found something different . . . something dangerous. It was just what he wanted. "Great art is always dangerous," Gifford wrote years later, "daring the reader, listener or viewer to go over the edge with the artist."

This no-holds-barred approach made Gifford the perfect collaborator for director David Lynch, whose deeply strange, oddly moving films either enchant or enrage; there is no middle-of-the-road response to his cinematic fever dreams.

First out of the gate was *Wild at Heart* (1990), Lynch's adaptation of Gifford's novel. Lynch approached Gifford about writing the screenplay. But, as the novelist told the *Los Angeles Times*, he was busy working on the sequel and was happy to leave that task to Lynch. "'You write it and send me the screenplay and I'll tell you what's wrong with it.' And he said fine."

The film follows Sailor Ripley (Nicholas Cage) and Lula Pace Fortune (Laura Dern) on a lurid and violent road trip through the South. The young lovers encounter a white-trash jamboree of eccentrics along the way. Sailor is in and out of prison, the couple is pursued by detectives and criminals alike, but he and Lula manage to survive in a world that's "wild at heart and weird on top." The film received the Palme d'Or at the Cannes Film Festival and remains Gifford's best known work.

Created for HBO, *Hotel Room* (1993) encompasses three discrete stories set in different eras but all taking place in room 603 of the fictional Railroad Hotel. Gifford wrote and Lynch directed the first segment ("Tricks," set in 1969, featuring Harry Dean Stanton, Freddie Jones, and Glenne Headly) and the third ("Blackout," with Crispin Glover and Alicia Witt, set in 1936). Both stories are heavy on atmosphere and filled with free-floating dread.

Dread is the keynote of *Lost Highway* (1997), Gifford and Lynch's finest collaboration. Lynch had an idea: "What if one day a person woke up and he was another person?" Bill Pullman plays Fred Madison, a middle-aged musician who is sentenced to death for the murder of his wife, Renee (Patricia Arquette), a crime he doesn't remember committing. One day he disappears from his death row cell; in his place a prison guard finds Peter Dayton (Balthasar Getty), a young auto mechanic. Dayton is released and proceeds to tempt fate by having an affair with a gangster's girlfriend (Patricia Arquette plays a dual role). Linking the two stories is The Mystery Man. Robert Blake — in white face, red lipstick, and no eyebrows — is an all-too-convincing embodiment of evil.

Gifford has referred to *Lost Highway* as "a psychogenic fugue," the symptoms of which are disappearance from one's usual surroundings and amnesia. The film has the logic of a nightmare and, like a dream, it's haunting, allusive, and sometimes puzzling.

But puzzles are right up Gifford's alley. As he noted in his coda to *The Phantom Father*, "I realized long ago that if forced to choose between revelation and mystery, I'll take mystery every time. Revelations solve very little; they serve only to preclude further thought, whereas mysteries continue to force speculation. The object, I concluded, is to encourage invention, not reduce possibilities."

Screenwriter/novelist Howard A. Rodman presented Gifford with the Anne Friedberg Award for Contributions to Noir and Its Preservation at the 2016 NoirCon in Philadelphia. Rodman spoke of the honoree's achievements. "Gifford did two invaluable things: he codified our canon; and he made it available, for the first time, to the larger audience. . . . I count myself among the honored band of those who can say that their own writing owes everything to the writing that Barry Gifford gave us — of others, and of his own. He is a used bookstore of the soul; he is the definition of noir."

Gifford's work as a publisher, novelist, and screenwriter brings us face to face with our own wildest and darkest dreams. It's an encounter as thrilling as it is disturbing. As Diane, a character in *Blackout*, muses, "It's kind of beautiful, though, the dark — don't you think?"

Ashley Weaver: A NEW GOLDEN AGE

Ashley Weaver's *Murder at the Brightwell* was published in 2014 to critical acclaim and received an Edgar nomination for Best First Novel. Set in a seaside resort hotel in 1930s England, *Brightwell* introduced readers to Amory Ames and her husband Milo. Both of them are young, intelligent and well-to-do, and Amory's life should be as peaceful and untroubled as a sunlit field. But the raffish Milo is the thundercloud that darkens her days; his roving eye and wandering ways push Amory's trust to the limit. When former beau Gil Trent asks Amory to visit the Brightwell Hotel to help him with a family problem, she encounters mayhem, murder — and Milo. His unexpected appearance throws Amory for a loop, complicating her investigation.

Amory's sleuthing digs up the secrets of her fellow guests and brings her face-to-face with a killer. It also shows the fault-lines that run through her marriage. Will Amory leave her charming but unreliable husband for the stolid Gil? Weaver mixes a delightful cocktail of menace and manners with a dash of bitter romance.

Amory returned in *Death Wears A Mask* (2015). Two months after the events at the Brightwell Hotel, she and Milo have reached a fragile truce. Amory's sworn off detective work, but she can't resist a friend's request for help. The clever Mrs. Ames finds herself embroiled in high-society shenanigans that start with jewel theft and end in homicide. While searching for the murderer, Amory is pursued by the amorous Viscount Dunmore, whose colorful past and less-than-savory reputation precedes him.

Mask is a worthy follow-up to *Brightwell*, offering lavish upper-crust locales for low-down activities. Amory Ames is a charmer, and her on-again off-again relationship with Milo provides an underpinning of real sorrow.

Ashley Weaver lives in Oakdale, Louisiana. She is the Technical Services Coordinator for the Allen Parish Libraries. In the summer of 2015, Ashley and I had a chance to talk about books, libraries, and her taste for the past and her plans for the future.

JOSEPH GOODRICH: When did you start writing? And why did you choose the mystery genre? Or did it choose you?

ASHLEY WEAVER: For as long as I've been a reader, I've always loved mysteries, so I naturally gravitated toward them when I started writing. I like the idea of all the little pieces of the puzzle that make up the whole picture. I wrote my first "book" in elementary school, complete with my own illustrations. I believe it was a mystery, though I can't remember the plot now. I wrote my first full-length novel in high school, a murder mystery with a romantic subplot set in Prohibition Era Chicago. I've ventured into other genres, but, no matter what I write, a mystery always manages to work its way into my plots. There's no escaping it.

JG: What prompted you to set your books in 1930s England?

AW: I was born in the wrong era. I love the sophistication and elegance of the early decades of the Twentieth Century. England in the 1930s kind of represents the Golden Age of Mysteries to me. When I got the idea for *Murder at the Brightwell*, it seemed like the time and place were already predetermined.

JG: It's clear that you're a fan of the classic mystery pioneered by such writers as Agatha Christie.

AW: I absolutely love her! The very first of her books that I read was *The Murder of Roger Ackroyd*, and it still ranks among my favorites. I also loved *The Hollow* and *Five Little Pigs*.

JG: Other mystery favorites?

AW: I'm a big fan of the Sherlock Holmes stories, and I've really enjoyed some of the hardboiled noir writers like Dashiell Hammett and James M. Cain.

JG: What kind of research did you do for *Brightwell* and *Mask*?

AW: Having enjoyed the novels and films of this era for many years, I feel I have a base knowledge of at least some elements of the era. At the start of each book, I usually gather enough information to set the scene, then I do additional research as the story develops. Being a librarian is very useful when it comes to research. I have a world of information at my fingertips.

JG: Libraries have played a big role in your life.

AW: As a child, the library was always one of my favorite places to visit. I absolutely loved browsing the shelves and carefully selecting an armful of books that I could bring home — for free! When I was a freshman in high school, an after-school job became available at my local library, and I decided to apply for it. At the time, I thought it would be a good way to make some spending money doing something I enjoyed. Little did I know that it would blossom into a career.

JG: What's next for Amory and Milo?

AW: I just finished the third book in the series, and the plans for book number four are beginning to take shape. I'm really enjoying exploring the way Amory and Milo's relationship is developing as they solve mysteries in their high-society setting.

JG: Ross Macdonald said that he wasn't his series character Lew Archer, but Lew Archer was definitely him. Along those lines, do you see any similarities between yourself and Amory Ames?

AW: I suppose there must be a little of me in Amory, but I don't think we're exceptionally similar in terms of personality. I do feel like I understand her very well, and I seldom feel conflicted about her motivations and behavior because I know instinctively how she responds to situations. We both enjoy mysteries, of course, but I wouldn't be quite as reckless as she sometimes is when searching for clues. She's a bit bolder and more decisive than I am. Perhaps she's who I would be if I knew I could write myself out of dangerous situations.

JG: *Brightwell* was nominated for a Best First Novel Edgar. How did you find out about the nomination?

AW: I belong to a group of mystery writers called Sleuths in Time, and they were actually the first ones to tell me that I had been nominated. It was a huge surprise.

JG: You came to Manhattan for the awards ceremony. Did you have a good time?

AW: I had a fabulous time! It was great to have the opportunity to interact with so many members of the mystery community. Everyone I met was absolutely lovely. And, as an avid mystery reader and librarian, it was an incredible experience to be in a room full of authors whose books I've read and seen on the library shelves for years.

JG: One final question: Will Milo ever settle down?

AW: Milo will probably always have a bit of a wild streak, but he's also starting to understand what's required of him in order to make his marriage work. I doubt he'll ever be perfectly well behaved — he wouldn't be as entertaining if he was — but he's growing as a person and as a husband, and readers can expect to see a different side of him in the future.

David Goodis: DRUGSTORE DOSTOEVSKY

Few genre writers make the journey from bus-station paperback racks to the acid-free pages of the Library of America. David Goodis made the leap in 2012, joining Dashiell Hammett, Raymond Chandler and Elmore Leonard as the only mystery authors to merit individual Library of America volumes.

French journalist Philippe Garnier's *Goodis: A Life in Black and White* was published by Black Pool Productions in 2013. Garnier's book first appeared thirty years ago in France and has long been a subject of discussion and speculation among Goodis fans. Its English-language debut marks the apotheosis of Goodis as a noir figurehead, long treasured by French critics but ignored or dismissed by their American counterparts.

Garnier's book is less a straightforward biography than a rumination on the facts of Goodis's life and work and the way both have been appreciated (and sometimes misunderstood) here and abroad. In the early 1980s Garnier interviewed many of the writer's friends and colleagues and, as he says in his introduction, mostly let them speak for themselves. He's gathered what can be known about the elusive Goodis, but doesn't embellish or distort that information to make a point or grind an axe.

David Goodis (1917-1967) was born into a middle-class Jewish family in Philadelphia. He attended Temple University, majoring in journalism, and moved to New York City in the late '30s, where he churned out hundreds of thousands of words for pulp magazines such as *Battle Birds*, *Daredevil Aces*, *G-Man Detective* and *Super Sports*. A mainstream novel, *Retreat From Oblivion*, found little success in 1939. In retrospect, it seems that oblivion was something Goodis sought. After a brief flurry of fame with his second novel *Dark Passage* and scriptwriting work in Hollywood, Goodis returned to Philadelphia. He lived with his parents until their deaths and remained in the family home to write and look after his mentally ill brother Herbert. From the early '50s onwards, he penned a dozen paperback originals for Gold Medal and Lion Books.

These novels — which include *Cassidy's Girl, The Burglar, Street of No Return* and *Down There* — serve as the basis for his posthumous reputation. Bleak and despairing, often set among the down-and-outers of Philadelphia's skid row, they are, in Garnier's words, "patented late-period Goodis, the drugstore Dostoevsky." Caught between a past too painful to remember and a future too painful to be imagined, his characters embody a particular kind of urban, masculine loneliness. Hemingway's influence can be detected; by and large the prose is swift, straightforward, spare. Goodis mostly avoids the hysterical implausibility that marks the work of Cornell Woolrich — a brother under the skin, as Garnier points out. Both were recluses with vivid fantasy lives and sexual proclivities they kept hidden from others. Woolrich has long been thought to have been a self-loathing gay man, and Goodis was by many accounts drawn to masochistic relationships with large, African American women. His books certainly reflect the polarized view of women typical of noir. In Goodis's world, two types of women exist: the slim, stylish belle who offers salvation, and the coarse harridan who dishes out hell.

For all the desolation and desperation the books contain, they also hold out a slender thread of hope. Lou Boxer, founder of NoirCon, a biennial festival of all things noir, remarks: "Goodis writes about those down on their luck. Miserable people in miserable places with miserable things happening to them. Do they give up? Do they look for an easy escape? No. These are the stories of people that life has been unjust to, but they continue on in spite of these inequalities."

D. H. Lawrence once warned readers to "trust the tale, not the teller." It hasn't always been easy to distinguish between the two when it comes to Goodis, and some prefer the line between life and art to be blurred. French publishers and filmmakers helped keep Goodis's work in front of the public but cast the writer in a romantic if misleading role. The French, Garnier writes, like "their artists *maudit* [doomed] — alcoholic, destitute, and of course unrecognized or unappreciated in their own countries." With almost no biographical material available (or, it seems, desired), French critics created a version of Goodis to fit the *maudit* profile. Goodis may have been highly eccentric, but he was neither destitute nor an alcoholic. Garnier believes the obscurity Goodis lived and worked in was a conscious choice. *Dark Passage* was published in 1946, became the third Bogart and Bacall movie a year later, and brought its author a measure of mainstream success. Goodis worked as a screenwriter for Warner Brothers, but he disliked Hollywood and left it around 1950 with few regrets.

During his time in the City of Angels, Goodis was better known for his eccentric behavior than for his work as a screenwriter. Instead of living in an apartment, he slept on a friend's couch, which he rented for four dollars a week. He not only wore the friend's old suits but would borrow a frowzy bathrobe and go out on the town, posing as a White Russian prince in exile. His ramshackle convertible was in such disreputable shape few wanted to be seen riding in it. His stinginess was legendary, as was his penchant for practical jokes.

Goodis's screenwriting credits are slim: he co-wrote (with James Gunn) *The Unfaithful*, a loose remake of *The Letter*, the Bette Davis vehicle based on W.S. Maugham's play and short story. *Up Till Now*, an ambitious, socially conscious project for Warner producer Jerry Wald, was ultimately abandoned by the studio. Two unused treatments were later turned into novels: *The Blonde on the Street Corner* and *Of Missing Persons*. It was time to head home to Philadelphia, and his own writing.

Goodis's books from that point on qualify as "termite art," in film critic and painter Manny Farber's phrase. Working on the margins of society with no pretensions to "taste" and high-art standards, the termite artist works, Farber writes, "where the spotlight of culture is nowhere in evidence, so that the craftsman can be ornery, wasteful, stubbornly self-involved, doing go-for-broke art and not caring what comes of it." Good, bad or indifferent — and Garnier admits that the quality of Goodis's work varies widely — his books could have been written by no one else. The particularity of his vision catches readers to this day. "When I began to read Goodis," Lou Boxer says, "I was magically transported back in time to the old Philadelphia. I could see, feel and hear the things Goodis saw, felt and heard . . . Cities, back alleys, bars all possess a throbbing vitality that tells the story of a place most of us never thought about, let alone ever thought of going to."

Goodis died in January 1967 at the age of 49 from a stroke. What caused the stroke is a matter of debate. Some reports claim it was due to a beating at the hands of a thief who was after Goodis's wallet. Others claim it was due to over-exertion from shoveling snow. Like so much concerning Goodis, one will never know for sure.

Garnier gives us as much as we're ever likely to find out. He packs a world of information into 215 pages. The reader is presented with sharply-observed portraits of Paul Wendkos, who directed the film version of *The Burglar*, which Goodis scripted; Warner Brothers producer Jerry Wald; Arnold Hano, an editor at Lion Books; and any number of Goodis's friends in Philadelphia and Los Angeles. Goodis's ambivalent years as a screenwriter are considered, and the history and economics of pulp magazines and paperback publishing are lightly and informatively related.

The book is lavishly illustrated with black-and-white photographs of Goodis and his friends; reproductions of vintage paperback covers; movie posters and stills; documents relating to Goodis's Hollywood work, drawn from Warner Brothers' archives; and the writer's marriage license.

Goodis's marriage to Elaine Astor is one more perplexing episode in the writer's life. Almost nothing about Astor was known until Laurence Withers, her son from a second marriage, discovered that she'd been married before. Astor and Goodis were, by all accounts, wildly mismatched. Married in October 1943, they were divorced in January 1946. Goodis rarely mentioned her, but the unflattering portrayal of some of his women characters may well reflect a lingering animosity toward his ex-wife.

Garnier's book is beautifully designed. A tip of the fedora to Eddie Muller, "the Czar of Noir" and the man behind Black Pool Productions, and book designer Michael Kronenberg for making this volume available. It's worth every penny. For Goodis fans and devotees of noir, it's priceless. It's been a long time coming, but well worth the wait.

What prompted Muller to publish it? "I'd been considering the idea of starting a publishing operation for some time," Eddie Muller says, "but I wasn't sure I wanted to start with my own books. . . . Garnier, who is largely distrustful of publishers, had passed on many invitations to have the book translated into English, but one day out of the blue he asked 'Why don't you publish it?' And it made perfect sense."

Once the decision to publish the book had been made, things came together rapidly. "Garnier did his own translation from the French and I edited it a bit to make it more American in tone without losing his distinctive voice. Michael Kronenberg turned the layout around very quickly. The copyediting, by Daryl Sparks, was the longest stage of the process. She's very thorough. All in all, [getting the book into print took] probably six months."

Like Boxer's NoirCon, Muller's plans for Black Pool Productions include but are not limited to Goodis. Both Boxer and Muller are interested in the entire noir spectrum. "I think all us noir-stained wretches come to these writers in the same general order," Muller says. "It always seems like Hammett, Chandler and Cain are the first, in some order, and then Thompson, Goodis and Willeford and the 1950s paperback writers." At which point, Muller adds, "If you're smart, you overcome the male bias and start reading Highsmith and realize she's as good as any of them."

Muller's already receiving queries about other Goodis projects, but he's not in the market for them, much as he admires Goodis' work, nor is Black Pool accepting other submissions.

Readers who aren't familiar with Goodis might wish to acquire *Five Noir Novels of the 1940s & 50s*, published by the Library of America. It contains some of his best writing (*Nightfall* and *The Burglar*) as well as some of his less effective (*The Moon in the Gutter*). All five novels are worthy of any noir fan's attention.

Garnier closes his book with a quote from Geoffrey O'Brien's *Hardboiled America* that sums up Goodis's achievement. His best books, O'Brien says, "have a unique poetry of solitude and fear, and even his lesser works come to life in violent patches of feeling."

Muller speaks of Goodis's appeal in a slightly different manner: "More bodily fluids spilled right on the page. The prose is a more direct conduit to his psyche than is the case with his peers."

It's ironic that, almost fifty years after his death, a man who sought anonymity is once again in the spotlight. Very likely Goodis would appreciate the humor of it. Of course acclaim would come long after his death. Why would fate work any differently?

Peter Quinn: MAN ABOUT TOWN

Readers of historical mysteries, take note: *Dry Bones*, Peter Quinn's third novel in a trilogy featuring private eye Fintan Dunne, was published in autumn 2013. It's a worthy successor to *Hour of the Cat* (2005) and *The Man Who Never Returned* (2010), Dunne's previous outings.

Like its predecessors, *Dry Bones* follows Dunne across the blasted heath of the 20th century. The novel encompasses the horrors of the Second World War and the sleeker, hidden corruption of the post-war world. Quinn's eye for detail and feel for history bring to life landscapes as disparate as battle-scarred Europe, pre-revolutionary Cuba and the glittering hustle of 1950s New York City.

Dry Bones is divided into two parts. The first takes place in 1945-46 and tells the story of an OSS mission into Nazi-occupied Czechoslovakia that almost costs Dunne his life. The second is set in 1958 and tracks Dunne through a labyrinth of governmental and sexual secrets related to that mission. It's a hell of an adventure tale that keeps the reader turning pages, as well as a rueful reflection on the great themes: love in all its varieties, and "the infinite incarnations in which death greets and embraces victor and vanquished alike."

Dry Bones is also about the nature of change. The wild-and-woolly OSS is transformed into the CIA. Dunne, the freelance private eye, sees his profession forsake individual cases for the more dependable and profitable field of industrial surveillance. Batista's Cuba is replaced by Castro's. The only constants are, as Quinn notes in *Cat*, "pain and politics. The perennials."

Fintan Dunne is at the heart of Quinn's books. An orphan who was raised in the Catholic Protectory in the Bronx, he served under "Wild Bill" Donovan in the war and, after his discharge, joined the police force. Too honest for his own good — or, at least, for a career in harness — Dunne struck out on his own. He scrapes a meager living out of divorce work until the events of *Hour of the Cat* force him to make a choice. A beautiful young woman asks Dunne to help free her brother, a Cuban émigré who's been convicted of murder. Dunne is tempted to tip his hat and walk away. Does he do what's easy . . . or what's right? Right and wrong matter to Dunne, even though he's no shining example to others. They matter because he's Catholic. Time and again, his moral sense impels this battered knight to take the more difficult path.

Cat finds Dunne grappling with Nazis, bent cops and twisted doctors. It covers two continents and the most tumultuous years of the last century, 1938 through 1945. *The Man Who Never Returned* has a tighter focus. It's an engrossing fictional account of the disappearance of Judge Joseph Crater in 1930. Two-and-a-half decades later, Dunne is hired by a Hearst-like media mogul to investigate the Judge's vanishing act. Dunne is presented with a very cold trail, but his initial skepticism fades when he gets the bit between his teeth. "No crime was a riddle beyond solution, a mystery with no answer [...] The only question was whether it was too late to gather the pieces of the puzzle, as well as how far those with the answers would go to stop the people trying to find them." Dunne pieces it all together, but the truth of Crater's disappearance remains, in every sense of the word, buried.

Quinn's books are thoroughly researched. "I'm a lapsed historian who stopped just short of a Ph.D.," he says. "I love to do research." All three books contain superlative period evocations of New York City, with its automats, elevated trains and newsreel theaters. Forgotten moments bring the era alive. In *Cat*, Dunne runs into Fuzzy Whalen, an old army buddy. They have a few drinks, then go their separate ways.

> They came out to a bruised and threatening sky. A thunderstorm seemed about to hit. But there wasn't a hint of moisture anywhere. The dryness coated throat and tongue. A few drops fell. Hard as sand. A minute later, the storm arrived. A shower of grit, the blown-away fields of dry, exhausted earth from a thousand miles away, from the busted farms of Oklahoma and Texas, descended on New York in a blinding swirl.

Bizarre as it may seem, this dirt storm actually occurred.

Quinn captures other locales with equal facility. In *Dry Bones*, Dunne remembers watching *Cover Girl* at a USO movie night in London. Gene Kelly and Rita Hayworth are singing Jerome Kern and Ira Gershwin's "Long Ago and Far Away" when:

> A lone soldier started to cry. Before long, muffled sobs filled the hall. Old-timers and newly arrived joined in. Technicolor beauty almost too much to bear, Rita could reduce any G.I. to tears. [...] When the

lights came up, tears had dried. Men skulked out, avoiding each other's eyes, like college boys leaving a Times Square peep show.

Quinn says Dunne is "an urban type wonderfully described by [novelist] William Kennedy as a 'cynical humanist.' He despises bullies. Though he's also sympathetic to people in trouble, he's a man of no illusions. Distrustful of all authority, skeptical of most causes, uninterested in heroics, he is reluctant to get involved. Whatever the case, he knows from the outset that there are no perfect endings, no spotless souls, and that some mysteries are better left unsolved. Still, despite his understanding of the futility of good intentions and the hopeless fallibility of everyone — including himself — Dunne can't help but try to see that some modicum of justice is done."

Quinn concludes: "Fintan Dunne is the man I want to be when I grow up."

Like his hero, Quinn is a product of New York City. Born in 1947, he grew up in the Bronx and remains a passionate defender of that much-maligned borough. He went to Manhattan College and Fordham University, where he studied history. His interest in politics is bred in the bone; his father, Peter A. Quinn, had a long and distinguished career in NYC's Democratic Party, serving as a district assemblyman, U.S. congressman, and State Supreme Court Justice. Quinn has dabbled in politics himself as chief speechwriter for New York governors Carey and Cuomo. He worked his way up the corporate ladder at what is now Time Warner, retiring in 2007 as corporate editorial director. A fourth-generation Irish-American, he's a well-known and much-admired figure in New York City's Irish community. His first novel, *Banished Children of Eve*, was published in 1995. *Looking for Jimmy: In Search of Irish America*, a collection of essays, was published in 2007.

Quinn's love of Raymond Chandler's work dictated the form Fintan Dunne's exploits would take. "Chandler's investigations are into character and soul," Quinn says, "into the American Dream and the nightmare wrapped inside it." But the form itself is a draw. "For me there's something innately attractive about the mystery/detective genre. At the risk of emphasizing the obvious, we're all sunk in trying to solve the mystery of our own lives, who we are, who our parents/ancestors were, what our fate will be, what will become of those who follow us . . . life as the great whodunit."

Quinn's sense of personal history and ethnic identity provide him with deep roots. No matter how far from the city he — or Fintan Dunne — may stray, he remains at heart a New Yorker. "My father was born over his father's bar on 11th Street," he says. "I rode on the 3rd Avenue El as a kid. The first baseball game I went to was in the Polo Grounds. The streets and sights and smells of New York are etched into the deepest crevices of my brain. But the city I write about is mostly gone — demolished, rebuilt, paved over, redeveloped."

This is the way New York City works, though, and Quinn admits it. "When it comes to their city, all New Yorkers — Dunne and me included — are hopeless romantics, always pining for what was."

Thanks to Peter Quinn, the reader can experience that vanished city in all its dirty glory

Dilys Winn: MAGICAL MYSTERY TOUR

Early in the summer of 1976, I was a 13-year-old boy in a small Minnesota town, and I was about to do something I'd never done before.

Everyone was occupied. The kitchen was empty. I eased the door shut. And then I did it.

I picked up the telephone receiver and held it to my ear. Nothing but the dial tone. Good. This meant the line was clear — we were on a party line, and I often had to wait for Mrs. Maday to finish her call before I could make one of my own.

The phone was mine.

I dialed the ten digits of a New York City phone number.

It was a mind-boggling thing to do. The world was larger then. Distances were greater. Especially if you'd never been farther from home than Sioux Falls, South Dakota, a whopping sixty miles away. No one called New York City, much less went there.

But I had to make that call.

I waited, listening to the phone ringing in some unimaginable other place. Ghost voices danced in the distance between the heart of the country and its East Coast.

Someone picked up at the other end of the line.

"Murder Ink," a voice said.

I cleared my throat, gathered my wits, and spoke.

~

A week before I made that call, I'd seen the latest *Mystery Monthly* on the magazine rack in Swanson's supermarket. I bought it, took it home, and devoured it. Along with short stories and book and movie reviews, that issue featured an interview with Dilys Winn, founder and owner of the world's first bookstore dedicated to mysteries. Punningly named Murder Ink, it was located on West 87th in Manhattan — Ellery Queen's old neighborhood. Winn spoke about the impulse that led her into the book business. Unhappy with her job as an advertising copywriter, she was looking for a change. She'd been impressed by expatriate bookseller Sylvia Beach, founder of the original Shakespeare & Company in Paris, and Beach's example offered a way out of Madison Avenue. "I'll open a bookstore, and call it Murder Ink," Winn said. "That was on a Wednesday. I found the store Thursday, and signed the lease Friday. I opened six weeks later."

Murder Ink was a success, rapidly developing a clientele composed of mystery readers and writers, as well as policemen, clergymen and psychiatrists. Winn eventually sold the store and left New York City. Murder Ink moved to a new location on upper Broadway and closed in 2006, a victim of the plague that's destroyed so many long-standing Manhattan businesses — death-by-rent-increase.

But back then, brick-and-mortar bookstores and the publishing houses that filled them with the latest mysteries were alive and well. Murder Ink was open for business.

If a customer asked for a recommendation, Winn was happy to oblige: *Such Men Are Dangerous*, attributed to Paul Kavanagh but really written by (as we know now) the one and only Lawrence Block; *The Red Right Hand*, Joel Townsley Rogers's cult classic; and anything by Dick Francis, "except the new one, which is sentimental." Winn had strong opinions and didn't mind sharing them. "I thought *Murder on the Orient Express* was one of the worst movies I ever saw. Same thing with *Chinatown*."

It's a good interview, but it wasn't what set my pulse racing and had me making long-distance phone calls. It was the notice that followed her interview for "The Mystery Reader's Tour of Britain":

Sixteen-day conducted tours, led by Dilys Winn, owner of Murder Ink, featuring lunch, tea, and cocktails with authors, book-buying binges, midnight train rides, walks on moors, ghost-hunting, bell-ringing, talks by firearm experts, newspaper reporters, practicing barristers, village bobbies, rare book dealers, theatre tickets to mystery plays, a suggested reading list compiled by Murder Ink. Sightseeing throughout England, Scotland, and Wales. Departure dates: June 27, 1976; September 1, 1976.

The cost of the tour included:

Round-trip jet flight from New York to London. Bed and breakfast accommodations. (Twin rooms with bath or shower.) Lunch, tea, dinner, cocktails where outlined in itinerary. Luxury coach transportation. Sightseeing tours. Tour escort. Airport taxes, local taxes, service charges.

The damage to one's wallet? $880.00.

A steal even by contemporary standards: $880.00 in 1976 has the buying power today of $3,700.00. That'll barely get a tourist to London, much less keep that traveler there for sixteen days, taxes, tips and book-buying binges most definitely *not* included.

~

"I'd like to speak to Dilys Winn, please."

"This is Dilys."

Heart in mouth, I said that I'd read about the tour of England she'd be leading, and told her how much I wanted to go. But there was a problem: my age. I was too young to go on my own. Would there be anyone on the trip who could keep an eye on me and thereby prevent my relatives from having nervous breakdowns while I was away?

Ms. Winn considered my dilemma. Yes, she said after reflection, there would be several ladies who could look after me on our journey through the United Kingdom. I'd be looked after. She'd see to that.

We talked a while longer, and she promised to send me further information about the trip. I could discuss things with my family and take it from there.

I thanked her and hung up, a jubilant, sweating mess.

My relief was immense. I'd be all right in England. The family wouldn't have to worry. Now all I had do was to convince my elders to not only part with me but with $880.00. I could deal with that later. The important thing was — I'd called Murder Ink! In New York City! I'd spoken with Dilys Winn!

I told the family at dinner, thrilled to share my news. I was sure they'd be thrilled, too. But as I looked from face to face, all I saw were puzzled expressions that quickly shifted into consternation. Never mind, I said to myself. They just need some time to get used to the idea. They can see how badly I want to go to England.

England: Just the sound of the word was an elixir to me. England. The home of Agatha Christie. Scotland Yard. The Tower of London. *The Mousetrap.* Earl Grey tea and buttered crumpets. History and murder everywhere.

I waited for further information about the trip to arrive. I was sure that the postman would bring it any day.

But he didn't.

That further information never showed up.

Or should I say . . . I never saw it.

I believe that Ms. Winn sent that information. I believe that it turned up in our mailbox. I also believe that the powers-that be in my house took that information, shredded it, and watched the pieces flutter into the trashcan.

To my great disappointment, I wasn't a part of the Mystery Reader's Tour, but I never forgot speaking with Dilys Winn, and the way she took me and my questions seriously. Her kindness meant everything to a mystery-obsessed boy who dreamed of Manhattan's spires and England's country houses.

Winn has long been recognized as a groundbreaking bookseller. She received a special Edgar Award in 1978 for her book *Murder Ink: A Mystery Lover's Companion*, a delightful compendium of essays by and about some of the greatest figures then working in the field. And speaking of awards, there's one named after her: The Dilys, which was created by the Independent Mystery Booksellers Association and is given each year to the book which IMBA members most enjoyed hand-selling.

Shortly after I joined the Mystery Writers of America in 2002, I sent out a message on the MWA list-serve. "Does anyone know where Dilys Winn is?"

She responded quickly. I sent her a long e-mail describing my youthful telephone call. "I remember you perfectly," she wrote, and invited me to visit her if I ever got within hailing distance.

A true lady, Dilys Winn.

I haven't met her yet.

But I'm still hoping.

Dilys Winn died in March 2016. We never had the chance to meet.

Gordon McAlpine: UNTANGLING *HOLMES ENTANGLED*

Holmes Entangled, Gordon McAlpine's captivating 2018 novel, takes the reader on a mind-bending excursion into an alternate world where an elderly Sherlock Holmes, disguised as a German scientist, teaches classical physics at Cambridge University; Sir Arthur Conan Doyle is a minor writer best known for his historical romances; and the truth about Edgar Allan Poe's mysterious death can be found in a curious Parisian bookstore. Holmes and Watson — *Mrs.* Watson, that is, the good doctor's widow — find themselves engaged in a fight-to-the-death with a ruthless and exceptionally powerful secret cabal whose nefarious goal is to…

I'll stop there.

Since his first appearance in 1887, Sherlock Holmes has been the subject of countless pastiches, parodies, and other brands of literary speculation. Nicholas Meyer's *The Seven-Per-Cent Solution* (1974) spawned hundreds of "lost" works featuring the world's greatest consulting detective in just about every conceivable time and place. The wide-ranging ingenuity of *Holmes Entangled* distinguishes it from its predecessors. It's something new under the Sherlockian sun, a story told with great speed and flourish that also embodies postmodern notions of authorship. The result is an engrossing work of speculative mystery fiction.

Recently I had the opportunity to discuss the book with Gordon, who spoke with great intelligence and passion about Holmes, Conan Doyle, and worlds within worlds.

JOSEPH GOODRICH: In *Holmes Entangled*, you bring Sherlock Holmes, Arthur Conan Doyle, Edgar Allan Poe, Charles Baudelaire, and Jorge Luis Borges into a universe of danger and intrigue. What prompted this fantastic mixture of people and ideas?

GORDON MCALPINE: A literary conceit presented itself to me unbidden: an author walks into a room and requests the help of one of his characters, the literary nature of their relationship being wholly unknown to both but evident to the reader. At this stage, I might have created a fictitious author and his character, but to do so would have required considerable backstory/set-up to establish the "unrecognized" literary relationship between the two as well as requiring an omniscient narrative voice capable of explaining what neither character could know. Contrarily, a single sentence, "Arthur Conan Doyle walks into a room to request the assistance of the great consulting detective Sherlock Holmes," economically accomplishes this meta-fictional setup with no explanation necessary. So, having arrived at the specifics of my unusual author/detective relationship — Conan Doyle and Holmes — I considered how such a metaphysical occurrence might be possible. The radical Everett interpretation of Quantum mechanics, which postulates the existence of many simultaneously existing worlds, came to mind. Subsequently, I recalled the short story "The Garden of the Forking Paths" by J. L. Borges and the essay, "Eureka" by E. A. Poe. As both Borges and Poe also created detectives of note, I included those authors and their respective characters in the novel too, variations on the author-seeking-help-from-his-own-unrecognized-fictional-detective theme. Hence, I arrived at a challenging and mysterious predicament.

JG: You offer a distinctly non-canonical portrait of the world's most famous detective. Would you call yourself a Sherlockian?

GM: I'm a great admirer of Conan Doyle's creation. And I share with Sherlockians the impulse to fancifully consider Holmes as real in the historical sense. However, for *Holmes Entangled*, I attempted to provide more than mere imitation, creating a Sherlock Holmes who was at each turn a plausible interpretation of the original while also providing readers with sufficient variation and personal nuance, expressed through Holmes's first-person narration, that a newly revealed character would emerge. My rationale was as follows: none of us would seem the same person by our own reckoning as we'd seem to be through someone else's (e.g., Watson's) interpretation. Likewise, we are all invariably altered by circumstance and the passage of time. The protagonist of *Holmes Entangled* is now 73 years old and living in the age of the "Moderns." Additionally, he has recently lost Dr. John Watson, his chronicler and friend. In this light, it seemed implausible to me that this *could* be a Holmes who is identical to the one portrayed by Conan Doyle/Watson in the decades before.

JG: The heart of the book is Holmes's grief over Watson's death and his relationship with Watson's widow. How did you approach Holmes's emotional life?

GM: I am so pleased you asked this question. Watson was the ever-sympathetic witness to Holmes's life, a life that Holmes himself never regarded quite so sympathetically. In the three years since Watson's death, Holmes has lost touch with his own identity, spending his time in various disguises teaching subjects at Oxford and Cambridge Universities that have little to do with his past life. To my mind, Holmes's grief is the primary motivation for him to write this novel-length account in the first place. True, the events depicted are sufficiently dramatic to inspire a telling of the tale, but, absent the emptiness that has assaulted Holmes since his friend's death, I don't know that the great detective ever would have embarked on such a task. But now, Holmes's writing makes him feel closer to the John Watson who was his chronicler, just as Holmes's investigative collaboration with the widowed Mrs. Watson makes him feel closer to the John Watson who was his friend. And this is to say nothing of how grief has opened Holmes to new possibilities that he'd have regarded before as unprovable and, therefore, hopelessly irrational and unscientific. New worlds, so to speak — even if the sadness persists.

JG: As in your two most recent books — the Edgar-nominated *Woman with a Blue Pencil* (2015) and *Hammett Unwritten* (2013) — a lost manuscript (or manuscripts) fuels the action. Why does the act of writing play such a large role in your work?

GM: I remain as enchanted today by what can be contained between the covers of a book as I was when I discovered reading for pleasure at eight years old. In that light, what could be more exciting than a lost book or manuscript that *I* might be privileged to discover . . . even if I have to invent it to do so? On a more practical level, a "discovered" manuscript provides a novelist an economical opportunity to lend context to the core story of his or her novel by the implicit acknowledgement that the book-within-the-book was, itself, written under particular circumstances, has been discovered in equally particular circumstances, and that these discrete circumstances, separated perhaps by decades, inevitably comment on one another. The layering of realities is of great interest to me.

REHEARSAL FOR MURDER:
CRIME ON STAGE AND SCREEN

William Link (L) and Peter Falk: "Just One More Thing" from a Classic Collaboration.

Anthony Shaffer (below): Grand Artificer.

Lucille Fletcher and Bernard Herrmann (above left); "No One's Idea of a Day in the Country."

Rex Stout (R): The Irresistible Force Meets the Immovable Object.

William Link: "JUST ONE MORE THING..."

It's a rare accomplishment for any mystery writer to create a detective so singular, so memorable, that the whole world instantly recognizes that super-sleuth's name.

William Link has done it twice.

As the co-creator of Columbo and Jessica Fletcher, Link has brought high-quality mystery storytelling to a national and international audience and introduced millions of viewers to the pleasures of the genre.

But that's not all he's done.

In a career that spans over 60 years, Link has been a groundbreaking writer and producer for network television; a long-time contributor to *Ellery Queen's Mystery Magazine* and *Alfred Hitchcock's Mystery Magazine*; a recipient of the Ellery Queen Award, multiple Edgar, Emmy and Golden Globe Awards; National President of MWA; and a genial elder statesman whose lifework has been honored by the Board of Governors of the Academy of Television Arts, the Bouchercon and Malice Domestic conventions, and the Southern California Chapter of Mystery Writers of America. In 2018 he received the genre's ultimate accolade: MWA named him as a Grand Master.

William Link was born in a suburb of Philadelphia in 1933. A passionate fan of radio crime dramas, pulp magazines and magic tricks, Link met Richard Levinson on their first day of junior high school. "Someone suggested I find this tall guy who liked to do magic and write mysteries," Link told J. Kingston Pierce in a 2010 interview, "and he was told to look for a short guy who did magic and wrote mysteries." It wasn't long before Levinson and Link were writing together

— a working relationship that lasted for over 40 years and which ranks among the greatest partnerships in the mystery world.

The young men's tastes in mystery were formed by such Golden Age giants as Ellery Queen, Agatha Christie and John Dickson Carr. Their influence can be seen clearly in Levinson and Link's own intricately plotted mysteries.

They made their first professional sale with "Whistle While You Work," which appeared in the November 1954 issue of *Ellery Queen's Mystery Magazine*. Written while its authors were still in high school, the story was published when they were attending the Wharton Business School at the University of Pennsylvania. But a career in business wasn't what they had in mind, and the sale to EQMM cemented their decision to pursue the writing game.

The Golden Age of Television was in full swing. Levinson and Link broke into the field in the late 1950s, crafting episodes of *Richard Diamond, Private Detective, Michael Shayne, The Third Man* and *Alfred Hitchcock Presents*, among others. ("We once had a three-hour lunch with the Master of Suspense in his bungalow at Universal," Link told Andrew McAleer. "Writing-wise, [Hitchcock] said that when you use coincidence it must occur early in the script and never again. Always go for the big, important scenes even if they defy logic.")

"Enough Rope," written for *The Chevy Mystery Show* in 1960, featured an eccentric detective with an offbeat way of questioning his suspects, a rumpled David who brought law-breaking Goliaths to justice. Columbo was his name — Lieutenant Columbo.

Levinson and Link brought Columbo back in the 1968 TV movie *Prescription: Murder*. This led to a critically lauded and vastly popular series that made the raincoat-clad detective a household name. The circle was completed with a number of made-for-television specials, the last of which aired in 2003. All but the first TV incarnation featured the inimitable Peter Falk as Columbo. Levinson and Link's collaboration with Falk is one of the all-time great fusions of writers, character and actor.

Each episode of *Columbo* followed the same pattern. Critic and novelist William L. DeAndrea described it in his *Encyclopedia Mysteriosa*: "We see someone commit what looks like the perfect crime . . . and then we see the seemingly bumbling detective take the perfection to pieces." As Link has pointed out, Columbo's foes are the rich and the powerful, and he attributes a portion of the show's popularity to the fact that the good Lieutenant is a working-class underdog. He represents the viewer, and the viewer exults in the piece-by-piece dismantling of the villain's smug belief in his (or her) invincibility.

Columbo is, as Gwen Inhat wrote for the A.V. Club's website, "the most iconic TV detective of all time." But he's not the only crime fighter Levinson and Link brought to the small screen. Other series include *Mannix, The Bold Ones, Tenafly, Ellery Queen, Blacke's Magic*, and (with Peter S. Fischer) *Murder, She Wrote* — which introduced the world to crime-solving mystery writer Jessica Fletcher.

Murder, She Wrote was a phenomenon, but the show's success was far from a sure thing. *Murder*'s stories had no sex, little violence, and featured a smart, independent older woman who, as Link said in an interview for the Archive of American Television, "wasn't bailed out by the men in the last reel." Jessica Fletcher can take care of herself. In *The Fine Art of Murder*, Margaret C. Albert offered an assessment of Ms. Fletcher's strengths: "Jessica is not an old lady. She moves comfortably through a house of prostitution, parades as a frumpy hypochondriac out to expose a phony doctor, and adroitly (and politely) upstages big-city cops who underestimate her skills."

Like Columbo, Jessica Fletcher was featured in a number of highly rated television movies after the series ended. She is, without a doubt, the second unforgettable character in Link's work.

Levinson and Link had a parallel career as pioneering writers/producers of television movies that dealt with racial prejudice (*My Sweet Charlie*), violence in the media (*The Storyteller*) and in life (*The Gun*). *That Certain Summer* was, according to the *New York Times*, "the first TV film to take a mature and non-remonstrative approach to the subject of homosexuality." *Crisis at Central High* dramatized the historical 1957 integration of a high school in Little Rock, Arkansas. *Terrorist on Trial: The United States of America vs. Salim Ajami* was a prescient look at Middle Eastern fundamentalism and the American legal system.

In 1961 FCC chair Newton N. Minow referred to television as a "vast wasteland." Levinson and Link definitively proved that the medium was capable of great and serious things, and could be used to illuminate and educate.

It can also mystify and delight, as evidenced by a trio of Edgar Award-winning TV movies: *Murder by Natural Causes, Rehearsal for Murder* and *Guilty Conscience*. These are fiendishly clever dramas that put the viewer through a wringer. They exemplify the pair's appreciation of what William L. DeAndrea called "the classical aspects of the mystery story: the clues and the solutions."

Richard Levinson died in 1987, but William Link is still working, still writing. His work has intrigued and entertained millions and upheld the highest standards of the craft. He truly deserves the title of Grand Master.

Anthony Shaffer: GRAND ARTIFICER OF MYSTERIES

Anthony Shaffer's tombstone in London's Highgate Cemetery bears the inscription: *Grand Artificer of Mysteries*. It's a fitting epitaph for the author of *Sleuth*. A staunch practitioner of and advocate for the classic mystery and a skilled player of practical jokes in real life, Shaffer (1926-2001) expended a great deal of energy in contriving deceptive circumstances. *Sleuth* — which won an Edgar and a Tony award, was twice made into a film and is regularly revived — and *Murderer* are his major works for the theater. His screenplays include *Frenzy* (Hitchcock's late-career return to form), *The Wicker Man* (a cult favorite that dabbles in paganism and the occult), *Absolution* (evil doings in a Catholic boys' school) and a trio of Christie adaptations: *Death on the Nile*, *Evil Under the Sun* and *Appointment with Death*.

Anthony Shaffer was born in Liverpool, England on May 15, 1926. His twin brother Peter, the future author of *Equus* and *Amadeus*, was born five minutes later to the surprise of all and the horror of some: "Lock the door and tell nobody," was their great-grandfather's advice. The Shaffer twins and their younger brother Brian were raised in comfortable circumstances in Liverpool and London. Twins Anthony and Peter were particularly close. They had their own language for a time, doubled for each other on occasion and served as each other's closest friend and confidante. All three brothers were educated at St. Paul's School and Trinity College, Cambridge. In the early 1950s Anthony and Peter collaborated on *How Doth the Little Crocodile?* and *Withered Murder*, mystery novels featuring the erudite Mr. Verity, a collector of ancient sculpture and a member of the Beverly Club, an organization dedicated to the appreciation of the more artistic variations of murder.

Following a checkered career as a barrister and a much more successful one as a producer of television commercials, Shaffer realized that if he was going to be a writer, it was time to get serious. *Sleuth* — the Main Event, as he called it — was born.

Though it wasn't his first play, *Sleuth* (1970) was Shaffer's first big success, racking up an impressive number of performances in London, New York and everywhere else. Speaking to *Plays and Players* in 1979, Shaffer described the elements of a mystery play as ". . . a mixture of fear and fun and puzzle. If you put these things together in the right proportions, people should be enormously satisfied." *Sleuth* provides plenty of fear, fun and puzzlement. Travel agent Milo Tindle has been invited to the country manor of mystery writer Andrew Wyke. Tindle's having an affair with Mrs. Wyke, but Wyke is willing to surrender his straying spouse — or is he? Shaffer puts his characters through an increasingly complicated game of cat-and-mouse. Audiences were riveted. "I don't know where ya just took me," a woman told the playwright after a performance, "but I've never known anything like it. If my house had been burning down, and if my children had been in that house, I would not have left your theatre!"

Sleuth is both a condemnation of and an elegy for the golden-age mystery and the often snobbish and repressive society that produced it. The aging, privileged lion Wyke engages the young *arriviste* Tindle in a civilized but deadly battle not only for possession of a woman, but for England. It's class warfare, pure and not-so-simple. Tindle is everything Wyke hates and fears and tries to keep at bay. But Wyke's elaborately contrived mystery novels, his obsession with games and mechanical toys can't keep his fears from destroying him. As Shaffer told the *New York Times* just before *Sleuth*'s American premiere, "If there is a focal point, it's that if people take fantasy for reality, and act upon it, it must end in disaster."

Sleuth was still running on Broadway and London's West End when the film version was made. Directed by the legendary Joseph Mankiewicz, *Sleuth* is a rare adaptation that improves upon the original. Shaffer's screenplay heightens the social differences between Tindle and Wyke and successfully opens up the play. The grounds of Wyke's country house — which include an elaborate maze — are memorably used. Ken Adam's designs for the interior of Wyke's house provide a highly detailed visual correlative for the complex, twisting action that takes place within it. Michael Caine and Laurence Olivier, Tindle and Wyke respectively, are both impressive. Caine's make-up during a crucial scene fails him; that and a few moments of strained slapstick are the film's only flaws. *Sleuth* brought Shaffer his second Edgar award. One of the MWA's statuettes of Edgar Allan Poe (Anthony Shaffer's first) makes a cameo appearance in the film, silently watching the action unfold.

Sleuth is the epitome of the well-made bourgeois entertainment, an elaborately carved 17th century Venetian dagger of a play. *Murderer*, Shaffer's next piece for the theatre, is a bloody ax. Where *Sleuth* is discretion and implication,

Murderer (1975) is violent and overt. It begins with an act of theatrical audacity. The very first stage direction informs us that "*Thirty minutes should elapse between the start of the play and the first spoken words* 'Open up. Police.'"

What happens in those thirty silent minutes is equally audacious. Shaffer told *Plays and Players* in 1979:

> I was prompted by the fact that in the thriller form the murder was always virtually left out. It was always the most casual thing in the evening. A shot was heard, or there was a quick smothering or strangling. But actually to put people into a house where they watched the process of dismemberment, and had to consider how to get rid of a body — it seemed to me that if we could get to a position where people were put face to face with those fantasies they have, that would be something new onstage.

In the first thirty minutes of the play, we watch Norman Bartholomew drug and murder his mistress, then dissect and destroy her corpse. Or do we? Shaffer pulls more than one rug out from under us in the course of the evening.

Norman's goal is uxoricide. The passion has gone out of his marriage and circumstances dictate only one way to end it. Obsessed with re-enacting famous murders from history, Norman plans to kill his wife and take up with a younger girlfriend. But things don't work out as planned. Two lives are ended and another irredeemably changed before the murderer is apprehended.

Murderer presages popular culture's intense interest in serial killers and their crimes; its plot has more twists and turns than *Sleuth*. Yet it achieved only a fraction of *Sleuth*'s *réclame*. Why? According to Shaffer, "the curiously tepid response" to the play owed to lead actor Robert Stephens's drinking problem and a tactical error concerning the gruesome opening scene. The producer thought it was "too ghastly for Brighton audiences." The scene was cut to half its original length, greatly diminishing its effect. *Murderer*'s West End run was fairly brief and the play is rarely revived.

Shaffer's next offering was *The Case of the Oily Levantine* (1977). It was rewritten and retitled *Whodunnit* in 1982 for its Broadway production. This send-up of the country-house-murder, with its archetypal starchy colonels, suspicious foreigners and sweet young things, ran for five months. There's a nice trick in it, but it doesn't add up to much. A critic for the London *Financial Times* found its parody elephantine and its solution trivial.

Widow's Weeds (Or For Years I Couldn't Wear My Black) was first produced in Australia in 1977. Ten years later it had its English premiere. *Weeds* is another comic thriller. A lower-middle-class housewife in suburban London has been selected by an ad agency to appear in a television commercial for Folliclean Shampoo. The arrival of a film crew, producer and director flusters her, and they in turn are flustered by *her*. Why won't Mrs. Collier let her son and daughter appear in the commercial? Is her husband at work or is he dead? Are her children cursed with morbid imaginations or are they bad seeds? The production successfully toured England but never played London.

Shaffer's last play, *The Thing in the Wheelchair* is "a rather cold-hearted melodrama," he told *Variety*. "A complete pathological bitch tortures an old woman in a wheelchair who is completely paralyzed except for her eyes." Although there'd been talk that film legend Nicholas Roeg would direct it in the West End in 1998, the play eventually premiered in Australia in 2001. Diane Cilento, Shaffer's third wife, directed the production at the outdoor theater she and Shaffer built on their property in North Queensland. Local reviews were favorable. There have been no other productions and the play has not been published.

Much of Shaffer's time and creative energy went into screenplays. Some were filmed; many others linger in that sad purgatory where unproduced scenarios languish for eternity. *Frenzy* (1972) remains his best-known work for the screen, along with *The Wicker Man* (1973) and the amusing series of Poirot films featuring Peter Ustinov. *Absolution* (1978) features Richard Burton as a priest in a Catholic boys' school who is driven to murder by one of his students. The shoot was troubled, parts of the script were rewritten by others, but Shaffer's story remains. The source for the script was Shaffer's unproduced work for the stage *Play with a Gypsy*. Its theatrical origins are apparent; the story's plot devices would have been better served in the theater, where disbelief is more easily suspended than in the all-too-real-looking world of film.

Hollywood provided Shaffer with a wealth of anecdotes that are featured in *So What Did You Expect?* Shaffer's memoir, published shortly after his death, is partial, slapdash, dotted with errors of fact and proofreading — and vastly entertaining. One gets a sense of how much fun it must have been to sit with "four fingers of the dark mahoganies" — Shaffer's doctor's phrase for scotch-with-a-splash — and enjoy an evening of droll reminiscences. Bette Davis's bad behavior on the set of *Death on the Nile*, an intoxicating lecture on the facts of life delivered by Shaffer's father, and how *Sleuth* found its title are only a few of the tales the memoir offers.

Shaffer died of a heart attack in London on November 6, 2001. A protracted battle over his estate began in 2004 when his mistress claimed she was entitled to a portion of Shaffer's fortune. Her claim was dismissed but other complications ensued. More than ten years after Shaffer's death, legal matters showed no sign of resolution.

The best of Shaffer's work continues to delight, engross and mystify the viewer. A firm believer in that old-fashioned virtue, entertainment, he worked hard to make it all look easy . . . and, when the final trick had been played, the final trap sprung . . . inevitable.

Lucille Fletcher: SHE HAS OUR NUMBER

We're all Mrs. Elbert Stevenson these days.

You remember Mrs. Stevenson. She's the main character in Lucille Fletcher's radio play *Sorry, Wrong Number*, a woman who can't leave her apartment and is subject to not only the fear pulsing through her overwrought nervous system but also to the unknown terror lurking in the street outside her Manhattan apartment building.

Fletcher (1912-2000) is a chronically underrated suspense novelist whose tales of fragile psyches and gaslighting villains seem more in tune with the zeitgeist than ever.

A bit of biography first. Violet Lucille Fletcher was born in Brooklyn on March 28, 1912. She attended Vassar, where the novelist Mary McCarthy was a classmate. Upon graduating in 1933, she went to work for CBS in various secretarial capacities. The Columbia Broadcasting System proved to be of critical importance to Fletcher in more ways than one: while typing out the radio plays of others, she decided she could write them herself; and it's there that she first met Bernard Herrmann, who achieved his own lasting fame as the composer of scores for such films as *Citizen Kane*, *Psycho* and *Taxi Driver*.

A prolonged courtship was followed by marriage in 1939. Photos from the mid-40s present a happy couple; I think specifically of a snapshot that captures the brash young composer sitting beside an attractive dark-eyed, dark-haired young woman who's reclining on a *chaise longue*. He's beaming with pleasure at his own good luck. She's beaming, too — at him. Fletcher and Herrmann had two daughters: Dorothy (who grew up to become a noted biographer) and Wendy.

Their marriage also produced several collaborations of a different nature. Herrmann provided scores for some of Fletcher's radio plays, and she wrote the libretto for *Wuthering Heights*, Herrmann's only opera.

In the late 40s Herrmann fell in love with Fletcher's cousin Lucille Anderson. A divorce followed, and Herrmann wed his second Lucille. In 1949 Fletcher married writer John Douglass Wallop, whose novel *The Year the Yankees Lost the Pennant* later served as the basis for a little musical known as *Damn Yankees*. Their union lasted until Wallop's death in 1985. Herrmann's marriage to Lucille Anderson did not last — but then, hot-tempered Benny Herrmann was never anyone's idea of a day in the country.

Suspense — "Radio's outstanding theatre of thrills" — first presented *Sorry, Wrong Number* in May 1943. It may be the "greatest single radio script ever written," as Orson Welles is quoted as saying; it is certainly one of the most effective. The set-up is simple. Thanks to a weird technical glitch, a querulous bed-ridden woman's telephone call to her husband is patched into a conversation between two strangers who are planning a murder that will happen later that evening. Mrs. Stevenson's attempt to find out who the men are, alert the authorities, and soothe her ruffled nerves is an exquisitely calibrated exercise in mounting hysteria, culminating in the final, fatal realization that she is the intended victim. Agnes Moorehead — best remembered these days as Endora on *Bewitched* — played Mrs. Stevenson. Her performance is a tour-de-force; almost 80 years after the first broadcast, Moorhead's neurotic intensity still takes one's breath away.

Sorry, Wrong Number was a phenomenal success, and Fletcher joined Norman Corwin and Arch Oboler as part of a select group of radio writers whose names were recognized by the listening audience. So striking was its effect that — aided by the 1948 film version with Barbara Stanwyck, whose performance was nominated for an Oscar — it continues to resonate in public memory. *Suspense* frequently repeated the program over the years, and a later iteration won an Edgar Award for Best Radio Play. It's a bona fide classic, a perennial testament to the power of radio.

Sorry remains Fletcher's best known work, but it's far from all she accomplished. There are close to a dozen more radio plays, all worth hearing; a stage play; and a handful of suspense novels that deserve re-evaluation and a new audience.

As a dramatist Fletcher was especially adept at furnishing strong women with strong parts. She gave Agnes Moorehead another star turn with *The Diary of Saphronia Winters*, then did the same for Ida Lupino with *Fugue in C Minor*. *Dark Journey* offered plum parts for Nancy Kelly and Cathy Lewis. As for male actors, Paul Muni and, later, Orson Welles were admirably served by *The Search for Henri Lefevre*. Welles alone brought *The Hitchhiker* to powerful, brooding life.

Fletcher's second-best known radio script, *The Hitchhiker* has the eerie feel of an urban myth. Ronald Adams sets off on a cross-country trip from his home in Brooklyn. In Lower Manhattan he spots a shabby, rain-spotted hobo. Later in his trip he sees him again. And again. And again. Who is this mysterious figure? What does he want? Adams finds out when, somewhere in the New Mexico night, he calls his mother from an auto-camp pay phone — and discovers the disturbing truth. Or as much of the truth as a man can know…

As radio drama entered its last years, Fletcher published *The Daughters of Jasper Clay* (1958), a novel set in Brooklyn during the Second World War. She returned to the mystery genre with 1960's *Blindfold*. Rock Hudson and Claudia Cardinale starred in the 1965 film version. Fletcher didn't care for the film; she wasn't alone.

Five other novels followed. . . . *And Presumed Dead* (1963), *The Strange Blue Yawl* (1964), *The Girl In Cabin B54* (1968), *Eighty Dollars To Stamford* (1975) and *Mirror Image* (1988).

. . . *And Presumed Dead* is a particularly strong outing for Fletcher, and a good place for those unfamiliar with her work to start. Novelist and critic Martin Edwards describes the book, which is set in Switzerland in 1951, as "the misadventures of Julia, whose beloved husband Russ was an airman who went missing during the war. She has followed Russ' mother to Alpenstadt, and it soon begins to look as though the older woman has something to hide." As the reader discovers, there's a lot to be hidden. *Dead* is the Fletcher novel I prefer — and so did she, it turns out. She wrote to a German correspondent in August 1979:

> It is still, in spite of its flaws, my favorite of the six suspense novels I have written since "Sorry, Wrong Number." It was based on a true story I heard from a friend of mine, and of course its background is the mountain of Birgenstock [sic] near Lucerne, Switzerland, where I spent about 6 weeks. The book was sold to the films many years ago and they were going to film it in Birgenstock with Bette Davis . . . but something happened and the picture was never made."

"You bury the secret," Fletcher once described her method to the *Washington Post*, "lead the reader down the path, put in false leads and throughout the story remain completely logical. . . . Mysteries are a challenge, a double task for the writer, for the reader is aching to solve the puzzle before you do." This is a fair description of her play *Night Watch*, which opened on Broadway in 1972. The *New York Times* called it "a most superior thriller" and "one of the most entertaining plays on Broadway." Elaine Wheeler, another of Fletcher's high-strung heroines, spots a body in the brownstone across from her own in the Kips Bay section of New York City. Or has she? The police find no corpse, no sign of a crime. Is Elaine losing her mind? Or is someone trying to drive her mad? Things are (of course) not what they seem. Despite *The Times'* review, the play only lasted four months on the Great White Way. It was made into a striking film with Elizabeth Taylor and has been frequently produced in community theaters across the country.

Night Watch shares a general pattern with Fletcher's novels. A typical Fletcher protagonist — often a woman, but not always — finds herself slowly drawn into an impossible, nightmarish situation that pushes her to the farthest reaches of sanity. That which is, cannot be; that which cannot be, is. Or so it seems until the truth is revealed — a truth more horrible than any illusion. (If you detect a tinge of the Gothic here, you're correct.) Her novels are filled with unscrupulous manipulators who prey on the innocent, the bereaved, the hurt, the lonely.

You see why I say she has our number?

One can only hope our own nightmarish situations resolve themselves the way they do in Fletcher's books, where turmoil and heightened sensation ultimately yield to reason. Order is restored. The schemers are unmasked and punished. Her world is not that of the eccentric, subversive Patricia Highsmith. In Fletcher's world, one fears for the worst; in Highsmith's, the worst is expected from the start. But Fletcher has a remarkable feeling for chaos, for the moment of blank panic, for the imminence of emotional collapse. Pulse rates rise — that of her characters, and that of the reader. Her books are expert entertainments, genuine bamboozlers with deep undercurrents of dark emotion.

Lucille Fletcher died on August 31, 2000, at the age of 88. *Mirror Image*, her last novel, ended her career on a high note in 1988. The plot is quintessential Fletcher: the daughter of a famous actress disappeared one day in Central Park. Twenty years later, a letter arrives from a small town in France. *I believe*, its writer says, *that your daughter has been found*. Filled with misgivings and forebodings, wishing for some sort of miracle, the older daughter goes to investigate. Her mother is dying of cancer and longs for one last glimpse of the daughter she'd lost so many years before. Fletcher masterfully evokes the way love and guilt intermingle, and shows how our capacity for hope can be used against us by the ruthless and deceitful.

Much of what we know about Fletcher comes from *A Heart at Fire's Center*, Steven C. Smith's marvelous biography of Bernard Herrmann. Her older daughter Dorothy Herrmann, biographer of Helen Keller and Anne Morrow Lindbergh, was once rumored to be working on a memoir of her parents. I hope she still is, for I suspect there's a great deal more to learn about the intriguing Ms. Fletcher, whose books are long overdue for a renaissance.

Amnon Kabatchnik: LIFE UPON THE WICKED STAGE

Theatre is the most ephemeral of the arts; it lives and dies in the moment. A dedicated cultural anthropologist is needed to dig up a vanished play and bring it back into the light to be remembered, read and — with any luck — brought to life again on stage.

Amnon Kabatchnik is one such intrepid explorer of the theatrical past. *Blood on the Stage*, his four-volume chronicle of "milestone plays of crime, mystery and detection," is the result of his explorations.

Spanning the years 1900 to 2000, Kabatchnik's books comprise a vast and detailed resource for devotees of theatrical mayhem. 458 plays are covered in over 2,500 pages. The great, the near-great and the now-obscure are all included. Classics like Eugene O'Neill's *Desire Under the Elms* (1924) and Sam Shepard's *Buried Child* (1978) rub elbows with once popular plays like Owen Davis's *Nellie, The Beautiful Cloak Model* (1906) and Elsa Shelley's *Pick-Up Girl* (1944).

Kabatchnik's focus is purposely broad. The reader is reminded that crime and punishment have long been a source of drama and have served the differing talents and ambitions of dramatists from ancient Greece to the present day.

Each play included in *Blood on the Stage* receives the same basic coverage. A synopsis of the plot (with spoilers) is followed by production details, critical response, a biography of the author(s) and, where appropriate, mention of any screen versions, revivals, and/or awards. Ample footnotes contain a wealth of information. For instance, the notes for Levinson and Link's *Prescription: Murder* (1962), in which a certain Lieutenant Columbo made his theatrical debut, features a succinct history of the inverted mystery in print and on stage.

Volume One of *Blood on the Stage* covers the years 1900-1925. Kabatchnik considers this epoch — with its plays full of "sheer adventure, excitement, and heart-pounding thrills" — the genre's "golden age." Such plays as Baroness Orczy and Montagu Barstow's *The Scarlet Pimpernel* (1903) and John Willard's *The Cat and the Canary* (1922) bear this conclusion out. But, Kabatchnik notes, the mystery play showed increasing depth and sophistication in works like Elmer Rice's dark, expressionistic *The Adding Machine* (1923) and Frederick Lonsdale's *The Last of Mrs. Cheyney* (1925), a charming comedy-of-manners about a lady burglar and her excursion into high society.

A series of appendices provide information on sub-genres: Twentieth-century courtroom dramas, Twentieth century Death Row plays, the phenomenon of Grand Guignol, and plays that feature deadly poisons.

Volume Two, 1925-1950 details the fading away of melodrama, an increasing number of mainstream playwrights and novelists working in the genre, and the initial appearances of some of the Golden Age greats. *Black Coffee*, Agatha Christie's first original work for the stage, premiered in London in 1930. This play launched a career as a dramatist that lasted until the final years of Dame Agatha's life. The prolific and popular Edgar Wallace penned a string of hits that include *The Flying Squad* 1928) and *On the Spot* (1930), which featured Charles Laughton as a Capone-like gangster. J.B. Priestley's *Dangerous Corner* (1932) used time in an innovative fashion. Daphne Du Maurier's adaptation of her novel *Rebecca* (1940) found greater success in London than it did in New York.

Golden age characters also made the leap from page to stage. Walter Butterfield and Lee Morrison brought Philo Vance to life in their version of S.S. Van Dine's *The Canary Murder Case* (1928). Mr. and Mrs. North, The Lockridges' amateur sleuths, came to Broadway in the aptly titled *Mrs. And Mrs. North* (1941); veteran playwright Owen Davis (author of the aforementioned *Nellie, The Beautiful Cloak Model*) was the author. Charlie Chan, Ellery Queen and Flashgun Casey trod the boards in *The Keeper of the Keys* (1933), *The Four of Hearts Mystery* (1949) and *Crime Photographer* (1950), respectively, though the original authors had nothing to do with the adaptations.

One hundred seventy-one plays are described and discussed in Volume Two. This is the Golden Age of the mystery play, if one judges by quantity alone. Quality (as evidenced by plays like *Dead End*, *The Little Foxes*, and *Night Must Fall*) isn't lacking, either. Volume Two repeats the appendices of Volume One and adds two more: plays about children in peril, and plays about Lizzie Borden.

Volume Three, 1950-1975 starts with *Guys and Dolls* (1950) and closes with Graham Greene's *The Return of A.J. Raffles* (1975). In between are some of the works that constitutes the gold standard of the mystery play. Frederick Knott's trifecta of *Dial "M" For Murder* (1952), *Write Me a Murder* (1961) and *Wait Until Dark* (1966), Agatha Christie's *Witness For the Prosecution* (1954) and Anthony Shaffer's *Sleuth* (1970) were all produced in this period.

A few less-than-classic curiosities came down the pike, too. The musical comedy *Dracula, Baby* (1970) had the cast of Bram Stoker's novel "singing and dancing in the plains of Transylvania, the pubs of London, and the catacombs of Carfax." The lyrics for *Dracula, Baby* were written by John Jakes, whose historical novels would soon sell millions of copies around the world. Kabatchnik's typically entertaining and comprehensive footnotes inform us that *Baby* is only one of almost a dozen musical versions of *Dracula*. Perhaps the most unusual musical mentioned is *Dragula*, which features a cross-dressing vampire.

Volume Four, 1975-2000 contains huge successes — Kander and Ebb's *Chicago* (1975) and Ira Levin's *Death Trap* (1978) — and embarrassing failures like Sidney Michael's *Tricks of the Trade* (1980) and Arthur Bicknell's *Moose Murders* (1983), both of which closed after a single performance.

Death Trap is the last big thriller to grace the Broadway stage. It marks the end of one age and the beginning of another: the shift to the regionals as the primary home and continuing source of new mystery plays. Los Angeles, Cleveland, Chicago, San Francisco, Denver, Tucson — these and other cities contributed productions to Volume Four.

The era encompasses shattering docudramas like Emily Mann's *Execution of Justice* (1984) and Moises Kaufman/Tectonic Theater's *The Laramie Project* (2000); hard-hitting straight plays like David Rabe's *Streamers* (1976), Charles Fuller's *A Soldier's Play* (1981) and Ariel Dorfman's *Death and the Maiden* (1991); comedies as different as Jerome Chodorov and Norman Panama's *A Talent for Murder* (1981) and Charles Ludlam's *The Mystery of Irma Vep* (1984); adaptations such as Stuart Gordon and Carolyn Purdy-Gordon's *The Little Sister* (1978), Giles Havergal's *Travels with My Aunt* (1989) and David Barr's *A Red Death* (1997); and a seemingly endless stream of Sherlock Holmes plays. Holmes's popularity as a character is a constant throughout all four volumes; his only competition is a certain Transylvanian count.

A new category is added in Volume Four's appendices: "Notable One-Acts of Mayhem, Mischief, and Murder."

One of Kabatchnik's goals in compiling *Blood on the Stage* was to "kindle interest in neglected plays and forgotten works." He succeeds mightily. His monumental work of love and scholarship gives us a new window onto the past, and proves that the mystery play is a rich, lively and still-vital form.

If assembling the four volumes of *Blood* wasn't sufficiently daunting, Kabatchnik also authored *Sherlock Holmes on the Stage*, subtitled "A Chronological Encyclopedia of Plays Featuring the Great Detective." Its scope is necessarily smaller, but it shares *Blood's* structure, thoroughness and erudition. It proves that, for a certain breed of playwright and theatergoer, there are no plays like Holmes.

All five books were published by Scarecrow Press between 2008 and 2012, and are the product of Kabatchnik's long-standing enthusiasm for the theatre and for the mystery genre. Born in Tel Aviv in 1929, Kabatchnik learned English from

American movies and from novels by the likes of Ellery Queen, Agatha Christie and Earl Derr Biggers. His years as a collector of mysteries began early. "I still remember vividly the cover of Biggers's *The Black Camel*," he says, and notes that "whenever I move to a new dwelling my first and upmost consideration is the wall space for bookcases."

An uncle in Lowell, Massachusetts invited the young Kabatchnik to come to America to pursue an education. He studied Journalism and Theater at Boston University, essaying the role of Hamlet at one point. After receiving his MFA in Directing from the Yale School of Drama, he moved to New York City and served as an assistant director for Sir Tyrone Guthrie and Tony Richardson. Kabatchnik worked Off-Broadway, in summer stock and university theatres, in Canada and back home in Tel Aviv for the Habima National Theatre. Though he staged plays by Chekhov, Shaw, Pirandello, Williams and Chayefsky, when the opportunity arose he'd choose a genre piece like *Arsenic and Old Lace* or *Gaslight*. Kabatchnik has had a lengthy parallel career as an academic. He's taught at SUNY Binghamton, Stanford University, Ohio State University, Florida State University, and Elmira College.

In the late 1960s Kabatchnik's interest in mystery book collecting led him to Marvin and Carol Lachman's apartment in the Bronx, a gathering place for mystery buffs. Fellow attendees at Lachman's parties included, at one time or another, Francis M. Nevins, Otto Penzler, Allen J. Hubin, and the late Chris Steinbrunner — all well-known names . . . or soon to be. (Lachman writes about this time in his book *The Heirs of Anthony Boucher: A History of Mystery Fandom*.) These enthusiasts encouraged Kabatchnik to "not only read and collect detective literature but also study its sources, history, and trends." This ultimately led to his magnum opus, *Blood on the Stage*.

"The project started as a checklist of milestone plays in the genre," Kabatchnik says, "and gradually developed into a full-scale endeavor." He searched libraries and used bookstores across the country for manuscripts, out-of-print plays, and old newspaper and magazine articles. Along the way a few surprises were encountered. The New York Public Library for the Performing Arts at Lincoln Center yielded the stage version of Gaston Leroux's *The Mystery of the Yellow Room*. At the Center for Motion Picture Study in Los Angeles, Kabatchnik unearthed *Everybody Comes to Rick's*, an obscure play by Murray Burnett and Joan Alison that served as the basis for the movie *Casablanca*. Kabatchnik also found a number of "obscure, pirated dramatizations of Arthur Conan Doyle's *The Sign of Four*, written and produced in America at the turn of the 20th century."

Kabatchnik has directed mystery plays from every period, but he particularly favors the "wild, unblushing, sensational melodramas" of the early decades of the last century. He relishes "the dark passages, secret panels and shadowy corridors" of a play like Willard's *The Cat and the Canary*. He's helmed *Canary* several times over the years, once with Abe Vigoda in the cast.

Whatever the era, the mystery play offers — in Kabatchnik's words — "strong plots; driving, relentless forward movement; issues of life and death; and nerve-wracking, heart-pumping climaxes." Such qualities will always find an audience, and Kabatchnik has no doubt that "a revitalization of the genre is waiting around the corner."

Stephen Sondheim: A WAY THROUGH THE MAZE

Stephen Sondheim is not only a much-lauded composer and lyricist, he is also a deviser of crossword puzzles and a long-time connoisseur and player of innumerable games ranging from acrostics, anagrams and charades to full scale citywide treasure hunts. It should come as no surprise that Sondheim is a mystery fan with a particular interest in the cleverly clued, fiendishly complicated classics of the Golden Age.

A small but distinguished part of his *oeuvre* fits neatly into the mystery genre: the operatic penny-dreadful *Sweeney Todd*; the comedy thriller *Getting Away With Murder*, co-written with George Furth; and the Edgar Award-winning film *The Last of Sheila*, co-written with actor Anthony Perkins. Other Sondheim works that might appeal to the discerning mystery fan are *Assassins*, with its probing look into the minds of a gallery of killers and would-be killers of United States Presidents; and *Road Show*, which tells the story of Addison and Wilson Mizner, brothers and hucksters extraordinaire in the first half of the 20th century. Sondheim wrote five songs for Warren Beatty's film version of *Dick Tracy*, one of which won a Best Song Oscar. He is also reputed to be the model for Andrew Wyke, the games-obsessed mystery writer in *Sleuth*, written by his friend and fellow games-player Anthony Shaffer. All in all, the mystery and Stephen Sondheim are old acquaintances.

Born in 1930, Sondheim had a privileged but emotionally chaotic childhood on Manhattan's Upper West Side. His father Herbert was a manufacturer of high-quality clothing; his mother Janet — known as "Foxy" — designed for the company. It was neither an easy nor a successful marriage.

When Herbert left the high-strung and emotionally demanding Foxy for another woman, the Sondheims' personal and business partnership came to an end.

According to Meryle Secrest — whose biography is the source for much of what follows — Sondheim's fascination with games and puzzles stems from this time. They offered "a reassurance he desperately needed that there really was a way through the maze, that magical secrets waited to be revealed, that a world in fragments could be reassembled, however painfully, and that a key existed to every riddle if he searched diligently enough."

Life had no dependable form or structure. But Sondheim, like so many other children affected by domestic conflict, found something that did: Art. "To me," Sondheim said to Anthony Shaffer years later, "the connection between puzzles and detective stories is all about order and solution. The nice thing about them is that there's a solution and all's right with the world — as opposed to life."

John Dickson Carr's *The Nine Wrong Answers* was an early favorite, and Carr and his contemporaries strongly influenced Sondheim's own mystery work.

This is most apparent in *The Last of Sheila* (1973). Choreographer-turned-director Herbert Ross kept asking Sondheim to write a murder mystery. Sondheim kept refusing. But Ross was persistent, and finally Sondheim gave in: "I outlined a plot about a group of people in a small Long Island community when they're all snowed in." He then asked his friend and fellow mystery fan Anthony Perkins to collaborate with him on the project. Perkins, who has a special place in the hearts of mystery lovers everywhere thanks to his appearances in *Psycho* and *Pretty Poison*, was looking for other career options, and readily agreed. They presented a treatment to Ross, who made a crucial — and welcome — suggestion. Sondheim quotes Ross as saying: "It's terrific, but I don't know why you're putting it in some dreary place like Long Island in the winter. Why don't we set it on a yacht in France and we can all have a wonderful time?"

They did, and they did. The result is a classic closed circle mystery set among the Hollywood elite. One night in Bel Air, producer Clinton Green's wife Sheila is killed by a hit-and-run-driver. A year later, Green invites the guests from the party to join him on his luxury yacht for a week-long cruise in (where else?) the south of France. Like his creators, Green is devoted to games, and he has quite a few of them up the sleeve of his French sailor's jersey. Everyone has to play, too — no exceptions. Not even when the games turn deadly.

Sheila's tone is bitchy, campy; the film's characters embody the film colony's pretensions and egocentricity. But the form is pure Christie. After Green himself is killed, the suspects are gathered together, the clues are assessed, deductions are made, and the truth is revealed. Or is it? Sondheim and Perkins lead us on a merry and complicated chase. Richard Benjamin as a screenwriter and James Mason as a director are particular standouts, and James Coburn's satyr's grin is used to great effect as the producer bent on revenge. Joan Hackett, Raquel Welch, Dyan Cannon and a very young Ian McShane round out the cast.

Sondheim and Perkins's script received the 1974 Edgar Award for Best Motion Picture. The competition was stiff; *Don't Look Now, Serpico* and *The Sting* were also nominated. While not a popular success, the film has developed a cult following over the years.

Sondheim and Perkins next collaborated on *The Chorus Girl Murder Case*. The film was never made, but the 53-page treatment, written in 1974, can be found at the New York Public Library for the Performing Arts at Lincoln Center.

Set in 1943, the treatment combines a backstage musical drama with a spy thriller. It's opening night for the celebrity-studded *Four Stars for Victory*, featuring the American comic Monty Morgan, Russian ballerina Natasha Volinskova, French dancer-magician Darius and English music hall performer Bessie West. A patriotic evening of comedy, song and dance turns to chaos when members of the cast and high-ranking military officers in the audience start dying during the show. Sure enough, there's a Nazi spy behind it all. Hard-working police detective Nate Petersen is determined to find out who that spy is. As you might expect, all is resolved before the show's triumphant conclusion and final curtain.

Sondheim and Perkins's treatment is great fun. Their love of old movies is palpable, their playful subversion of crime film conventions genuinely amusing. If it had made it to the screen, *The Chorus Girl Murder Case* would likely have been an entertaining addition to the spate of period films that grew out of the nostalgia boom of the early 1970s that includes films like *Paper Moon, Movie Movie* and *The Cheap Detective.*

Sondheim's work as a composer and lyricist brought new intellectual and emotional depth to the American musical. His choice of subject matter has been similarly bold, ranging from the bittersweet ironies of love in 19th century Sweden (*A Little Night Music*) to the origins of Western incursion into Japan (*Pacific Overtures*). With *Sweeney Todd* (1979), he brought blood, gore and a very unusual kind of meat pie into the mainstream.

Sweeney Todd, the demon barber of Fleet Street, made his debut in Thomas Prest's newspaper serial *The String of Pearls: A Romance* in 1846-47. Todd has proven to be an enduring character, and numerous versions of his story have appeared in print and on stage and screen.

In 1973, Sondheim saw English playwright Christopher Bond's take on Sweeney Todd during a stay in London. This version, Bond said, "crossed Dumas's *The Count of Monte Cristo* with Tourneur's *The Revenger's Tragedy*" for an evening of crimson mayhem and black comedy. Sondheim procured the rights and asked Hugh Wheeler to help him adapt Bond's play. It was a canny choice. Wheeler (1912-1987) was a playwright known in mystery circles as one of the writers behind the Q. Patrick/Patrick Quentin pseudonyms. Sondheim, Wheeler and director Hal Prince reimagined *Todd* as a work of operatic size and force.

Sweeney Todd returns to London many years after a corrupt judge sent him to Australia and pursued Todd's young and naïve wife. Mrs. Lovett, baker of "the worst pies in London," tells Todd that his wife killed herself and that his daughter, now a young woman, is in the care of the evil judge. Todd seeks revenge, but when he loses his chance to slit the judge's throat, his madness blooms. Bodies pile up — and are turned into meat pies by the ever-ingenious Mrs. Lovett, who finds herself with a thriving business.

Like its protagonist, the musical possesses a ghoulish wit and a grieving heart. The murderous barber's journey approaches something akin to tragedy. He loses the woman he loves not once, but twice. "To seek revenge may lead to hell," says one of the lyrics, and before Sweeney is destroyed he feels the flames.

Sweeney Todd was a major hit, running at the Uris Theatre for 557 performances. It's had two major revivals on Broadway and has been performed in theatres and opera houses around the world. Tim Burton's film adaptation featuring Johnny Depp hit the big screen in 2007.

In striking contrast to the dark and dangerous beauty of *Sweeney*, Sondheim's next major foray into the genre was the comedy thriller *Getting Away With Murder* (1996). Seven analysands gather on a dark and stormy evening for a group therapy session in a soon-to-be-demolished building on the Upper West Side. Two differences mark this meeting: there's a new member in the group, and the doctor is late. Before too much time passes, they discover the doctor is in his office—dead. After determining that one of the seven has to be the killer, the group goes through its alibis, sifting truth from lies, until the murderer is discovered. He — or is it she? — offers the others a plan that might let them all walk away scot-free.

Originally titled *The Doctor Is Out*, the play debuted at San Diego's Old Globe Theater in 1995. A revised version with the present title opened on Broadway in 1996 and featured New York theatrical stalwarts John Rubenstein, Josh Mostel and Christine Ebersole. Its 17-performance run reflects the mostly negative reviews the play received. It deserved better. *Murder* is an ingenious, neatly plotted piece of work. Its characters are sharply drawn New York types — the unscrupulous real estate speculator, the suave political manipulator, the politically correct academic, the sex-starved airhead, the angry ex-cop, the canny Russian émigré, the fashionable woman of a certain age.

Publicity for *Getting Away With Murder* included a conversation between Sondheim and the playwright Anthony Shaffer that was published in *The New York Times*.

Their discussion of the ways and means of the mystery play includes this behind-the-scenes gem. Sondheim asks:

Did I ever tell you about the time I met Sir Laurence Olivier? I was at a play in London, and during the interval [the British director] John Dexter said, "I have somebody here who'd like to meet you." And he dragged over Sir Laurence — this was right after *Sleuth* had finished filming. I blushed appropriately as Olivier said, "Oh, Mr. Sondheim, I'm so delighted to meet you. I've been playing you." Of course I thought he meant records of my musicals. So I said, "Which show?" And he replied, "No, I've been playing you in the movie." Because he had heard that you had based the character on me.

Shaffer neither confirms nor denies this, but merely says: "I'm sure you'll admit that the *Sleuth* character's obsession with games-playing accurately describes a certain aspect of your personality, Steve."

Will that aspect of Sondheim's personality make another appearance on stage or screen? Is there another Sondheim mystery in the works? Sadly, the answer appears to be no. In a note to the author of this article, Sondheim stated: "I no longer have the interest in the mystery field that I used to have." This is a shame, as the genre is always in need of a sharp mind with a penchant for devious complexity and a killer wit.

Foyle's War: TELEVISION'S FINEST HOUR

Detective Chief Superintendent Christopher Foyle is, in every sense of the word, an arresting figure.

Created by novelist, screenwriter, and dramatist Anthony Horowitz and brought to life by actor Michael Kitchen, DCS Foyle represents the most felicitous melding of actor, writer and character since Richard Levinson and William Link met Peter Falk.

Between 2002 and 2015, 28 hour-and-a-half episodes of *Foyle's War* were produced by England's ITV network and, in later years, by the American media group Acorn. Foyle's investigations during and after the Second World War provided riveting mystery fare and trenchant English social history for audiences on both sides of the Atlantic. The feature-length format and high-quality production values of the series allow us to inhabit Foyle's world and follow him through the rigors of a nation under siege.

It all began, as Horowitz pointed out in a 2002 interview, with an impending absence. *Inspector Morse,* the enormously popular ITV series featuring the late John Thaw, was coming to an end. ITV was looking for a new detective series to fill the gap. Several hundred ideas were submitted but only a handful made the grade, and one of them was Horowitz's.

The Blitz Detective was Horowitz's working title for the series, which would take place in London during the Second World War. But he soon realized that both title and location would have to change; turning 21st century London into its wartime self was far too expensive an endeavor. And, as Horowitz wryly observed in an e-mail to this author, "the series would last longer than the Blitz itself." Rechristened *Foyle's War* and relocated to Hastings on the South Coast of England, the show went into production.

Even with the changes, production designers had to work overtime to disguise street signs, hide satellite dishes, digitally remove modern road markings and other reminders of the modern world. Marvels were performed without a great deal of money. The ingenuity and effort paid off. One of the series' strengths is the accuracy of the wartime setting. The period details are flawless, from suspenders to Spitfires, from fire trucks to reading matter (in one episode, Foyle's son Andrew is perusing a paperbound edition of Graham Greene's *Brighton Rock*). The sense of the past is palpable.

The crimes that Foyle must solve are war-related. Foyle goes up against dealers in Black Market goods, saboteurs homegrown and foreign, British and American war profiteers, anti-Semites, Fascists, xenophobes and opportunists of every stripe. The series clearly illustrates the way war disrupts lives, heightens feelings, and brings out the best and the worst in people. "What sort of world is this, Mr. Foyle?" asks a young man whose Italian-born father has been killed in a fire set by an angry mob. It's a world of extremes. Prejudice and violence flare like incendiary devices, but extraordinary acts of bravery and kindness are also possible. Danger lurks just across the Channel . . . and in the heart of your next-door neighbor. Altruism and sacrifice vie with expediency and greed for the upper hand on the home front. DCS Foyle is there to see that law is maintained in an increasingly lawless and brutal world — a world in which, Horowitz notes, "murder had actually become devalued."

He's a marvelous creation, Mr. Foyle, though the material he's made of is familiar. Foyle's keen intelligence and taciturn nature are qualities he shares with many other detectives. His devotion to fly-fishing is straight out of Josephine Tey's Inspector Grant. Like Columbo, he's a David who fights the upper-class Goliaths who populate the governmental and business worlds. I also detect a bit of Georges Simenon's Maigret in Foyle's ability to simply watch and wait and listen. What distinguishes him from his fictional peers is the strength of Horowitz's writing and the depth of Michael Kitchen's performance. "He made the show," Horowitz writes. "He was always my first choice for the role."

Foyle is the role of Kitchen's life. Kitchen is a quiet, meticulous craftsman who's been active in film, television and stage since the late 1960s. Prior to *Foyle*, he was best known for his appearances in *Out of Africa* (1985) and several of the James Bond movies featuring Pierce Brosnan. He's performed with everyone from John Gielgud to Roger Daltrey. Horowitz once said that Kitchen is the only actor he's ever worked with who asks for *fewer* lines. Kitchen has a gift for silence, effortlessly conveying the act of thinking and evaluating. It keeps criminals — and viewers — guessing what his next move will be.

There's an additional reason for Foyle's reticence. T. S. Eliot wrote: "Poetry is not a turning loose of emotion, but an escape from emotion; it is not the expression of personality, but an escape from personality. But, of course, only those who have personality and emotions know what it means to want to escape from these things." Substitute "police work" for "poetry," and you've got DCS Foyle. He keeps a great deal hidden, and one senses his struggle to keep all that he feels in check. Whether it's questioning a killer or almost — but not quite — embracing his son who's heading off to be a pilot in the RAF, Kitchen skillfully reveals the wealth of emotion that reserve conceals.

One of the emotions Foyle hides is grief. Foyle is a widower; his wife died in 1932, and he regularly visits her grave. One feels that if his sorrow were unleashed, it would flood the world.

Yet another factor lends gravity to Kitchen's portrayal: Moral force. Like a Hemingway character, Foyle lives by a code. "I'm a policeman," he says near the end of the first episode. "I'm here to do a job — simple as that. If I start bending the rules, I might as well pack it in. . . . Murder is murder. You stop believing that and we might as well not be fighting a war — because you end up like the Nazis."

Foyle was speaking to Samantha ("Sam") Stewart, his driver. Sam is young, enthusiastic, idealistic, the product of a family rife with vicars. Due to the shortage of able-bodied men, she was transferred from the Mechanized Transport Corps to serve as Foyle's driver. Played by the pert Honeysuckle Weeks, Sam quickly became an audience favorite. In 2008 Horowitz told the *Daily Mail*:

> Honeysuckle was utterly perfect for the part, and I knew it the moment I met her. She's a 1940s woman in a 21st-century world. She has that extraordinary clipped, slightly eccentric quality, not to mention the bearing that takes you straight back to the war. She's also terribly nice. These are dark, sometimes depressing stories. What we needed was someone with a relentlessly positive quality, an optimistic outlook. And that's exactly what Honeysuckle supplied.

Sam's relationship with Foyle is spiky at first. She's not content to merely chauffeur Foyle from one crime scene to another. She asks questions. She wants to be a part of the goings-on. Foyle simply wants her to be quiet — until she coshes an escaping criminal with a trash can lid, and he realizes that Sam is no ordinary driver. The trust and affection that develop between the older detective and the younger woman is one of the pleasures of the series. We watch Sam grow into a resourceful, highly competent part of the team.

Sam and Sergeant Paul Milner are Foyle's closest colleagues on the Hastings police force. Milner (played by tall, wide-eyed Anthony Howell) lost part of his left leg during the Battle of Trondheim. Recuperating in Hastings, he's listless and despondent. Foyle coaxes the young man out his depression and back into harness. Like Sam, he and Foyle take some time to adjust to each other. In "The White Feather," Milner — feeling useless and plagued by a failing marriage — flirts briefly with British Fascism. Guy Spencer (a reptilian Charles Dance) finds a potential convert to his pro-Nazi organization in the confused and worried Sergeant. Milner inadvertently blurs the line between the personal and the professional by sharing information about Foyle with Spencer. Foyle feels betrayed and calls Milner onto the carpet. A chastened Milner redoubles his efforts to live up to Foyle's expectations.

Milner's brush with Fascism is only one instance of how the series weaves individual stories into the larger historical narrative. We come to know and love Foyle and his cohorts. We delight in their idiosyncrasies and share in their troubles. Sam's lodgings are destroyed by a German bomb; with no place else to stay, she discreetly camps out in one of the jail cells. Foyle discovers this and offers her temporary lodging under his own roof. Milner's wife Jane is frightened and disgusted by his amputated leg and deserts him. In her absence, Milner begins seeing Edith Ashford, the sister of an old school friend. Their romance is heating up when Milner's wife unexpectedly returns after a two-and-a-half year absence. She wants Milner to take her back. He's understandably reluctant. When Jane's dead body is found in a secluded byway, Milner is the main suspect. Foyle is forced to investigate his right-hand man.

As the end of the war approaches, change is in the air. Foyle and his colleagues stand on the verge of a new landscape: the post-war world, with its atom bombs and a new enemy — the Soviet Union. Foyle reluctantly joins MI5, British Military Intelligence, and changes his center of operations from Hastings to London. The greens and blues of the South Coast give way to the greys and blacks of an exhausted, smoke-stained city. The clear-cut moral values of the war are replaced with the shifting allegiances of the Cold War. Foyle's new job brings him into contact with Russian defectors, American and Arabian oil barons, spies foreign and domestic, and NKVD assassins.

Sam Stewart also makes the transition to London. Married to a young Labour Party politician, she works for Foyle at MI5. The demands of her job are often a source of conflict with her husband Adam. Sam's troubles reflect the situation of many women at the time, who found it difficult to return to the drudgery of nappies and food queues after the danger and excitement of the war years.

ITV canceled *Foyle's War* in 2007. "We missed out a whole year of the war (1944) when ITV decided to axe us," Horowitz writes, "and it's a shame because of course there were all sorts of stories I could have told." Public demand brought the series back. When the time came to bring Foyle's adventures to an end, the decision was made by its creators.

In January 2015, in an article for England's *Radio Times*, Horowitz wrote:

> Every year when we think about a new series of *Foyle's War*, I meet with Michael Kitchen and producer Jill Green. We always ask the same question. Are there any more stories to tell? Together, we've travelled

from the start of the war and the disaster of Norway to Dunkirk, the Blitz, Pearl Harbor, Dresden, the D-Day landings, VE day, VJ day — and then into the Cold War with Soviet spies, traitors, war criminals and the atomic bomb.

Were there more stories to tell? Horowitz and company decided there were not, and the 28th episode was the last.

It might not be the end of Foyle, however.

At the end of the fifth episode, "Fifty Ships," industrialist Howard Paige gets away with murder because he plays a crucial role in winning American support for the British war effort. Foyle vows that justice will ultimately be served. At the beginning of episode 23, "The Eternity Ring," Foyle returns from America where, we learn, Paige has committed suicide. The full story of Foyle's sojourn in the States tantalizes. How this viewer would have loved to see the good inspector in post-war Manhattan, with its neon-lit luxuries, its surging crowds and looming skyscrapers. Horowitz would have liked it, too — but once again, money was the problem. "As to Foyle in America, it was simply too expensive to shoot the episode when he brought down Howard Paige," Horowitz says. "I might one day write it as a novel."

Foyle's return in the pages of a book is a prospect to relish. But whether or not that novel is ever written, the 28 episodes remain. Stunningly designed and photographed, incisively written and performed, *Foyle's War* is a jewel of a series that bears repeated viewings, a feast for mystery lovers with a taste for historical detection. Horowitz, Kitchen, Weeks *et alia* are to be complimented for their sterling achievement. After a dozen years, Foyle and company seem like old friends. And why shouldn't they? We've gone through a war together.

Pushing the "Panic" Button, Or:
HOW PLAYS GET WRITTEN

In 2011, Wisconsin's Peninsula Players — the oldest resident summer theater in the country — produced my play Panic. *Would I come see the show? And could I be persuaded to give a talk about the play? The answer to both questions was: "Yes."*

On occasion a playwright will be brought in to see a production and then asked to talk about it. This is a wonderful state of affairs. Most playwrights love to travel, and I haven't yet met a playwright who doesn't love to talk. It's wonderful in another, more important way, too: a play only lives when it's performed, and such an opportunity gives the writer a chance to see the play in question brought to life.

But where did that life begin? Where does a play come from? What triggers the process that culminates in a hundred or so pages of dialogue and action?

The answer is as varied as there are playwrights to answer it. Sometimes it starts with an image. Sometimes it starts with a title. Sometimes it starts with the simple desire to write a play. All of those things have prompted me to put words on a page.

I've rarely done research for a play; a play tends to grow out of an existing interest, an obsession that I've had for years — sometimes for many, many years. That's certainly the case with *Panic*.

Alfred Hitchcock has been an abiding passion of mine for four decades and counting. I have vague memories of seeing *Notorious* and *Vertigo* on late night television, and images from these early viewings — I'd have been about ten years old at the time — remain with me to this day. In the years that followed I've seen the films again and again, but these vestigial, almost pre-conscious viewings still haunt me. They demonstrate the power and beauty and strangeness of Hitchcock's work. It *is* strange, you know, all these deadly, gorgeous films, imbued with fear and guilt, these bad dreams made real.

Hitchcock shared his nightmares with us, and made them ours. He's shaped the way I experience things. This is a sign of how deeply his work has made its way into the culture. I can't take a shower without thinking of a certain scene from a certain film of his . . . birds on playground swing sets make me very, very nervous . . . the Statue of Liberty reminds me of other things than immigration . . . and I never talk to strangers on trains.

I exaggerate a trifle, but I hope I've made my point.

Around the time I first saw Hitchcock's films, I started reading mysteries.

Apart from the thrills and chills they provided, I liked mysteries because they reflected the world I knew. The adult realm is mysterious to children; my family had its share of secrets that no one wanted to talk about, and dark places no one wanted to visit. Everyone was guilty of something: the church taught me that. I was brought up as a devout Lutheran with a ridiculously over-developed sense of right and wrong, of good and evil. I have a very strong idea of how Hitchcock, with his Catholic upbringing, must have felt. When one is raised to be "a good boy" (as both Hitchcock and I were), one is awfully tempted to find out what the bad boys and the bad girls are up to. Hitchcock's attraction to and fear of violence and sex, the illicit and the covert, made perfect sense to me.

As I got older, I realized something that many other people — from New York City to Paris, where the young François Truffaut first saw the films after the Liberation, to London and divers points all over the world — had already figured out: Hitchcock is one of the seminal figures of the 20th century, on a par with Stravinsky and Picasso, a man who so imprinted his vision of the world on our own that his name has become an adjective: Hitchockian.

David Ansen wrote in *Newsweek* at the time of Hitchcock's death:

> For years, Hitchcock was unanimously hailed as a master manipulator, a prankster-craftsman whose sole purpose was to capture his audience in his elegant traps [. . .] But there have proven to be as many ways of looking at Hitchcock films as there are Hitchcock films to look at. Where one critic salutes *North By Northwest* as "a prime example of contentless virtuosity," another produces a 100-page analysis of its intricate Oedipal content. To his detractors he was a soulless, sadistic technician; to his admirers everything from a profound moralist to a Catholic metaphysician.

Regardless of how one views him, Hitchcock's continued presence on the cinematic scene is undeniable. To this day if someone says, "it was like something out of a Hitchcock film" we know what that person means. "It was like a Hitchcock film" immediately communicates the feeling of a situation. Even today, when the cultural scene is so fragmented and disparate.

I watched these films when I could, I read about them, I bought whatever books were available. There weren't many: Robin Wood's critical exegesis — how's that for a ten dollar word, as Emma Lockwood says in the play; a book called *Focus on Hitchcock*, a collection of rather academic essays on various aspects of the oeuvre; a couple of heavily illustrated books for the general reader and film fan, and, of course, *Hitchcock/Truffaut*, the transcripts of lengthy interviews with Hitchcock conducted by his adept and colleague François Truffaut. And then, just before or just after Hitchcock's death in 1980, two biographies appeared: John Russell Taylor's *Hitch* and Donald Spoto's *The Dark Side of Genius*.

I read Taylor's book when it came out, and haven't looked at it since. As I recall, it's a standard biography; it gives you the facts, a few considered opinions, a couple of caveats and there you have it. Spoto's book, on the other hand, is something else. It's only a small exaggeration to say that it did for Hitchcock what Rufus Griswold did for Edgar Allan Poe: it thoroughly blackened his image by creating a pernicious portrait of the artist.

Spoto's Hitchcock is a tortured, deeply perverse, misogynistic voyeur who is the living embodiment of all that is nasty, sordid and disgusting in his films. Spoto's version has since been modified (and, I hope replaced) by Patrick McGilligan's *Alfred Hitchcock: A Life in Darkness and Light*. McGilligan's book is a marvel, and I highly recommend it to anyone interested in Hitchcock. I read it in great gulps. McGilligan benefited from new research and offered the reader a far more balanced and just appraisal of Hitchcock's work and character . . . a character with which I've long been fascinated.

One day in early 2004, I was on the phone with Nick Faust, a director with whom I've worked many times over the years. Nick is an enormously talented director and a film buff beyond compare. If it's been made, he's seen it — and he'll tell you why you should see it (or why you shouldn't) and, for no extra charge, place it in the context of the director's work with a shot-by-shot critique. We were talking that day about McGilligan's book. I was about halfway through it by then, and sharing my impressions of it.

And that's when it hit me.

An idea.

An idea — a glimmer, really — that there was a play about Hitchcock and Truffaut.

This idea became, eventually, *Panic*.

Certain elements of the play were drawn from what I knew of Hitchcock's life. The initial flash of idea was exciting; playwrights love initial flashes. But what to do with it? How to develop it? Utilize it? What to do with this inkling, this flash, this tantalizing glimpse of an idea?

What to do with the idea was answered very quickly, and relates to an episode that occurred in 1964 during the making of *Marnie* and involved Hitchcock and actress Tippi Hedren. Each of Hitchcock's biographers tells the story differently, but the gist of the story is that Hitchcock tried to force his attentions on Hedren. Rebuffed, the vengeful director made the rest of filming as difficult as possible for the confused and upset young woman.

Did Hitch try to kiss Hedren? Did he proposition her? Did he attack her? No one can definitively say what exactly happened between the two. [Hedren published a memoir in 2016 in which she claimed Hitchcock sexually assaulted her. Her claims have been disputed.] I have no brief to turn Hitchcock into a saint, or Hedren into a liar. What I find intriguing about this event — whatever it was — is how it raises questions: What is truth? How is it determined? Who do we believe, and why? This is rich dramatic material.

I drew upon other aspects of Hitchcock's life, as well, primarily on the working relationship with his wife Alma. The Hitchcocks started off as friends, fellow workers on a film. Alma quickly became Alfred's right-hand woman and co-wrote a number of his movies. To the end of Hitchcock's life she served as a sounding board and, sometimes, as a censor for his ideas. She must have been extraordinary. If you've seen the 1979 American Film Institute tribute to Hitchcock, you know how much he loved her. What he says about her is tremendously moving. Hitchcock is not well, he has trouble getting up and sitting down; he's an old man. He looks, frankly, miserable; this is not the droll host of *Alfred Hitchcock Presents*. Alma is seated to his right, and is in very poor health herself. She's had at least one stroke by this time, and is even frailer than her husband. But the love you see in her poor, ravaged face as Hitchcock tells the world how grateful he is to her, how much he loves her — though being an Englishman, he doesn't say it directly — the love you see is a testament to the closeness and longevity of their bond. We should all be so lucky.

I also drew upon my sense of Hitchcock as one of Hollywood's insiders, a respected master of his craft and a friend of the famous and wealthy. The play refers to other directors such as Billy Wilder as well as various stars of the screen: Cary Grant, Jimmy Stewart, and Grace Kelly. I hope I've included something of the loyalty Hitchcock's co-workers and colleagues felt for him.

All of these things I used to help delineate the character of the film director, Henry Lockwood, in my play. At the risk of sounding disingenuous, though, I will stress at this point that *Panic* is *not* a biography of Alfred Hitchcock. What it is might be called a dramatic speculation — informed speculation, I hope, but speculation all the same. No one knows the exact nature of the relationship between Hitchcock and his wife. Nor about what actually did or didn't happen between Hitchcock and Tippi Hedren. But I can make certain surmises about these things based on what we know . . . or strongly suspect.

So I had a version, a speculative version of the Hitchcocks.

Who else?

Well . . . Truffaut. François Truffaut, the French critic who did indeed become a filmmaker. Truffaut was insanely ambitious and madly in love with film and would have, I suspect, *considered* killing someone to get a film made. Luckily, his wife just happened to be the daughter of a wealthy film producer, so no blood was shed to get *The Four Hundred Blows* made. I gave this character the name of Alain Duplay. Duplay smacks of *duplicitous*, which pleased me, and is why I settled on that as a name for the character.

Miriam Stockton is not drawn from any particular real-life character. Joan Harrison, a screenwriter and later a producer of Hitchcock's television show, played a somewhat analogous role in Hitchcock's life, but it's not a close match at all. I don't recall why I chose the name Miriam, but Stockton comes from Jo Stockton, the name of Audrey Hepburn's character in *Funny Face*, which is set, as you may recall, in Paris. This is an oblique tribute to that film and the beautiful and charming Miss Hepburn.

Hepburn, by the way, almost made a film with Hitchcock, but backed out due to certain aspects of the script which Hitchcock refused to change. It's a shame the two never worked together. Hitchcock loved stars because they brought with them a depth of association and audience goodwill. His later films are less satisfactory in part because the star system had dimmed, and charm and charisma are far less available to carry the viewer over any holes in the plot.

Later on, I threw in other references: Jimmy and Cary, of course, but also mentioned Whit (that's Whitfield Cook, a friend and a screenwriter who worked on several of Hitchcock's films); Miss Kahn (that's Joan Kahn, a well-known editor of mystery novels who worked for Harper and Row for many years); Eric and Claude (Rohmer and Chabrol, respectively, French film directors who both loved Hitchcock's works); and Patty (as in the gloriously perverse novelist Patricia Highsmith).

All that came later, as I wrote. But what did I begin with? I had a few characters: the Hitchcocks and company, and a setting: Paris. I got to work.

That means I sat in a room, smoked — I was still a smoker, then — and played a one step forward, two steps back kind of game. I knew the elements, knew there was a mystery, but I wasn't sure what the mystery was, exactly. I wrote, I thought, I sketched out possible versions of events. I combined, I discarded, I found a plan of action rising from the chaos. I had to change or cut or add certain things to fit the emerging picture. I don't plot in advance. I'm generally a step or two ahead of myself, but that's about it. One trusts that the jigsaw puzzle one is making will not only have all the pieces, but that all the pieces will fit together. And, though it can be hell sometimes to make it happen, it always does.

When I had the first act done, I sent it to Nick, who thought it was intriguing, but thin; that comment led to what I hope was a 'thickening' of the characters and their responses to the situation they find themselves in. Nick loved the Hollywood shop talk, and urged me to put more of it in; that helped thicken things, and it buttressed the idea that the Lockwoods were Hollywood royalty. He also found Emma Lockwood too much of a grande dame, and reminded me that Alma Hitchcock was a down-to-earth woman and probably more Americanized than her husband. So I worked on Emma Lockwood's language. I cut out a lot of upper-class rhetoric and made her much more direct and plain spoken.

I had some more-or-less specific ideas about the form the play should take. Over the last several years questions of form have intrigued me, and I've consciously been exploring various categories of the well-made play. This is, in brief, a play with a beginning, a middle and end; with a clear dramatic shape: inciting incident, rising action, crisis, resolution, and denouement. It's provided dramatists with a handy form for, oh, several hundred years, I'd guess. And — if you go by certain arbiters of theatrical taste — it's a dead form. Dead as a dodo. Dead as the playwrights who have used it so well over the years. The great plays of the golden age of Broadway are all well-made plays. Today, however, these plays are thought to be mechanical in form and emotionally unrealistic. And some of them are. Some are just pieces of fluff, albeit well-made pieces of fluff, trifles that had their moment in the sun and faded into nothingness when that sun set. Other plays, however, have endured, with good reason.

Have you seen *The Little Foxes* recently? Or *The Man Who Came to Dinner*? Or *Biography*? Or *Dead End*? When these plays work, they offer a theatrical satisfaction that very few modern plays can match, in my opinion. It's the pleasure of craft, of structure, of an artistic alchemy that transforms the raw stuff of life into theatrical activity. We are free to relax and enjoy the evening because we know we're going to hear a well-told story.

I wanted to write the kind of mystery play that had given me so much enjoyment over the years. *Sleuth*, for instance, Anthony Shaffer's brilliant embodiment of and farewell to the traditional mystery play. Agatha Christie's *Witness for the Prosecution*. Frederick Knott's *Dial M for Murder*.

I wanted to create something in the classical vein. I wanted cocktails and dinner jackets and evening gowns. I wanted wit and glamour and banter. I wanted stylish surroundings for sordid secrets. I wanted to excite and delight.

I had come to realize that, among the many things the theatre can do, one of its aims — perhaps its greatest aim — is to entertain. I came to see that there is nothing wrong with entertaining an audience. Now, this may sound like a strange confession from a playwright, but in the context of 20th century drama, entertainment is undervalued and underappreciated these days. Works of art must gouge. They must tear. They must push boundaries of all sorts — esthetic, communal, personal boundaries. I spent any number of years writing plays that did just that. I like those plays, I'm proud of those plays, but they're not the plays I want to see anymore. Or write. The rock critic Greil Marcus described one of the Beatles albums as the moment the Beatles shifted from assault to seduction. I think that's an apt way of describing the change in my work over the last six or seven years. I, too, have shifted my tactics from assault . . . to seduction.

There was something else I wanted quite consciously to address in the writing of the piece, and that's the subject of suspense. Hitchcock was a master of it, after all, and a mystery play should have plenty of it, so I decided that I'd make it an overt part of the play. It's the subject, or one of the subjects, of Duplay's interview with Lockwood. The means by which suspense can be created are openly discussed and then utilized in the course of the play. I'd liken this aspect of the play to one of those buildings that have been constructed with the heat pipes and air conditioning ducts not disguised, not hidden, but left on display as part of the design. It's a modernist idea to show the workings. It's a way of acknowledging the artifice involved in any artistic endeavor, and especially one like the mystery play. That's what I did with *Panic*.

So there I was. Given that subject (Hitchcock, to one degree or another) and that form (the well-made play), I started writing. I wasn't merely going to refer to the mystery form, or draw upon it, I was going to do my best to write an out-and-out, no-holds-barred mystery.

Given my years as a mystery fan, I wonder why it took me so long to put my two great loves, the theatre and the mystery, together. It's a natural combination. Crime and the theatre have always had a mutually beneficial relationship. As an extremity of human behavior, crime is dramatic. We see this in plays that we might not immediately think of as mysteries. *Oedipus Rex*, of course, and *Medea*, which could be viewed as an ancient Cornell Woolrich revenge story: *The Bride Wore Poison*. O'Neill's *Mourning Becomes Electra* is, among other things, a rip-roaring murder melodrama. And Pinter's *The Birthday Party* is a version of *The Killers*: a man with a past tries to hide from it, but can't. Neither of these plays is exactly a mystery, but they demonstrate that both O'Neill and Pinter knew their sensational literature.

There are certainly fewer mystery plays being written these days (or at least being produced) than in the golden age. The situation can be compared to that of the pulp magazine when radio and television essentially took the pulps' audience away by providing short-form mysteries you could listen to or watch. But mystery plays are still being written and produced, though their home is no longer on Broadway. The form thrives in regional and community theatre. Audiences love a good mystery, whether it's one of the seemingly inexhaustible supply of plays about Sherlock Holmes, or a new adaptation of a classic mystery novel, or an original taking place in New York City. In a good mystery play there's always a moment when the entire audience leans forward. They want to know — they *have* to know — what's going to happen next. It's one of the prime experiences an audience can have. And to be the author of that moment is just as thrilling.

That's what I wanted to do: create those thrilling moments.

In July of 2004 I had a draft of the play. I flew to Los Angeles for a two-week work session with Nick Faust. Nick had moved to LA earlier in the year. I'd lived there in the '90s and would have a chance to see some old friends, so Los Angeles was the obvious choice. Very appropriate, too, for a play about a film director.

Nick had scheduled two readings. One took place shortly after my arrival, the next ten days later. This was smart planning. I'd get to hear the play, then work on revisions based on what I heard, then we'd read it again. With any luck the play would find its final shape by the end of my stay.

It seemed to be working. The first reading was private. Nick, a group of actors and I spent a pleasant and productive day in a theatre in Beverly Hills reading and talking. The play held up well. There were some cuts to make, perhaps, and some things to add here and there, but by and large the play was in great shape.

Except for one thing.

The ending.

This is the problem I mentioned a while back, the one sticking point.

The ending. And, more specifically, how to convey the culprit's explanation of the who, what, where, when, how and why of the play. I'll try not to give anything away about the ending for those who haven't seen it, but I was looking for a way to reveal all that much-needed information in a natural — that is, unforced — way. No criminal just stands there and relates his or her crime. There has to be some compelling reason for the villain to do so, otherwise it smacks of contrivance. It becomes nothing more than an ungainly heap of exposition that stops the action in its tracks.

I knew what the problem was, and had wrestled with it through various versions before I arrived in California. I wrestled with it there, too.

None of the versions solved the problem. I knew it as I read each version aloud to Nick. He didn't have to say a word for me to know that I hadn't reached it. It was driving me to distraction. I honestly couldn't see a way out of the quandary I found myself in. The date of the next — and last — reading was quickly approaching. I was a glum and touchy fellow.

One evening, after Nick and I had gone to see a friend's play, we went to eat at a place across the street from the now-demolished Ambassador Hotel. We were kicking the dilemma around. I'd say, "Well, how about . . ." And Nick would say, "I don't think so . . ."

Desperation is a highly motivational force. I was pushed up against a wall. I was running out of time. I was angry at myself. I was angry at Nick for not just telling me the ending I had was perfectly fine. I was angry at — well, what *wasn't* I angry at?

And the solution appeared.

Looking back, it seems to me to be such an obvious answer to the question that I'm surprised I didn't think of it before. It parallels the opening scene of the play. It bookends the piece, you might say, and balances everything out in what I believe is a clever and satisfying manner.

I blurted it out, and waited. I trust Nick, so if he didn't like it, I'd accept that and reluctantly return to the drawing board.

He thought it over. He asked me a question or two.

And then he said:

"I love it."

I knew I was home free.

I put the idea into motion, and the draft was finished.

Then the hard part began: getting it produced.

But I had the play.

I had the play…

Hearing Voices

As a dramatist and a writer of fiction, I spend a lot of time alone in a room talking to myself. It's only natural that the question of voice fascinates me.

When I talk about voice, I'm talking about two things, really: the voice of an author, and the voices of an author's characters.

The first is a subtle combination of subject matter, language, experience, and perspective — the sum of all the choices a writer makes in the creation of a work. Those choices are as singular as fingerprints, and also serve as identification. It's why Hammett doesn't sound like Christie, and why Christie doesn't sound like Highsmith. Another word for this is style, which Raymond Chandler once defined as "the projection of personality."

A character's voice is a lot like an author's: it reflects the age, background, likes and dislikes of that character, and serves to distinguish one character from another. For me — and this is a result of years of working in the theater — the key to a character's voice is *sound*. Marty Kaplan, the narrator of my short story "Red Alert" (*Alfred Hitchcock's Mystery Magazine*, November 2014), is an East Coast wisecracker of a certain age who was once in show business. His sound is snappy, irreverent — and what he says is (I hope) entertaining.

When I'm moving words around at my desk, or contemplating notes scrawled in a Moleskine, or walking down the street with a head full of jangling story fragments, one of the things I'm doing is listening for the *sound* of the piece in question. Sound isn't separate from sense, of course. The two are related. But "Call me Ishmael" creates a different effect than "Hey, man, it's Ishmael. 'Sup?"

Voice is what draws us to certain writers and characters. It's the single most important factor in appreciating (or not appreciating) an author's work.

An editor once cut some lines from one of Raymond Chandler's stories because they didn't advance the action. Chandler begged to differ. He believed that what readers really cared about was

> the creation of emotion through dialogue and description; the things they remembered, that haunted them, were not for example that a man got killed, but that in the moment of death he was trying to pick a paper clip up off the polished surface of a desk, and it kept slipping away from him, so that there was a look of strain on his face and his mouth was half opened in a kind of tormented grin, and the last thing in the world he thought about was death.

We're all aiming for that golden combination of language, psychological truth, and urgent circumstance that makes for great reading.

Heraclitus said that character is fate. Our fictional creations reveal their fates through the language they use. Voice is fate.

I'd better get back to mine.

It's time again to start listening…

Nero Wolfe: FROM PAGE TO STAGE

My adaptation of *The Red Box*, the fourth novel in the Nero Wolfe series, had its world premiere at Park Square Theater in Saint Paul, Minnesota in June 2014. It marked the stage debut of Rex Stout's corpulent, orchid-fancying crime solver and his irrepressible Man Friday, Archie Goodwin. Moving the inhabitants of a certain brownstone on West 35th Street from the page to the stage was a process that took, from first thought to lights up, three-and-a-half years.

The initial part of that process reminds me of the great lyricist Ira Gershwin, who was once asked, "Which comes first? The words or the music?"

Gershwin's answer: "The contract."

Before I set pen to paper, I needed permission from the Stout estate to dramatize one of the Wolfe stories. It turns out that Rex Stout's younger daughter Rebecca Bradbury manages the estate, so we were soon corresponding. Obtaining the dramatic rights took the better part of a year, and I understand why. It was not a small decision to make. Legal documents do not grow overnight. But they do grow, and eventually terms were agreed upon, and a contract was signed.

With the question of dramatic rights settled, another question presented itself: Which book to adapt?

I considered a number of titles before deciding on *The Red Box*. The novellas I'd contemplated using didn't have quite enough action for theatrical purposes, and many of the novels had too much. *The Red Box* struck me as having the right amount of plot and number of characters. I could trim and condense where necessary without fatally damaging the story. The fact that it was one of the lesser-known titles was also a strength; it would be unfamiliar to many, and perhaps even offer a few surprises to Wolfe aficionados. It's a strong early outing with Wolfe and Goodwin that possesses all the charm and zing we expect from them.

The Red Box. All right. How to — where to — begin?

I began by reading and re-reading the novel until the paperback threatened to fall apart. I must have read it a dozen times before I started writing. Certain aesthetic considerations shaped how I viewed the novel. *The Red Box* was first published in 1937, and it seemed appropriate to utilize the mainstream theatrical conventions of the era: one set, a limited number of characters engaged in recognizable, psychologically motivated behavior. The play should be compact, fast moving, intriguing — above all, it should be entertaining.

Based on these choices, I decided that Wolfe's office in the brownstone would be the sole setting. I shortened the time frame from a week to three days to heighten the tension. I eliminated several smaller characters and simplified certain aspects of the plot. I moved the action of one scene from upstate New York to Brooklyn because Archie could get to Brooklyn faster.

Even with these alterations, I believe my adaptation is true to the spirit of the book and to the larger issues of character and relationships that animate the series. Archie Goodwin is the irresistible force. Nero Wolfe is the immovable object. Crime sets the conflict between the two in motion and lends gravity to their struggle — a struggle that's resolved by the solution of the crime. Wolfe and Archie meld their different personalities, their different gifts, and by doing so restore a kind of order.

The penultimate part of the process occurred in fall 2013, when Park Square Theater held a three-day, in-house workshop of the play. I heard it aloud for the first time; met the director and cast; and, most importantly, made revisions based on what I heard and saw. I made many small changes and cuts, added material here and there, fleshed out a character or two, straightened out a sentence. The play is sharper and clearer because of those three intense days, and clarity is essential for a mystery play.

The final part of the process began on May 30, when previews commenced, and reached another level on June 6, opening night. The play ran through mid-July 2014.

It's hard to believe that three-and-half years had elapsed since I'd first asked myself, "Would it be possible to bring Nero Wolfe to the stage?" and opening night. Luckily, the entire process had been, as Wolfe himself would say, "satisfactory." My hope is that all who had the chance to see the play agreed.

Flummery, Flapdoodle, and Balderdash:
NERO WOLFE IN THE AGE OF ALTERNATIVE FACTS

In 2017 I was asked to be the Keynote Speaker at the Nero Wolfe Literary Society's Black Orchid Weekend.

Before I share a few thoughts concerning the residents of a certain brownstone on West 35th Street, I'd like to express my thanks to the Wolfe Pack for inviting me to speak at tonight's gathering; and to Rebecca Stout Bradbury, for the gift of her friendship and for her continuing support of my Wolfean theatrical activities. It's a source of great pleasure to me that so many Pack members made the trek to Saint Paul to see one or both of my adaptations.

I would also like to acknowledge the illustrious men and women who have preceded me at this podium. It's a remarkable group of writers, critics, performers, and artists. I'm honored — and humbled — to be included, if only for the evening, in their company.

In thinking about what I might speak of this evening, I contemplated the two main philosophies concerning public speaking. The first approach warns against controversy and advises that sex, religion, and politics are to be strictly avoided. The second is perhaps best epitomized in a famous remark attributed to Alice Roosevelt Longworth: "If you can't think of something nice to say . . . sit next to me."

I hope to steer a course between controversy and contumely, but I will delve, however, into one of the forbidden topics: politics. I believe I'm justified in doing so because Rex Stout was involved himself in political matters and had any number of strongly held beliefs about the world and the way it was run. As an enemy of cant and hypocrisy, as a lover of language, and as a man who made his living by the skillful use of his pen, Mr. Stout was attuned to the ways in which language can exalt or pervert, reveal truths or obscure them; there is an inescapable political dimension to how it's employed — and for what reasons.

Working on my adaptation of *Might As Well Be Dead*, I invented the following exchange between Nero Wolfe and Archie Goodwin. It's late in the evening and Archie has returned to West 35th Street. Mr. Wolfe is reading *The New York Times*.

ARCHIE: Anything in the papers?

WOLFE: Perfidy.

ARCHIE: Isn't that a French perfume?

WOLFE: It is the very stuff and substance of the world. Those pages are filled with tales of cheats, frauds, dissemblers — the light-fingered and the larcenous.

ARCHIE: A typical day in New York.

WOLFE: A typical day in the world.

HE TAKES A BOOK FROM A SHELF AND READS ALOUD.

"Falsehood flies, and truth comes limping after it, so that when men come to be undeceived, it is too late; the jest is over, and the tale hath had its effect; like a man who hath thought of a good repartee when the discourse is changed; or like a physician who hath found an infallible medicine, after the patient is dead."

Those lines are from an essay by Jonathan Swift entitled "The Art of Political Lying." That essay was written over three hundred years ago but it remains, alas, as timely a statement on world affairs now as it was then. If lying — in any form, on any subject, at any time — could be considered an art form, it is safe to say we live in a golden age, a veritable renaissance of liars and the lies they tell.

I beg your pardon. Did I say lies? What I meant to say was: "alternative facts."

Kellyanne Conway, an advisor to the current President, introduced this phrase in January 2017 on *Meet the Press,* NBC's venerable current affairs program. Shortly after Conway first employed this risible expression, astrophysics Professor Adam Frank shared his thoughts on the subject with National Public Radio. The world, Frank states, "is a jumbled barrage of sights, sounds, impressions and intuitions."

Given this chaos, Frank notes that we make sense of the world in two ways: private opinions and public facts. He offers this example: If I think I'm in love with someone, who's to tell me I'm wrong? That's my opinion. But if I believe the object of my affection is an alien, we then enter the realm of public fact. The object of my affection either is or is not from another planet. Frank continues:

> Just as important, we should be able to do something to prove the fact of the matter — one way or the other. And that's it in a nutshell. It's 'the facts of the matter' that matter. That's why we came up with science. We needed a way to figure out which facts were truly public. We needed a method to determine which statements about the world were ones we could *all* agree were, indeed, facts of the matter. And the essence of the method we came up with, the one called science, hinged on something absolutely remarkable in the history of humanity.
>
> It all depended on an agreement.
>
> Over time, and as a society, we decided to agree what the rules of the fact-finding method called science should look like. It went something like this: *Public facts will be accepted as public facts, if and only if you can show multiple and independent lines of public evidence to support them.*

Evidence . . . the more, the better, and from as many different sources as possible. This seems like an eminently sensible way to perceive the world. There's only one flaw here: agreements can be broken. Frank writes: "That is a danger of living in a 'post-truth' world. The agreement that we'd all play by these rules because they gave us solid ground to stand on is not carved in stone. Instead it's etched in standards of behavior."

Frank concludes:

> This civilization we created is really complicated — just like the natural world. That means all of us, regardless of how we voted, need all the help we can get to keep it working. In a functioning democratic, technological society, public facts act as a kind of glue ensuring we're all playing on the same ball field. They help us ensure that our public facts are as close as possible to the true facts of nature and the world — *the true facts of the matter.*

The parallel between the scientist and the detective is clear. Separating fact from flummery is the essence of the detective's job. (It is, at least, in what might be called the optimistic mystery, in which law and order and the punishment of crime are generally considered worthwhile activities; the pessimistic mystery views both cop and criminal as equally corrupt. But even this brand of mystery acknowledges the strength of the truth; the only problem is that no one believes the truth does any good.)

Optimistic or pessimistic, the mystery is an endlessly fascinating genre. The mystery is both moral allegory and sociological document. It captures the mores, language, and values of the era in which it was written. At the same time it is overtly concerned with matters of right and wrong that stretch back at least as far as Cain and Abel.

The Wolfe stories embody both the timeless and the time-bound aspects of the Mystery to a high degree. Because Nero Wolfe and Archie Goodwin do not age but are rooted in the present, they remain contemporary, and the stories in which they are featured offer the reader a vivid picture of more than 40 years of American life — from the New Deal to the Cold War and on to Watergate. The length of their mutual careers and the probity with which those careers were conducted lend Mr. Wolfe and Mr. Goodwin an unmatched moral authority. There are no "alternative facts" in Wolfe's world. "Alternate facts" are what crooks and killers use to muddy the waters and hide their crimes. Simply put, they are lies.

I have spoken in the past of my belief that the Wolfe stories are comedies of manners. Wolfe is the immovable object, Archie the irresistible force; crime sets the two in conflict. When the crime is solved, peace is restored and the two forces are balanced, if only momentarily — hence, the stories are comedies in the grand Shakespearian sense of the word. I stand by this notion, though I'd alter it slightly by saying that it describes the *form* of the Wolfe stories but not the *content*.

The heart and soul of the stories are drawn directly from the heart and soul of their creator. In *Bloody Murder*, his history of the mystery genre, Julian Symons describes the gentleman I refer to in these words: "In person Rex Stout was an astonishingly energetic man with multifold interests. He was indefatigable in support of many causes relating to authors, and remained to his death a committed radical of a distinctly American kind."

In preparation for this evening, I re-read *The Doorbell Rang* and *A Family Affair*, two of the most overtly political of the Wolfe stories. I was struck again by their zest, their élan. *Affair* is only secondarily concerned with Watergate, though President Nixon receives his fair share of opprobrium. There's much to admire in *Doorbell*; the quality I admire most is its audacity. Publishing a tale in which Wolfe takes on (and bests) the FBI is a provocative act . . . and a brave one, too. Who would choose to do battle with the Federal Bureau of Investigation and its paranoid, racist homophobe of a director?

No one but Mr. Stout and Mr. Wolfe. Hoover's reign at the FBI lasted for decades and ended only with his death. He abused his power repeatedly, gathered material illegally, persecuted and prosecuted those he deemed his enemies. Stout was well aware of the danger the autocratic and vindictive Hoover posed to the body politic. In McAleer's biography, Stout says of the Head G-Man: "I think his whole attitude makes him an enemy of democracy. I think he is on the edge of senility. Calling Martin Luther King the 'biggest liar in the world' is absurd. He is getting sillier and sillier…"

Stout certainly portrays Hoover as a figure of fun. At the end of the novel, as we all know, he is left forlornly ringing the doorbell of Wolfe's domicile. No one will answer. Ring all you please. Wolfe's door will never be opened to such a man.

Stout didn't feel that the FBI would take any action against him because of the book. I believe that Stout's eminence as a writer, civil libertarian, and staunch advocate of democracy made attacking him a losing battle.

The Wolfe stories can be read and re-read for any number of reasons: the pleasure of Archie's wry narrative voice; of returning to a world so lovingly created over so many years; of once again encountering old friends and foes. They can also be read for the wisdom they contain. Stout wove his moral, political, intellectual, and gastronomic convictions into his stories. Mind and Body must each be nourished. Eat Well. Read Widely. Search without cease for the facts of the matter. Truth is superior to falsehood.

For these reasons, *all* of the Wolfe stories have political dimensions. McAleer points out that *The Doorbell Rang* revealed "that the dual careers of Rex Stout were not mutually exclusive. He was not a champion of civil liberties who also wrote detective stories for profit or diversion. The Wolfe saga all along had served him as a vehicle for stringent social commentary."

In an age when flummery, flapdoodle, and balderdash dominate public discourse, it is more important than ever that we separate the fraudulent from the factual. It is one of the duties of being a citizen. Rex Stout and Nero Wolfe provide us with fine examples of how to live in the land of the free and the home and the brave . . . and how to keep it that way.

Killer Tunes: MUSIC FOR MYSTERY WRITERS

In the 1950s and 60s Alfred Hitchcock's celebrity as a film director and television host prompted a number of enterprises bearing his name. These include the *Three Investigators* series for younger readers; *Alfred Hitchcock's Mystery Magazine*; and a curious little record titled *Alfred Hitchcock Presents Music to be Murdered By*.

First released in 1958, *Music* is a collection of standards such as "I'll Never Smile Again and "After You've Gone," as well as Gounod's "Funeral March of a Marionette" (the theme music of Hitchcock's TV show). Jeff Alexander arranged the songs and conducted the orchestra. James Allardice penned Hitchcock's comically lugubrious narration — a job he also performed for *Alfred Hitchcock Presents*.

Each musical selection is prefaced with a few macabre observations. The listener is invited to lend an ear to this album of "mood music in a jugular vein" and to "relax, lean back and enjoy yourself — until the coroner comes." As the record spins to its close, Hitch says with regret, "If you haven't been murdered, better luck next time. If you have, goodnight . . . wherever you are." The album is an amusing addition to Hitchcock-related items, completely in keeping with his image as a tongue-in-cheek connoisseur of the gruesome.

It also got me thinking: if this is music to be murdered *by*, what about music to commit murder *to*?

Fictional murder, of course.

Writing has a great deal in common with magic. The invisible is made visible; something is created where nothing existed before. And just as the magician requires the proper ingredients — eye of newt, wart of toad — so the writer obsesses over the tools of the trade.

The variables are immense. Pencil or pen? Legal pad or spiral notebook? If the choice is paper, should it be lined or unlined? What about graph paper? Moleskine notebook or big Chief tablet? If the choice is computer, what font? Are you a Times New Roman devotee, or does Calibri do the trick? Once the proper tools have been obtained, the question of locale arises. Alone at home, or with others in public? Some happily scribble away in the midst of a café's tumult; others would rather die than write in a crowd. Time of day? Some writers are up typing before the sun's ascent; others can only work deep into the night, when the world is still and interruptions are at a minimum.

Whether a writer uses a fountain pen, Blackwing pencil, or laptop, whether she works by sunlight or moonlight, the goal is the same: to coax a few more words onto the page or screen. Rituals must be strictly observed if the writing gods are to be appeased.

Some authors make music a part of their ritual. In *Letters to a Young Writer: Some Practical and Philosophical Advice*, Irish novelist Colum McCann urges the tyro to: "Play music. If you have a favorite writing album . . . put it on auto-repeat so that the music seeps into the background and becomes then part of the landscape of your language."

Not all agree with McCann. An informal poll of a quartet of award-winning writers — Rupert Holmes, S. J. Rozan, Jonathan Santlofer, and KC Trommer — revealed a variety of attitudes on the subject.

Mystery novelist Rozan works to music, though "sometimes I just want birdsong, which luckily I can get outside my window. As we New Yorkers say, I live in the back." Rozan favors classical music, "but not Baroque. I'm partial to piano and to cello. Occasionally I'll put on something else, to set the mood for what I'm specifically working on: Mongolian throat singing, Chinese erhu."

Artist and author Santlofer notes the difference between his two disciplines: "When I was a full time painter I lived for music, with a predilection for rock, though just as often great jazz singers like Dinah Washington or Billie Holiday. When I first started writing I couldn't listen to music at all, which upset me, but lyrics always got in the way of writing sentences."

Rozan seconds that point. "Vocal music is okay, but if the words are in English I start to listen with the writing part of my brain, and that screws everything up."

Santlofer envies "writers who can listen to people like Bruce Springsteen or Amy Winehouse, which I do whenever I'm drawing or painting, but I could never do that when I'm writing."

Composer, songwriter, novelist, playwright Holmes prefers silence. "Writing dialogue is really a form of composing, as our characters have their own cadences and rhythms, at least in our mind's ear. Someone once asked me if I could make a musical out of David Mamet's play *Glengarry Glen Ross* and I said, 'That's absurd — *Glengarry Glen Ross is* a musical.' I could no more write dialogue for disparate characters while music is playing than I could teach synchronized swimming during a tsunami."

Poet and essayist Trommer needs quiet, too — at first. "During the early drafts, I have to write in whatever passes for silence in my corner of Queens. I'll put music under it once I have some text in place." At that point, Trommer echoes McCann's habits. "If I'm writing with a particular person (in the case of non-fiction) or character (in the case of fiction) in mind, I will often put a song on repeat so it can inform the work I'm doing."

For Holmes, "There is no such thing as background music." This has an effect both on the page and off. "Dining in a posh Knightsbridge supper club with a jazz trio playing tasteful sounds in a far corner of the room, Joan Collins once asked me how I would categorize a play of mine she'd been taking under consideration, and I thought, *G minor 7 going to an E7 with a flatted fifth? What a nice way to approach an A minor 9.*"

Music is mandatory for me, whether it's WQXR in the background, an internet jazz station, or a scratchy old LP spinning on the turntable. I've put together a list of some of the albums I've listened to while committing murder — fictional murder, of course. I love them all, and I hope they might be useful to others who are looking for some killer tunes to accompany imaginary misdeeds. It should come as no surprise that these are low-key, contemplative records; creating a world on paper is a delicate business, and one must tread softly. Mechanical tasks like proofreading or formatting a manuscript can be done to the Rolling Stones, for instance, but not the initial writing.

Five albums, for your listening — and, perhaps, writing — pleasure:

John Lewis, Volume 2: J. S. Bach, Preludes and Fugues from the Well-Tempered Clavier, Volume 1. An unwieldy title for an album of sublimely graceful music. Lewis (1920-2001) was the musical architect behind the Modern Jazz Quartet, composing, arranging, and playing piano with the group for over twenty years. He was a rare mixture of scholar and hep cat. His interest in classical forms such as the fugue and his delicate touch at the keyboard are matched by his bebop bona fides; he was a graduate of Dizzy Gillespie's big band and a friend and collaborator of Miles Davis. He was an early proponent of Third Stream jazz, defined by music critic and composer Gunther Schuller as "a new genre of music located about halfway between jazz and classical music."

Schuller might have been describing Lewis's Bach recordings. Accompanied by guitar, bass, violin and viola, Lewis at the keyboard reflects on and responds to the German composer's work, one moment pensive, another lightly swinging, a third mournful. The album is the aural equivalent of shifting sunlight and shade on a summer's day.

93

Always Say Goodbye, Charlie Haden and Quartet West. From a sunny field we move into the perpetual night of the urban jungle. *Goodbye* opens and closes with a snippet of music (by Warner Brothers stalwart Max Steiner) and dialogue (by tough guy Humphrey Bogart) from *The Big Sleep.* It's clear that we're in Noirville, a place of lost love and broken dreams, a town built on the bones of 1940s Los Angeles. Haden (1937-2014) was one of the jazz world's most influential bassists, fluent in a number of musical genres, and the recipient of a 2012 NEA Jazz Master Award. *Always Say Goodbye* mixes covers of period material ("Everything Happens to Me") with new versions of jazz standards (Charlie Parker's "Relaxing at Camarillo") and Hayden originals ("Nice Eyes"). Haden and Quartet West, to quote T. S. Eliot, breed "lilacs out of the dead land, mixing memory and desire" into a richly atmospheric evocation of a vanished place and time.

From Gardens Where We Feel Secure, Virginia Astley. We abandon the streets of L.A. and return to nature's pastoral calm. Astley (born 1959) was in several 1980s indie bands and played piano on one of her then-brother-in-law Pete Townshend's albums, but *Gardens* is her major musical accomplishment. Allmusic.com describes it as "a lovely 35-minute meditation built around field recordings Astley made of the ambient sounds of the rural English countryside. . . . These nine songs are melodically rich and varied; mood pieces in the truest sense of the term." The chirping of birds and a simple piano melody open the album, effortlessly transporting the listener to summer in England. I'm reminded of William Wordsworth's poem "I Wandered Lonely as a Cloud," wherein the poet recalls a "host of golden daffodils" he encountered on a solitary country walk, and how the memory of those flowers returns to him:

> For oft, when on my couch I lie
> In vacant or in pensive mood,
> They flash upon that inward eye
> Which is the bliss of solitude;
> And then my heart with pleasure fills,
> And dances with the daffodils.

On the Other Ocean, David Behrman. A student of Stockhausen's, a peer of Robert Ashley and Terry Riley, Behrman (born 1937) has been active in the new music scene for more than five decades. He's worked with John Cage, written music for Merce Cunningham's dance company as well as for various art installations. His experiments with computers and other technology during the '60s and '70s mark him out as a pioneer of electronic music. Behrman's album notes describe *Ocean* as "an improvisation . . . centered around six pitches which, when they are played, activate electronic pitch-sensing circuits connected to the 'interrupt' line and input ports of a microcomputer. . . . The relationship between the two musicians and the computer is an interactive one, with the computer changing the electronically produced harmonies in response to what the musicians play, and the musicians influenced in their improvising by what the computer does."

That may sound daunting, but *On the Other Ocean* is entirely accessible. Following the slowly shifting tones creates a meditative state — an effect Behrman finds tonic. "The world is filled with busy noisy music and noise in general," he said in an interview with Jason Gross published in the online magazine *Perfect Sound Forever*, "and I'd rather contribute to the quieter end of the spectrum most of the time." If you're a fan of Brian Eno's ambient music, you'll find much to savor in *On the Other Ocean*.

La Belle Époque: The Songs of Reynaldo Hahn, Susan Graham. These songs from France's "beautiful era" — an era destroyed by the conflagration of the First World War — are redolent of the drawing rooms and concert halls of *In Search of Lost Time*. For good reason: composer Hahn was Marcel Proust's lover and, in later years, his cherished friend. Sensitively accompanied by pianist Roger Vignoles, mezzo-soprano Susan Graham illuminates these *chansons*. Settings of poems by Verlaine, Daudet, and other French writers, they remain Hahn's best-known works. He was also a conductor, music critic, and director of the Paris Opera. Hahn outlived Proust by a quarter of a century, dying in 1947. His songs endure.

> *…Un vaste et tendre*
> *Apaisement*
> *Semble descendre*
> *Du firmament*
> *Que l'astre irise...*
> *C'est l'heure exquise.*

> …A vast and tender
> Consolation
> Seems to fall
> From the sky
> The moon illumines...
> Exquisite hour.

(Paul Verlaine; Richard Stokes, translation.)

Many thanks to Rupert Holmes, S. J. Rozan, Jonathan Santlofer, and KC Trommer for sharing their thoughts with me — I sing their praises, whether or not they listen to music when committing murder.

Fictional murder, of course . . .

ELLERY QUEEN, MASTER DETECTIVE

Ellery Queen shoulder-to-shoulder: Lee and Dannay

A Challenge to the Viewer

I first met Ellery Queen in 1975.

I don't mean Ellery Queen the author. Nor do I mean Ellery Queen — here I pause to take a deep breath — the editor, the anthologist, the radio scriptwriter, the lecturer, the collector of mystery fiction and, arguably, the single greatest friend and advocate the mystery genre has ever had.

I'm referring to Ellery Queen the TV star. "Star" might not be quite the right word, as *Ellery Queen* only lasted for one season on NBC. But one season was enough for the Queenian magic to take hold — at least for this viewer. My initial encounter with Queen was as momentous for me as was Queen's encounter with Sherlock Holmes six decades before. The series led me to Ellery Queen's books, and the books led me into the mystery field. My fate, as they say, was sealed. Not even John Dickson Carr could have figured a way out. And I wouldn't have taken it if one had been offered. As a reader and, eventually, a writer, I have dwelt happily in the genre ever since.

Developed by Richard Levinson and William Link, this video incarnation of Queen began life as a TV movie (based on *The Fourth Side of the Triangle*) which aired in March 1975. *Ellery Queen* garnered big ratings and, not unnaturally, a series followed.

Beginning that fall, Jim Hutton and David Wayne reprised their respective roles as Ellery and Inspector Queen. The series was canceled due to low ratings, the last episode was broadcast in April 1976, and the small-screen adventures of EQ disappeared from sight.

With the exception of a few scattered airings on A&E and The Mystery Channel, *Ellery Queen* has lingered in limbo for 30 years now, fondly remembered but unseen.

The series was released on DVD in 2010. I approached with caution. I wasn't sure what to expect; how would the series, viewed through adult eyes, hold up? As it turned out, *Ellery Queen* held up just fine.

Certainly nostalgia has something to do with my present-day appreciation, but I find it easy to agree with much of Mike Madrid's 1976 review in the short-lived *Mystery Monthly* magazine:

> obvious elements of appeal to mystery buffs, including elegant surroundings for murder — penthouse apartments and black-tie nightclubs. Lanky Jim Hutton plays a boyishly unpretentious detective, and veteran actor David Wayne plays a likeably cranky but ineffective inspector. Moreover, the guest cast is routinely excellent...and the charm of the Forties sets, costumes and overall milieu is a refreshing change from the "asphalt jungle" of contemporary New York and the endless freeways of modern Los Angeles.

Madrid went on to fault the series for its lack of danger — "Ellery goes about his sleuthing with impunity . . . as if he's playing a parlor game after dinner" — and a concomitant lack of suspense, concluding that *Ellery Queen* was like "a gun without bullets. Decorative, perhaps, but hardly effective."

Madrid's point is generally valid; all I would say in the show's defense is that it was more of a champagne cocktail than a boilermaker, an exercise in stylish ratiocination that made no claims to "gritty authenticity." As such, there's much to enjoy: the period details that Madrid mentions, the byplay between Ellery and Inspector Queen and, more often than not, the twists and turns of the mysteries that Ellery is called upon to solve.

My only real objection stems from certain aspects of the way Ellery's character is handled. Jim Hutton's otherwise-admirable portrayal errs a little too often for my taste on the side of comic absentmindedness. This character trait was obviously chosen to "humanize" Ellery, to make him more "appealing" to the audience. Amusing as it can sometimes be, it has little to do with the EQ of the books. Hutton is at his best when he's simply allowed to do what Ellery did best: apply his sympathetic intelligence to the solving of a crime. I wish the series had drawn upon some of the fierce and agonized moral conscience that provides such depth to *Cat of Many Tails* and *Ten Days' Wonder*.

But to wish for that is to wish that *Ellery Queen* had been something other than what it was, to rue a missed possibility rather than appreciate what is there. Though the series is set in 1947, well into the third period of the Queen canon, its format owes more to the golden-age days (and even more to the EQ radio show) than anything else. The game is all, the puzzle takes precedence, and a challenge to the reader — or, in this case, to the viewer — is issued when all the clues to the solution of the crime have been presented.

It's interesting to note that the only Queen story used as the basis for one of the episodes was 1934's "The Adventure of the Mad Tea Party". The crimes themselves are not exceptionally difficult to figure out, but they do require keeping a close eye on the action and a bit of reasoning . . . a recipe for death in the ratings then as now.

Levinson and Link kept the books' triumvirate of Queen *pere, fils*, and Sergeant Velie. David Wayne's Inspector Queen, though missing his print counterpart's silvery mustache and given to arresting suspects on less-than-rock-solid evidence, is indeed superb, and Tom Reese's Velie is a stolid addition to a long line of head-scratching, cigar-chewing Man Fridays. Created for the series to provide competition for Ellery and grief for his father are the stylish radio sleuth Simon Brimmer — played with sardonic élan by John Hillerman — and the pugnacious news-hawk Frank Flanagan, brought to brash and bristling life by Ken Swofford. Brimmer and Flanagan can be counted on to provide the wrong answers to whatever case Ellery is involved in, and their comeuppance is a ready source of humor. No Nikki Porter is to be found lurking about the Queens' brownstone, a blessing or a curse depending on how you feel about Nikki. A few women vie for Ellery's attentions in the course of the series, but he remains essentially the world's oldest, tallest and smartest boy. Dashiell Hammett's famous question concerning Ellery's sex life (" — if any") remains unanswered. The emphasis is on deduction, not seduction.

Little more than a year elapsed from the pilot's first showing to the last aired episode. *Ellery Queen* remains, to date, the last time Dannay and Lee's creation has appeared on the home screen. If only PBS would do for Queen what the BBC has done for his British counterparts. Think of, say, *The Roman Hat Mystery* done up in all the period trappings of the late 1920s; think of *Calamity Town*'s town square (which was round), the changing seasons of Wrightsville's weather and the changing fates of the Wright family; think of the sweltering claustrophobia of New York City roamed by the serial killer of *Cat of Many Tails*; think of *And On The Eighth Day*'s isolated desert Eden that comes to know the greatest sin of them all. The mouth waters at the prospect.

Until this happens, the modest and intelligent pleasures of the Levinson and Link series will serve admirably. It constitutes a relatively minor but charming addition to Queeniana. I use the word "relatively," well, relatively. For one 12-year-old boy in a small Minnesota town, *Ellery Queen* was a major event. It opened up a world.

No — *worlds*.

A Kind of Triumph

William Butler Yeats observed: "Out of the quarrel with others we make rhetoric; out of the quarrel with ourselves we make poetry."

He might have added: "Out of the quarrel with our cousins, we make mysteries."

But Yeats never met Frederic Dannay or Manfred B. Lee, the notoriously fractious first cousins from Brooklyn who created Ellery Queen. Known for their legendary differences of opinion on just about any subject under the sun, Dannay and Lee were proof that conflict is not only the essence of fiction but also the very nature of collaboration.

Or, should I say, of *their* collaboration. Ample evidence of the *Sturm und Drang* that animated their professional and familial relationships can be found in *Blood Relations: The Selected Letters of Ellery Queen, 1947-1950*.

Blood Relations covers the years when Lee was living in Los Angeles, where he was writing the Ellery Queen radio show, and Dannay was living in Larchmont, New York. For the better part of their careers, the two collaborated at a distance, communicating through letters and telephone calls. The letters afford us the chance to watch Dannay and Lee at work — a rare opportunity to see some of their greatest novels forged in the fire of their disputes and debates.

Ellery Queen the author has been my favorite mystery writer since I discovered him when I was 12 years old; Ellery Queen the character, my favorite fictional detective. A portion of my affection for Dannay and Lee's creation stems from that youthful fascination, but I've re-read the books many times since then and they hold up marvelously well. My enthusiasm was warranted.

In the summer of 2008 that enthusiasm led me to approach Richard Dannay, one of Frederic's sons, about an obscure piece of Queeniana: the stage play *Danger, Men Working*. Written with Lowell Brentano in 1935, the play closed out of town and was subsequently forgotten. Richard Dannay was kind enough to pass along a copy of the play. I arranged a staged reading of it at the New York Conservatory for Dramatic Arts in January of 2009.

Richard mentioned that the correspondence between his father and Lee — housed at Columbia University — offered a unique view of their collaboration. A trip to the Butler Library's Rare Book and Manuscript Room proved that he was absolutely right. I spent the next six months transcribing those letters. By the time I'd finished, I'd amassed almost a quarter-of-a-million words. I assembled and edited a selection of letters that illustrates how Dannay and Lee wrote *Ten Days' Wonder, Cat of Many Tails, The Origin of Evil*, and provides a glimpse into their troubled private lives. Both men suffered psychic and physical distress; both desperately needed the money that Queen made for them; both were sensitive to the point of morbidity and each felt undervalued by and resentful of the other.

Dannay did the plotting, Lee the actual writing. But these strictly demarcated tasks were never wholly separable, and each felt the other was poaching on his terrain. Dannay thought Lee didn't treat his plots with enough care. Lee chafed at the constraints of Dannay's storylines. They needed each other to make their books, and bitterly resented it.

How bitterly, I came to discover as I worked my way through their letters. I had no idea that these vital and complex works were born out of such struggle, such anger and doubt.

For all the sorrow and sadness in Dannay and Lee's lives, their story is a kind of triumph. Against the odds they managed to collaborate successfully for over 40 years, merging their separate strengths into a cohesive, meaningful whole. They played a vital part in the creation of the Golden Age of mystery fiction. They responded intelligently and creatively to the challenges of the post-Golden-Age world, a world wracked by the chaos of war and the madness of genocide, and created their finest work. No matter what external or internal catastrophes befell them, like Samuel Beckett's wanderers they kept going.

Adventures in Radioland:
ELLERY QUEEN, ON (AND OFF) THE AIR

As someone who's been reading Ellery Queen since the Ford administration, it's gratifying to note the recent revival of interest in the work of Frederic Dannay (1905-1982) and Manfred B. Lee (1905-1971), the two cousins from Brooklyn who created the fictional detective/author Ellery Queen.

Renewed attention to EQ has manifested itself in a number of ways. In the fall of 2010, the 1975-1976 NBC television series starring Jim Hutton as a tall and boyish Ellery was released on DVD. In the winter of 2013 Francis M. Nevins, the Magellan of Queen studies, published an expanded version of his groundbreaking study *Royal Bloodline: Ellery Queen, Author and Detective*. Many of the EQ titles are back in circulation, be it in print or electronic form, thanks to the Mysterious Press/Open Road Integrated Media, and to James Prichard's Langtail Press. Biographer Jeffrey Marks is at work on a tome about Dannay and Lee. My own efforts include editing and annotating *Blood Relations: The Selected Letters of Ellery Queen, 1947-1950*, which details the writing of three of the greatest Queen novels, and was published in the winter of 2012; my stage version of *Calamity Town* had its premiere at the Vertigo Theatre in Calgary, Alberta in January 2016.

These are palmy times for the Queen fan. But such was not always the case. Ellery Queen, character and author, largely disappeared from popular culture after the cancellation of the 1975-1976 television series. The books went out of print and, with the exception of a handful of Queen enthusiasts, Dannay, Lee and EQ were largely forgotten. Many reasons have been offered for this, ranging from changing tastes in popular literature to the decline of Western civilization. Critic Jon L. Breen has written quite insightfully about Queen's eclipse, and finds its roots in a simplistically bifurcated vision of the mystery novel's development that divides the genre into upper-class English female classicists and working-class American hardboiled males. This view leaves male classicists such as Queen out in the cold.

Whatever the reasons, the result was the same: Ellery Queen — once a synonym for "detective" — languished in obscurity.

One of those who remembered EQ was Douglas Greene, the founder of Crippen & Landru. In 1999 Greene published the invaluable *The Tragedy of Errors and Others*. Marking the 70th anniversary of *The Roman Hat Mystery*, EQ's debut, *Tragedy* contains a half-dozen uncollected Queen stories; almost two-dozen recollections of Dannay and Lee by friends, family members and colleagues; and, most tantalizingly, Dannay's last outline for a Queen novel, *The Tragedy of Errors*.

For the reader who may not know how the cousins collaborated, Dannay provided the intricately crafted plots that Lee turned into full-fledged novels. The division of labor between plotting and writing played to their respective strengths but was more honored in the breach than in the observance, and was a continual source of friction between the two. Dannay felt that Lee treated his story constructions with a cavalier indifference. Lee felt hard pressed to enliven what he considered to be outlandish and unbelievable characters and premises. They clashed frequently and disagreed about almost everything. That the novels and short stories and radio plays got written is a testament to the determination of both Dannay and Lee; proof in its way of the strength of their bond. Their personal and working relationship may have been, as Lee described it, "a marriage made in hell." But the "marriage" lasted for over 40 years and produced some of the finest mystery novels of the 20th century.

Dannay's outlines were highly detailed affairs, running into tens of thousands of words. *Tragedy* is no exception, and provides the reader with an intriguing glimpse into Dannay's contribution to the collaboration. Lee died before he could transform the outline into a novel.

The personal reminiscences contained in *Tragedy* expand our understanding of the two cousins and their lives on and off the page. Dannay, Lee and Queen are viewed from a number of angles — as writers, as parents, as public figures (or, in Lee's case, as someone who hated public appearances with a passion). Of particular interest are essays by family members. Douglas and Richard Dannay write with clarity and affection of their father's love of poetry and book collecting. Rand B. Lee poignantly examines his troubled relationship with a father who died too soon.

Greene brought out another volume of Queen material in 2005 to mark the 100th birthdays of Dannay and Lee — and of EQ, who was also "born" in 1905. *The Adventure of the Murdered Moths and Other Radio Mysteries* gathers together

14 scripts from the *Adventures of Ellery Queen* radio show, which aired from 1939 to 1948.

Moths does a great service by making the scripts available. Out of the dozens of shows produced and aired over the course of its run, only a handful of broadcasts have survived. Thanks to *Moths*, we can now imagine over a dozen more.

The Frederic Dannay Papers at Columbia University contain a fair amount of correspondence concerning the radio show. It comes as no surprise that — like everything else involving their brainchild — Ellery Queen's portrayal on radio was a subject of dissension. Should he be a social critic solving crimes of injustice and intolerance (Lee's view), or should he leave the do-gooding to others and stick to pure detecting (Dannay's)? The cancellation of the radio show in 1948 effectively ended the debate, but while it lasted it burned hot and bright. Lee was not a man for half-measures; nor, in his quieter, more subdued manner, was Dannay.

The Adventures of Ellery Queen was, for a good portion of its existence, primarily Lee's bailiwick. Faced with the death of his first wife and the pressures of editing *Ellery Queen's Mystery Magazine*, Dannay stepped aside from the task of providing Lee with plots for the show; critic and mystery writer Anthony Boucher and journeyman radio writer Tom Everitt took his place. Lee moved to California in 1947 to supervise the show. He not only wrote the scripts but also served as a quasi-producer, dealing with radio sponsors, advertising agencies and recalcitrant actors and directors.

Despite his best efforts, the show was cancelled. In a long letter dated June 28, 1948, Lee aired his grievances to William Morris agent Alexander ("Sandy") Stronach. Lee's blunt, impassioned letter offers an insider's look at the radio business as it reached its terminal stage. It is quoted in full.

> Dear Sandy:
>
> Dannay writes me that he had a long talk with you the other day about the Queen radio situation and he gave me in some detail the substance of that conversation. Recriminations are pointless and I am not going to indulge in them, but you and William Morris have the job of selling Queen for radio and that's very much to the point. It seems to me you can't do the job properly unless we are all clear and agreed on the facts. After carefully reading Dannay's report on the "facts" as transmitted to him by you, I am far from satisfied that we are all clear on them and certainly we are not in agreement.
>
> As I understand it, you "finally got the story out of ABC" as to why they dropped Queen: They had been pressed for some time economically, decided to drop some shows, conducted "a sort of survey, or inquiry" on mystery shows to determine which they should retain and which they should drop, their survey revealed that the only popular

mystery shows have two characteristics in common — a central character and a quality or qualities in that character which make "listeners feel that they are participating in the adventures of a real person, one they know and like and want to hear about, watch," etc. — and that, measured by this test, the Queen show "failed" on the second count: that is, ABC concluded that Ellery was not "a real living person with human qualities in the sense that other central detective characters on radio are"; and that, as a consequence, they dropped Queen.

If the above paragraph represents in essence what ABC told you, Sandy, as their reason for dropping Queen, it is extremely important for me to go on record with you — and the Morris organization — as characterizing it as pure, unadulterated horse shit. It may well have been their reason — they may even believe it, although I submit that the facts of record cast the strongest doubt even on that — but it isn't the truth about Queen and I don't see how you can try to sell Queen if you believe this about Queen. And that, not ABC, is what chiefly concerns me.

First, as to ABC's veracity: ABC put us on sustaining last November, at considerable budgetary cost to them. In a talk I had with [radio executive] Bud Barry out here before we set the deal, at which Murray was present, Barry revealed that the main pressure for ABC's putting Queen on the network came from the ABC sales organization in New York: he said, and I quote, "they consider Queen the most saleable mystery property in radio today." Queen was hardly a new show last fall; we had been on the air more than eight years at that time; a radio sales department could hardly have based their opinion on Queen's saleability upon hearsay or a misconception — it could only have been from a thorough knowledge of the Queen show and the Queen character and the Queen record on the air. (This last, I might add, consistently under and in spite of uniformly adverse conditions.)

We were on for ABC a total of 27 weeks. During 21 of those 27 weeks I had at least half a dozen reports from [William Morris radio agent Phil] Weltman regarding ABC's "satisfaction" with the show, two expressions directly to me from [ABC Radio's West Coast head of production] J. Donald Wilson to the same effect, and some 6 weeks before they dropped us, another personal talk with Bud Barry in which he said, and again I quote (Weltman was present): "We are thoroughly satisfied with the show; the only beef we have is against ourselves, because we haven't been able to sell it." And — mark this well, please — in this same talk, with Weltman present, Barry said to me, "In fact, *if you are willing*, we would like to continue with the Queen show at least through this summer. We still feel it is a valuable property and that, if we can ride out the current anti-mystery show cycle, we can sell it." I repeat: this conversation took place 6 weeks before they dropped us.

I submit that in the face of all this enthusiasm for the Queen show, consistent and without a sour note, it is strongly open to doubt that, suddenly, in the last few weeks, a "survey" revealed to ABC what none of them had ever known before: that Queen was not a character in the same way as other radio detectives and therefore he wasn't, after all, saleable. Who conducted this survey? When? How? Who was "surveyed"? Who said Queen had insufficient human qualities? And why were "human qualities" suddenly so important when for some nine years previously an apparent "lack" of them had not kept Queen off the air? My present records go back only to October, 1942; but *between October 10, 1942 and September 21, 1947 — a total of 5 years — we were off the air exactly 14 weeks!* I doubt if many mystery shows can match that record. Then we were off the air for 2 months to make the switchover from New York to Hollywood and were on 27 weeks for ABC. And even in that 5-year period 6 of the 14 weeks were a layoff enforced when Anacin switched from CBS to NBC and the switchover couldn't be effectuated sooner. And I want to point out, further, what I think it is most important for all of us to remember: *that every single broadcast in those all-but-solid 5 years was a commercially sponsored show.* Add to this fact that in those 5 years we had only 2 sponsors, and I think the score adds up to a damned successful Queen show, human qualities or no human qualities. And I want to point out further that before October 1942, with the sole exception of our first sustaining series for CBS as a 1-hour show, we were also uniformly sponsored. And I want to point out further that we would have continued being sponsored after September 21, 1947 — by Anacin, who wanted us to continue this past winter and spring, in the Sunday 6:30 spot on NBC — if not for the refusal of Niles Trammell to allow our sponsor to keep a mystery show in that spot during the regular broadcasting season.

So, as I say, survey or no survey, ABC believing it or not believing it, the question of Ellery's having "human qualities" or not is irrelevant, absurd, and a dangerous red herring.

My personal opinion, Sandy, based on the above facts, is that — contrary to your belief — you have still not got out of ABC the real reason for their having dropped the Queen show. I think they've handed you a line of double-talk. I think, in view of the facts, their integrity and veracity are widely open to question. As confirmation: They notified us of their decision not to renew *and in the same notification they assured us that their decision was in no way dictated by dissatisfaction with the show.*

I have a copy of their official notice to us of cancellation. I quote the pertinent paragraph:

"This cancellation is due to a complete rearrangement of our evening schedule, and while this formal notice of cancellation is necessary because of the four weeks' notice required, *we are going to make every effort to find another time for the program* before the final broadcast in which case *we would reinstate the series if you are willing. The program has been a successful series and this cancellation has nothing to do with the merit of the program and we continue to have faith in the property.* It is entirely a question of time availability. We certainly hope we can work the problem out within the next few weeks. (Italics mine.)

By May 5, the date of the cancellation notice, just 3 weeks before the last broadcast, ABC was still having "faith in the property" and "the merit of the program," still thought it had been "a successful series" — to such an extent, in fact, that they would "reinstate the series" if we were "willing"! Did their survey post-date May 5? And, no matter what the findings of that survey, how could they have possibly changed the facts which dictated their statement — on May 5 — that the series had been successful? Success is not a matter of opinion but of facts.

Either on May 5 they were lying in that letter, in which case they're liars and nothing they say can be believed, or they were telling the truth as of May 5, in which case their survey story is — as I said — a lot of equine foecal matter.

Whichever way you smell it, it stinks.

I don't know, as I say, their real reason for dropping us; but whatever it was, it had nothing to do with any "survey." And it certainly had nothing to do with Ellery's "lack of human qualities." As a matter of fact, even this latter charge is not true. It is true that Ellery is not an eccentric; but for at least the last 3½ years, on an increasing scale, he has been a human being, recognizable as such, with extremely likeable qualities, and moreover he has engaged in cases which for the most part told stories of human interest about people you could care for. And his relationship with Nikki has been one of alternating conflict and attraction. This is not open to contradiction. The scripts and the recordings exist to back up my statement. I am astounded that anyone at all familiar with the week-in, week-out adventures of Ellery for the last several years could seriously entertain for a moment credence in the ridiculous charge that during that considerable period Ellery has not been a human being in radio.

But apparently at Morris some credence is given to this. And since Morris has to sell Queen for radio at present, it is highly important, as I said before, for your office to be set straight. Certainly Weltman out here is in a position to do so: he can at least testify to the quality of both Ellery as a human being and the show as an entertainment feature for the past ABC series. But, as I say, the shows speak for themselves. Apparently they spoke pretty convincingly to ABC up to May 5.

I am told by Dannay that your personal explanation for Queen's radio success for years — in spite of, presumably, Ellery's lack of human qualities — is that we brought a unique format to radio mysteries; and for Queen's present radio "failure" your opinion is that by now the format has simply worn out. This is not merely an oversimplification in my opinion; it just isn't true. By "unique format" I presume you mean the challenge-to-the-listener device. If the format has worn out, why has CBS recently put a mystery show on the air called *Find That Clue* which uses a variation — may I say a swipe? — of the identical device? I have only recently heard of another program using another variation of the same theme. If anything, the trend seems to be *to* the device, not away from it. Have you, for your side, any evidence that our format is worn out? For myself, I have no objection whatever to scrapping a format that is passé; but I'd have to be convinced by facts that it's so before I'd agree. I am certainly not going to let the format take the rap — or Ellery's "character," or any other integral factor of the show itself — when there are a dozen other possible explanations for the present standstill in the Queen operation. The first impulse of people in and around radio, when things don't go right, is to blame the show. It's too easy.

What are these "other possible explanations"? Certain things seem to be true. According to Bud Barry, the mystery show in radio has for some time been "in the doldrums," to use his phrase. As of the date of our last talk, which was in March, Barry said ABC had been unable to sell a single mystery commercially except *Gang Busters*, and even that one, he said, was sold only by the most extraordinary concessions and pressures on ABC's part. He blamed the organized groups which have been propagandizing against mystery shows, and especially [NBC Radio President] Niles Trammell and NBC. He said the whole atmosphere scared sponsors off mysteries, or tended to. He did say he thought it was a "temporary condition," and that was when he said ABC would like to keep Queen on at least through the summer — "to ride it out" if we were willing.

Secondly — as for the Queen show itself — the record shows that, considering the length of time we have been on the air, we have not got out of that long tenure what we should have got out of it. A favorable record in radio is made, as everyone in the business knows only too well, by factors other than the show itself. One is network. Another is time. Another is position in relation to other shows.

The record will show that in all of Queen's tenure on the air since our first half-hour show, commercially, for Gulf Oil, many years ago, we have not once had (a) a really good network coverage; or (b) a choice broadcast time; or (c) a favorable position in relation to other successful shows on the same network on the same night. The sole exceptions to this have come during certain summer series, when we had good broadcast spots — the only trouble being that we had them only during the summer, when ratings go down to zero. As soon as the regular broadcast season began, we would be yanked to go elsewhere.

Queen's record has been made *in the face of, and despite*, this terrible handicap.

The greatest number of network stations we have ever had during any commercially sponsored period was under 60.

We have never had a really choice broadcast time for a show like ours. As I have explained times innumerable to everyone concerned, including the Morris office, the various advertising agencies involved, etc., our show has always called for concentration on the part of the audience, consequently it demands a time late enough in the evening not to be threatened by the normal hazards of early-evening listening, such as dinner, putting-the-kids-to-bed, etc.

We have never had a favorable position, by which I mean being preceded by or followed by a high-rating show on the same network. On the contrary, we have been used to build up a spot for others to benefit by. This we have managed to do with monotonous regularity. (In this connection, I would like to point out that even during the late ABC series of 27 weeks, twice we built up a spot which ABC took away from us promptly for the sale of another property. ABC had us in three different time-spots in 27 weeks. How can you build up a rating when you can't get set long enough to have any chance of doing so? Even so, we managed to build them up sufficiently for ABC to sell them elsewhere.)

If you are looking for a reason for Queen's present deplorable condition on radio, don't you think the above makes a little sense? I do. And where would you say the responsibility lies for the above facts? I would say in the hands of those entrusted with the job of selling the show.

In fact, I do say so.
Sincerely,
Manfred B. Lee
4560 Carpenter Avenue
North Hollywood, Calif.

Lee never shied away from speaking his mind.

I believe that both Dannay and Lee would speak quite freely---and favorably---about Douglas Greene and Crippen & Landru. Greene shares Dannay's avid interest in the mystery short story and Lee's devotion to good writing. Greene has preserved work from such neglected figures as Queen, John Dickson Carr, Christianna Brand and Margaret Millar. He offers us some of the best contemporary short mystery fiction from writers such as S.J. Rozan, William Link, Clark Howard and Marcia Muller.

Hats (or deerstalkers, if you prefer) off to Douglas Greene!

All of us — not just Queen fans — are in his debt.

Confessions of a Literary Safecracker

2016 marked the 75th anniversary of *Ellery Queen's Mystery Magazine*. It also marked the 74th anniversary of *Calamity Town*. Mike Nevins, grand explicator of all things Queenian, has divided Frederic Dannay and Manfred B. Lee's work into four distinct periods. *Calamity Town* opens Queen's third and arguably greatest era, the years from 1942 to 1958. This period, Nevins writes, "saw Dannay and Lee at the peak of their powers and popularity, selling millions of copies a year, praised as highly by critics and their fellow writers as by their immense audience."

Calamity Town is the first of Queen's novels set in the fictional New England town of Wrightsville, ten thousand souls in the shadow of the Mahoganies. *Give Me That Old-Time Detection*'s editor Arthur Vidro has proven that Claremont, New Hampshire is the real-life model for Wrightsville, right down to the town square (which is round).

The novel is one of my very favorite EQs. I vividly remember the first time I read it. The year was 1976, and I'd checked out *The Wrightsville Murders* omnibus from my local library. My affection for the book has only grown over the last 40 years. I never had the opportunity to meet Dannay or Lee, but I feel I know them. I've read their books and I've read their letters. I got to know them even better when I decided to adapt one of their novels for the stage.

Turning a book into a play involves the deepest kind of study and sympathetic magic. One becomes a literary safecracker, seeking the combination to unlock a book's secrets and transpose them into another medium. A successful work of art is like a successful crime; it is an accomplished fact, something as beautifully constructed and functional as a Chase Manhattan bank vault.

Given its place in the canon, *Calamity Town* would seem like the natural choice for an adaptation. However, I'd originally been drawn to the second Wrightsville novel, *The Murderer Is a Fox*, in which Ellery reconstructs — and finds the real solution to — a murder that took place over a decade before. The book has a dual time frame that struck me as very theatrical, with the past and the present existing at the same time.

But there was also *Calamity Town*, a novel I knew well. I must have read it a dozen times over the years. Repeated exposure to the book fostered a greater appreciation of Frederic Dannay's brilliant use of seasonal celebrations as an organizing principle. Patty Wright tells Ellery near the end of the book: "Every last awful thing that's happened — happened on a holiday!" Dannay contrasts the warmth and nostalgia we feel for the holidays with cold-blooded criminal behavior.

Manfred B. Lee's evocative prose captures the look and feel of the town and the emotional highs and lows of its characters. Lee often felt he was the undervalued half of the EQ team, and with some justification. Although Dannay's awe-inspiring ability to conceive brain-busting plots attracted a great deal of attention, the books wouldn't exist without Lee. At his best Lee was a fine writer, equally capable of making a Grand Statement and selecting the telling detail.

While I was contemplating which novel to adapt, I saw the Broadway production of *The 39 Steps*. The show is a very amusing, 90-minute in-joke about Alfred Hitchcock's film. I was taken with the unabashed way the production used narration, multiple casting, lighting shifts and an ever-changing, non-realistic setting. What if that approach was used to tell a more serious story? Wrightsville is a town torn apart by murder. *Calamity Town* presents a panoramic portrait of a town, and it made sense to me to use overtly theatrical devices to characterize Wrightsville and its inhabitants. A theatrical model existed long before *The 39 Steps* that used similar techniques. I'm speaking of Thornton Wilder's *Our Town*, a play of simple means and dark truths. My adaptation would be *Our Town* — with murder.

Vertigo Theatre in Calgary, Alberta, produced *Calamity Town* in January 2016. Co-directors Craig Hall and Nathan Pronyshyn staged the play masterfully. On a raked stage of a blood red-brown, the nine-member cast moved light, specially made chairs and tables to indicate various locations. A sensitive soundscape provided period music and ambient sounds: train stations, crickets, ambulance sirens, the crackle of a tube radio warming up for one of FDR's fireside chats. Stunning state-of-the-art projections transported the spectator from courtroom to jailhouse to moon-drenched midnight lawn; the effect was highly cinematic. The period-perfect costumes and, above all, the superb acting ensemble, made Wrightsville as real and familiar as your own backyard. Ellery and Patty Wright, dancing to Glenn Miller on the porch of Calamity House . . . John F. Wright's understated and deeply moving graveyard recitation of Christina

Rossetti's poem "When I Am Dead, My Dearest"... Ellery, panama hat on head, suitcase in hand, silhouetted against a vivid blue sky of farewell. . . . These and dozens of other moments and images still resonate with me.

Directly or indirectly, every mystery reminds us that actions have consequences, time is on the wing, death is inevitable, and life is precious beyond belief. Near the end of the novel, we find Ellery

> looking at the old elms before the new courthouse. The old was being reborn in multitudes of little green teeth on brown gums of branches; and the new already showed weather streaks in its granite, like varicose veins. There is sadness, too, in spring, thought Mr. Queen.

Reading the Wrightsville novels and short stories that followed *Calamity Town*, one is saddened by the changing physical landscape of the town and the surrounding countryside and by the deaths of characters one has come to cherish. The truth of Ellery's observation is unmistakable.

Calamity Town, the novel, is dear to me. It cemented my affection for Queen's work. I grew up in a town just about Wrightsville's size and, even though my hamlet was in southwestern Minnesota, I saw its darkness and light reflected in Ellery's New England.

Calamity Town, the play, is a labor of love, my tribute to two cousins from Brooklyn whose work is once again finding new readers and admirers. To those who are making their first visit to *Calamity Town*, I say:

Welcome to Wrightsville, my friends. Ten thousand souls in the shadow of the Mahoganies . . .

On the Road with Manfred B. Lee, Part One:
"WE COULDN'T EVEN GIVE TICKETS AWAY"

In the early 1960s, Manfred B. Lee, the "writing" half of the Ellery Queen team, went on the lecture circuit to raise some extra money. Lee had six children to take care of, and a recent heart attack added medical expenses to the monthly bills. So he took to the road, speaking at colleges and various professional and civic organizations. A number of his notes — typewritten on index cards — recently came into my possession thanks to the generosity of Rand B. Lee, the youngest of Lee's surviving sons and an author in his own right.

Lee's lectures were advertised as "The Misadventures of Ellery Queen," and focused on the mishaps and mistakes that dotted Queen's career. The tone is ostensibly comic, but an unmistakably melancholy note is never far from the surface. Lee was a man of great — if mostly unexpressed — feeling, and it's likely he suffered from chronic depression.

Lee's notes will be of interest to Queen fan and mystery scholar alike; they offer new details concerning well-known EQ anecdotes as well as an all-too-rare opportunity to hear Lee's "voice." As the editor of *Ellery Queen's Mystery Magazine* Fred Dannay — Lee's first cousin and the "plotting" half of the EQ team — was the public face of the collaboration. Lee's death by heart attack at the age of 66 in 1971 also contributed to his relative obscurity. Dannay lived another eleven years and was the figure journalists and historians of the genre turned to when writing about Ellery and company. Lee never had the chance to weigh in on matters Queenian.

Dannay and Lee achieved conspicuous success in print but labored to lesser effect for the stage and screen. *Danger, Men Working*, their only play, was written with Lowell Brentano and closed out of town early in 1936. The piece is far from a disaster; with judicious editing and a sensitive director and cast, it would hold a stage nicely. Not much is known about the circumstances surrounding the creation of the play.

Until now — thanks to Lee's lecture notes.

It was a nightmare. Such theatrical legends as producer Jed Harris, the actor and director Thomas Mitchell (best known today as Uncle Billy in *It's a Wonderful Life*), and future Academy Award-winning actor Broderick Crawford are part of the saga. In Lee's account, dramatist Lowell Brentano is disguised as "John Doe." Burk Symon, the play's director-of-record, remains nameless, as does the show's hapless producer. A great deal of hard work and even larger amounts of frustration, confusion, and chaos led to a big dramatic goose egg of a show — one of Ellery Queen's greatest misadventures.

Imagine this: you're sitting in a college theater or a municipal auditorium in the early 1960s. A short, white-bearded man with heavy black spectacles stands at a lectern, a stack of index cards in front of him. He flips to the next card, which is headed "HOW E.Q. BECAME A PLAYWRIGHT":

> Agent sends "John Doe" to us — has an idea for a mystery play. Characterize: Office in the Fisk Building — first morning we met — Doe whispers in partner [Fred Dannay]'s ear, partner whispers something back, and Doe goes out. I ask Fred: "What on earth could he possibly have to ask you that he doesn't want me to hear?" Fred: "He asked me to tell him how to get to the men's room."
>
> This fellow pretended to be hard of hearing. Fred and I, from years of working together, had developed a rapid-fire kind of dialogue — we'd toss ideas at each other like machine guns. Our collaborator, Mr. Doe, would let us rattle on for fifteen minutes — and then he'd cup his ear and say: "Would you mind repeating that, please?"
>
> His idea discarded — unworkable — plot entirely ours — in the finished play script, when we went over it in privacy, we discovered that he had contributed exactly one line of dialogue.
>
> Agent sells play to Jed Harris in twenty-four hours. Our interview with Harris… Tells us: "Now write the play."
>
> Twelve days and nights in Hotel Edison, N.Y.C. Our third partner's sole contribution was to pop in occasionally and ask, "Is there anything I can get for you boys?"
>
> Finished re-write. Harris: "Fine. Good work. Now we'll all go out to the Half-Moon Hotel in Coney Island and rewrite the play."
>
> Exhausted — pleaded for vacation — while gone, agent took play away from Harris — he was temporarily "out of funds" and didn't have

the $500 necessary to bind a producing contract. . . .Biggest mistake of our lives. Play sold to — I'll call him Mr. X — who had been running a successful summer theater for years but whose greatest ambition was to produce a Broadway play. I might add, "with a very wealthy old lady's money," and say no more.

Talk about a misadventure! Everyone who's ever written a play insists that *his* maiden experience the most horrible of all — but I submit that for sheer, vomitous ineptitude — for bungling and fumbling and stumbling — by any test you care to set up — our play — "Danger, Men Working" — takes the all-time booby prize.

Our try-out was in Baltimore. Baltimore is where I learned to drink brandy. I was taught by a master, a young member of the cast whom you may still recognize under the name of Broderick Crawford. I'll always remember Brod Crawford with gratitude, but I think I'd have learned to drink brandy during our prison sentence in Baltimore even without Brod's expert teaching and encouragement.

Rehearsals — twenty hours a day. *Our* hours were even worse than the company's, because we not only had to sit through rehearsals, but when the cast was dismissed to snatch a few hour's sleep we had to rewrite scenes. I remember one stretch of rewriting when we went thirty-six hours without going to bed.

How shall I begin to describe what went wrong? Mr. X, our producer, who was extremely generous with his wealthy backer's money, suddenly decided he didn't like the sets, and he called in another set designer and had all new sets built — at mere extra cost of $20,000. This was in 1936, remember, when $20,000 was $20,000.

Our director . . . He was Mr. X's summer theater director, a dignified and pathetic little fellow who was still living back in the days of David Belasco, whose assistant he had been. I draw a merciful curtain over his so-called direction of our play.

On opening night in Baltimore, during the intermission between the second and third acts — so help me, ladies and gentlemen — our leading man got a heart attack. This is something that happens only on TV. But it happened to us — years before TV was anything but a gleam in a few far-sighted eyes.

I'll tell you something else — and I know you won't believe it: the actor who got the heart attack between the second and third acts insisted on the play going on . . . with him, heart attack and all, still playing the lead! And he did. He finished the play, God bless him.

Needless to say, the Baltimore critics skinned us alive. After a few days of playing to empty houses — we couldn't even *give* tickets away — Mr. X decided that Baltimore didn't deserve our play, and we moved on to Philadelphia.

Some weeks ago on David Susskind's "Open End" TV show, the actress Bette Davis referred to the disgraceful dressing rooms American theaters provided for actors in legitimate plays. She used vigorous language. Miss Davis could never have seen the dressing rooms in the theater *we* used in Philadelphia, or she'd have been cut off the air.

This was the second oldest theater in the U.S. The dressing rooms looked like cells in some medieval dungeon — as Jack Paar would say, I kid you not. They even had bars on the windows — those that *had* windows. The dust and grime of generations were ground into the seats, the walls, the floors. I have never seen a dingier, filthier place for a public performance.

It was in this throwback to the Middle Ages that Fred and I wrote, and rewrote, and re-rewrote and the company re-rehearsed, and we opened, and what little hide the Baltimore critics had left on us the Philadelphia critics finished removing.

Was Mr. X daunted? Not he. He closed [the show] — fired director — hired Thomas Mitchell — to redirect. Mitchell sits in the orchestra and orders a run-through. We watch his face. It seems in great pain. He slowly rises and says, "Boys and girls, this play must be entirely redirected — from curtain to curtain."

And Tommy Mitchell tried. He tried very hard. But then something crumbled inside him, and he spent the rest of his directorial engagement in his hotel room — you guessed it — drinking brandy with Brod Crawford.

So we reopened in Philadelphia, and of course we completed the flop. But Fred and I would have been through even if some Philadelphia dream critic has been drunk enough to say a kind word about our play. We'd had it, we told Mr. X. You can do what you want with "Danger, Men Working" — *these* men are throwing in the towel. We went back home. All we had to show for investing eight months of our lives in the theatre was that we had actually set a theatrical record.

This is a fact. Ours is the only play in the history of the American theatre to open in Philadelphia, close in Philadelphia, re-open in Philadelphia, and *re-close — in — Philadelphia*. It never did get to Broadway.

Time and distance may have blurred Lee's memory. The February 11, 1936 issue of the Philadelphia *Inquirer*, for example, featured a review that had kind words for both play and cast. But overall, his account of the crash-and-burn of EQ's only stage play rings true. The playwright S. N. Behrman has noted: "There is really nothing in this world so heady for a writer as theatrical success. It is unmistakable. It is instantaneous." So, alas, is theatrical failure. Luckily Dannay and Lee had other irons in the fire and survived their "prison sentence" in the theatre relatively unscathed.

On the Road with Manfred B. Lee, Part Two:
"THE MOST PROFOUND MYSTERIES..."

In the early 1960s a cash-strapped Manfred B. Lee took to the lecture circuit. His talk was called "The Misadventures of Ellery Queen," and focused on some of the strange, unexpected, or downright disastrous events experienced by Lee and his cousin Frederic Dannay in the course of their writing careers. Lee had a wealth of material to draw upon; their brainchild Ellery Queen found success not only in print but also in radio, film, and television and provided them with a plenitude of adventures . . . and misadventures.

Rand B. Lee, Lee's youngest surviving son and a widely published science fiction writer, kindly provided me with his father's lecture notes. In the following excerpt, Lee turns his attention to the mystery genre itself — its relation to real-life crime, its appeal to readers, its social and political implications, and its connection to "the most profound mysteries" we face as human beings. Manfred B. Lee's notes:

> One of the penalties you pay for being a mystery writer is that everyone thinks you can solve any crime, anywhere.
>
> A mystery writer has no more authoritative opinions about real-life criminals and crimes than anyone else. He can't have. For one thing, the really important facts of, say, a murder case are simply not available to him. If the investigating police have a clue that looks promising, you may be quite sure they're going to keep it to themselves. Without all the

facts — even if we were natural-born bloodhounds, which very few of us are — how can we be expected to arrive at significant conclusions?

But even if the mystery writer had all the facts, the chances are he wouldn't do as well with them as any run-of-the-mill precinct first-grade detective.

A mystery writer usually works from conclusions backward and builds the facts that make the conclusions stand up. He also knows in advance — because he makes them up — which facts mean something and which don't. Confronted by a real-life case, where anything can mean something, or nothing, he's at as great a loss as any layman.

Just as the reality of real detectives is quite different from the fantasy of fictional detectives, so the reality of writers is a long, long distance away from what the public fondly believes. A writer's life consists chiefly of staring at four walls, a floor, and a ceiling, before his paralyzed fingers a typewriter with a sheet of blank paper in it, and for company nobody but his own miserable, abandoned self.

The worst of it is that a writer usually has to work — like an actor — when everybody else is either having a good time or is sensibly in bed, asleep. If you've ever pounded a typewriter at three o'clock in the morning, with the wind howling down the chimney, the mice scurrying in the walls, and not a light showing anywhere, you'll understand why mystery writers write the kind of stories they do — and why it's a much more satisfactory way of earning a living to drive a garbage truck or drill holes in people's teeth. Why does a writer write at three o'clock in the morning? Because at three o'clock in the afternoon Junior is being Marshal Dillon [hero of TV's *Gunsmoke* series] chasing bad guys, playing all the parts at the top of his lungs. The wife is demanding to know why, in April, you still haven't taken down the outdoor Christmas lights, and you'll please do it right now! And the phone keeps ringing, and the doorbell, and your head . . . all in all, three AM is a much better time. You don't get much sleep that way but oh, the blessed silence!

You may well ask — in fact, the question comes up with dismal regularity — "Why write mystery stories at all?" Or: "If you have to be a writer, why don't you write something quote serious unquote?"

Well, for one thing, we can't all be William Shakespeare. For another, who knows what "serious" writing is and what isn't? A great deal of what passes as great writing today, given the full Pooh-Bah treatment of critical analysis and acclaim, is far trashier than many of the mystery stories at which critics elevate their dainty noses.

The mystery writer has something to communicate, too, and while I wouldn't for a moment make more of him than he is, what he has to communicate is not without importance. And at times his work has been a lot more significant than it's ever given credit for. A pretty good argument can be made, for example, that the so-called Hemingway school of writing owes its origin not to Hemingway but to a mere mystery writer — the late Dashiell Hammett.

It has been said that the characteristic that most distinguishes man from the lower animals — second only to his consciousness of God — is his restless, never-satisfied curiosity. Since most of the mysteries we're curious about we can never solve in this life, the mystery writer performs a valuable service for us. He invents situations that seem to defy explanation, and then he *gives us the answers*. He fills a genuine human need.

He performs another service for us. Almost always the situations he invents are situations of *violence*. This has caused a great many well-meaning people to label mystery stories a bad influence, especially on youngsters. Some of these stories — I won't particularize — undoubtedly are. But we have merely to watch the nearest blue-eyed, golden-haired little angel enthusiastically tearing her dolly to shreds to realize that the human animal is born with some very violent instincts. And the problem is, as law enforcement agencies know all too well, how to control them. Oddly enough, reading well-written stories of violence does tend to help us control our own violent tendencies. It gives them a harmless outlet. Nobody gets hurt but a character in a book, and he can't bleed.

Without attempting to go lofty on you, I submit also that the mystery story serves the cause of law and democracy. Not many people know that among the first books burned in Nazi Germany, when the barbarians consigned the world's greatest literature to the flames, among the first books they burned were detective stories. My partner and I have in our libraries probably the only copies extant of the German editions of Ellery Queen books published before Hitler seized power.

There was a reason for Hitler's hatred of mystery stories. They are a peculiarly Western institution; and in most of them an individual private citizen, working outside the established agencies of the law, solves crimes the regular police cannot. *The totalitarian cannot permit the individual free man to triumph over the State.*

In the same way, it's significant that no mystery story has been published in the Soviet Union. The individual making a monkey out of the established forces of law and order is sheer heresy to the totalitarian system.

The mystery story performs one other important function: entertainment. Or, as it's sometimes called, "escape." Like everything else in this life, overindulgence means trouble. Two or three pieces of candy are fine, but eat two or three pounds at a sitting and you'll wind up on the other end of a stomach pump. TV has brought a great many problems of overindulgence into our homes. The same thing can be said of so-called "escape literature."

But I always remember at such times what happened between 1942 and 1946. I first became aware of it in 1943, when I picked up a book written by a war correspondent named Richard Tregaskis called *Guadalcanal Diary*. It was the true story of the invasion of Guadalcanal, and it began with a description of the men outward bound on the Pacific for a destination unknown even to the officers — except that they all knew they were going somewhere to fight the enemy who had devastated Pearl Harbor. There was great tension among the men. Every Marine on those crowded decks knew that he might be going to his death.

Each man reacted in his own way. Some cracked jokes. Some wrote letters home. Others were studying maps. And one officer Tregaskis noticed was utterly absorbed in an Ellery Queen novel.

I was terribly touched. And before the war was over, I was to get that same feeling many times. We received literally thousands of letters from fighting men from every theater of war — written in billets, foxholes, on warships, in submarines and bombers — thanking Ellery Queen for this book or that, and telling us how much our books meant to them.

Four years ago — 13 years after the war — I was unexpectedly carried back to those wartime letters. One of my daughters was attending a school in Massachusetts and I was asked to be the speaker at their annual Red Cross fund drive. When my speech was finished and I sat down, the Red Cross representative rose and said how thrilled she was to have met me at last; during World War II she had been sent into North Africa with our troops, and the only books she carried in her duffel bag were two Ellery Queen novels which, she said, tided her over many a bad night of blood and death. These two books, she said, she had brought back with her and they still occupied an honored place in her library.

There can't be much wrong with "escape reading" that performs a function like that!

The unique quality of the mystery story lies hidden in the word itself. Life, love, God: a mystery. We're born, we live, and we die among the most profound mysteries; and very few of us dare suggest that we've solved them.

On the Road with Manfred B. Lee, Part Three:
"THE SAME BLOODY IMAGINATION..."

A thick stack of index cards is all that's left of Manfred B. Lee's appearances on the lecture circuit in the early 1960s. In need of money for medical bills and food, clothing, and shelter for his wife and children, Lee signed with the prestigious W. Colston Leigh Bureau, whose other speakers included Eleanor Roosevelt, Indira Gandhi, and William L. Shirer. Lee's subject was "The Misadventures of Ellery Queen," a wry recounting of the vagaries of the authorial career he shared with Frederic Dannay.

His lecture notes provide a welcome opportunity to hear Lee's point-of-view on Queen's often checkered past — and, in this excerpt, EQ's beginnings:

> I'm the only two-headed author in captivity — although, as you see, I've left the other head at home. I refer, of course, to the head attached to the shoulders of my partner-in-crime, Frederic Dannay. Mr. Dannay and I together form that monstrous fictitious entity known as "Ellery Queen."
>
> I speak of Ellery Queen as if he were someone else entirely, and in a horrible sense that's true. You'll recall the famous chiller written about 150 years ago by Mary Wollstonecraft Shelley — the story called "Frankenstein." In that story the hero creates a monster without a soul, and in the end the monster turns on his creator and makes boarding house hash out of him.

In creating Ellery Queen I'm afraid my partner and I are condemned to share Frankenstein's fate. Who ever heard of Manfred B. Lee? Or of Frederic Dannay? Yet tens of millions of people on this and five other continents know who Ellery Queen is, and some of them may even have read two or three of his books.

The creature's output is disgusting. Almost three-dozen novels — over 60 short stories — a dozen Omnibuses in the English language, and numerous others in foreign translation. Several very learned — they tell us — critical works. Over 100 true-crime articles. Over 350 radio shows. Not to mention TV (which I won't) or the three-act play we gave eight months of our lives to.

It's been estimated that the number of books bearing the name Ellery Queen stands somewhere between 80 and 100 million copies. Queen mysteries have been translated into every important modern language except Chinese and Russian. Since World War II ended we have even been translated extensively into Japanese. Japan's swing from feudalism to modern democracy is nowhere better illustrated than by the fact that today it is one of the leading nations in the world in its consumption of Western-style detective stories; and my partner and I take considerable satisfaction in EQ's being called Japan's favorite American mystery author.

Let me tell you how Ellery Queen came to be created.

His very birth was a misadventure of the literary delivery room — a birth that came perilously close to strangling on its umbilical cord.

Dannay and I are first cousins. Our mothers were sisters; we are not only related by blood, but from childhood we shared the same bloody imagination.

In September of 1928 Fred was working for an advertising firm in NYC and I was doing publicity and advertising in the NYC office of a motion picture company. Because our offices were in the same neighborhood, we used to meet almost daily for lunch. One day, one of us came armed with that morning's copy of Mr. Pulitzer's famous newspaper, the *New York World*, in whose pages could be found the modest announcement of a mystery novel contest. A book publisher, Frederick A. Stokes Company — like the *New York World* itself, long since defunct — was offering a $2,500 advance against royalties for the winning manuscript, and a magazine named McClure's was offering $5,000 for the serial rights. The publisher and the magazine had arranged with a well-known literary agency, Curtis Brown Ltd., to handle the contest for them. One of the rules was that you had to submit your manuscript under a freshly invented pen name. This was because the contest was open to any and all writers, even professionals, and the judges didn't want to be influenced by a well-known name. Your real name was to accompany the manuscript in a sealed envelope retained by the Curtis Brown Company. The deadline for submission was Dec. 31st of that year — less than four months away.

The more Fred and I talked about it, the more tempted we were to enter the contest. We'd always been interested in mystery stories. In fact, at about the age of 15, we had actually planned one, to feature a detective named — hold your hats! — Wilbur See. S-double-E. It never got past the planning stage, but the bug had been incubating ever since.

I can remember how we sat in that restaurant, our food growing cold, saying, "Well, of course it's silly to think of trying a thing like that. What chance would we have against thousands of contestants, a lot of them old pros? Anyway, we don't have the time, BUT . . . just for laughs . . . suppose we *were* going to enter the contest — how about this for an idea?"

Before we paid the check we were committed.

How we managed to produce that novel I've never understood. We'd work nights, either in his office or mine — weekends — in subways — over lunches. I don't how many times we were on the verge of throwing the whole thing away. But we didn't. There's no known cure for authoritis. They'll identify and overcome several dozen suspected viruses of cancer before anyone comes up with a specific cure for the writing bug.

By the exercise of the kind of inhuman energy only the very young are able to summon up, we just made the deadline; we slipped the manuscript into the post office slot a few minutes before closing time on Dec. 31st, 1928. The only emotion I can recall is sheer relief. It was pure cussedness that had made us stick it out. Fred and I knew perfectly well that we'd wasted four months of our lives; now the nightmare was over, and we could forget the whole bloody thing.

But youth is made of rubber. By early March we had bounced back. One day, over lunch, one of us said to the other, "Say, whatever happened about that contest? Have you seen an announcement of the winner yet?" Well, no, we hadn't, so we went to a pay telephone and, pretending we didn't really care, called up the office of Curtis Brown Ltd.

The moment Mr. Rich, the office manager, heard the name under which we had submitted our manuscript, he got very excited. No, the winner had not yet been announced, but . . . could we come right over to his office?

Could we come right over to his office! That was the fastest trip made by man until the invention of the space rocket.

I don't remember much about the rest of that afternoon. I don't think we went back to our offices at all. I do recall that as we dazedly walked up Fifth Avenue we planned how we were going to spend the $7,500 in prize money. We were going to quit our jobs, of course, and go to the South of France, and really Write, with a capital W. And I remember that we stopped into the Fifth Avenue shop of swanky Dunhill's, and we bought identical briar pipes and had the initials E. Q. stamped on them, and then, with solemn formality, each of us presented his pipe to the other. We still have them.

Two days later, Mr. Rich phoned us. Would we come over to his office immediately? He sounded like a clergyman about to give the last rites to a couple of condemned men.

A few minutes later in the Curtis Brown office, frozen, unbelieving, with mice nibbling away at our giblets, we faced Mr. Rich and the horrible news. In those two days the magazine that had co-sponsored the contest, *McClure's*, had gone into bankruptcy. That took care of $5,000 of the $7,500.

But the agent's news was worse than that. A magazine named *The Smart Set* was taking over *McClure's*. This was not *The Smart Set* of the heyday of Mencken and George Jean Nathan — it had degenerated into a cheap love story magazine; in fact, on its cover it carried the byline, "A Magazine for Young Women." And therein was the rub. *McClure's* had been a man's magazine, and so we had deliberately designed our story to appeal to men. *Smart Set* was willing to assume *McClure's* share of the contest, but only if it had the final say over the winning manuscript. They had already picked the winner, Mr. Rich told us — a novel that was the work of a Chicago housewife. She had written a romance-type detective story that was right up *Smart Set's* feminine alley. Gone was the $7,500. Gone was the South of France. All we had left were the two Dunhill pipes — and they tasted mighty bitter. Frederick A Stokes had been caught in the middle; they still thought our story was the best, and they offered to publish it anyway. Do you know we almost turned them down? Especially since, instead of $7,500 Stokes could only offer us the usual advance in those days — $500.00. How were the mighty fallen.

But we picked ourselves up from the floor. After all we had to recoup the cost of those expensive pipes, and we'd used a lot of paper, carbons, and typewriter ribbon in the creation of our opus. We signed the Stokes contract. That first Ellery Queen novel, *The Roman Hat Mystery*, originally published in August of 1929, has just been published in its 14th Pocket Book reissue, 33 years young and still going strong.

The bankruptcy of *McClure's* — the misadventure that launched Queen's career — was prophetic. It's set the tone for everything that's happened to us since . . .

REQUIEM FOR A DANDY

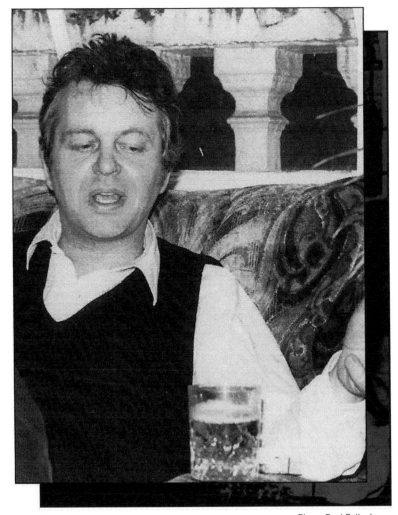

Photo: Paul Gallagher

Derek Marlowe

Requiem for a Dandy:
REMEMBERING DEREK MARLOWE

"These fragments have I shored against my ruins"
T. S. Eliot, *The Waste Land*

1.   UNCERTAINTY

This is provisional, partial, contingent.
A story — if not the whole story.
So much remains unknown.

2.   COORDINATES

Los Angeles, 1991-1995.

Home was a studio apartment a few minutes' walk from Santa Monica and Western. Like the neighborhood itself — a stretch of desiccated palms and cracked stucco in the shadow of a freeway overpass — the apartment wasn't lovely. But at 385 dollars a month it was affordable. The landlady was a kind-hearted eccentric who invited me in for rock-hard cookies, tepid hot chocolate and, at Christmas, carols sung to a record of the Percy Faith Orchestra. She provided a lyric sheet just in case I didn't know the words.

The apartment was at the back of the building on the second floor. The sun filtered through leaves and gave the room a cool green light. I'd grown up in a house with too few rooms for too many people; to have a place to myself was tonic.

I liked the place, truth to tell. I even cleaned it, every once in a while, though not often enough to become a habit. Something Quentin Crisp once said profoundly affected my housekeeping in those days: "After the third year, the dust doesn't get any worse." Practical experience proved he was right.

The apartment came with a bed, a desk and chair, a wardrobe on wheels, and a table and chair in the kitchen. Most of the furniture eventually disappeared into one theatre production or another. Jeff Phillips helped me sneak the item in question down the steps and into the back of his ancient red pick-up and thence to the Lost Studio on La Brea. We were part of a company there, a workshop/laboratory that produced the work it created.

Theatre is almost always done out of love and brings its participants very little money. I scratched out a living as a clerk at a bookstore on the Sunset Strip, answering phones, ordering books for customers, and looking after the film and television sections.

Working in a bookstore meant that I had no shortage of reading material. I'd line up the books on the dresser in the alcove next to the bathroom. I spent two months reading *Ulysses* aloud to myself after work. Joyce's words blended of an evening with the heavy gray rains that constitute a California winter.

It wasn't a bad place to work, by and large; one was surrounded by books and by people who liked them. I think of the raven-haired S. and her taste for gothic tales of despair and degradation. Of T., who specialized in Italian fascist literature and decadence of any nationality. Of G., the day manager who ran the outdoor newsstand and started every morning with a mournful look at Sunset Boulevard and a basso profundo *Oh, the air we breathe*. Of J., a Londoner obsessed with the American South and its music. "I don't believe anyone has listened to more pre-war acoustic blues in the last three years than I have," he told me once, and I had no reason to doubt him. There were others who worked at the store for shorter or longer periods of time. Some became friends. Some still are.

The only real problem about working there was the owner. Socially inept and chronically insecure, he toadied to the celebrities who frequented the store and treated his staff like peons. His lack of regard for those in his employ was shocking. He left his Sotheby catalogues lying about, marked up with his latest rare book purchases, but wanted to stop serving the staff meals on Easter because "it wasn't an eating holiday."

He was dissuaded from implementing this no-food policy, but it made no real difference. Everything he said or did displayed his contempt for us. I actually heard him say: "Anyone over 30 who's still working in a bookstore deserves whatever they get."

I wasn't yet thirty when I started working there, but I was close. I was naïve enough to be impressed by the celebrities I found books for, and sharp enough to be amused by the film industry's saucheries. Some of the telephone queries I answered epitomized every cliché about Hollywood ignorance. "Who wrote *Death Comes for the Archbishop*?" someone's assistant asked me one day.

"Willa Cather," I said.

"Who's her agent?"

I explained that Ms. Cather had been dead since 1947.

After a pause, the assistant asked: "But who's her agent?"

"Alfred A. Knopf." I said, and hung up.

Not all customer/clerk exchanges were like that. Sir Michael Gough, in town to play Alfred the Butler in the Batman films featuring Michael Keaton, was British class and charm incarnate. Marianne Faithfull was a delightful co-conspirator in jolly fantasies about emptying the cash register and heading to Las Vegas; I can still see her eyes light up and hear her husky rasp of a voice saying, "Oh, yes, let's *do*…" And it's hard to forget the occasion a few days after Kurt Cobain's suicide when a tear-stained Courtney Love approached the information desk with a plaintive: "Do you have any books on death?"

We did, and she was gently escorted to the Psychology section.

Looking back, it's hard to say if these were happy or unhappy years. They were busy, I know that. I worked at the bookstore during the day and wrote and acted in plays at night. They were also angry years; I was at war with the city. My goal was to have as little to do with Los Angeles as possible. I didn't have a telephone for most of my time there. I didn't have a car. I worked in the theater, the redheaded stepchild of the entertainment industry. I had a transistor radio for the news. Halfway through my stay I broke down and got a cd/radio combination and started buying compact discs — a major concession to then-current technology. Until then I'd made do with a cheap Panasonic tape recorder. I'd lie on the tobacco brown carpeting, ear next to the recorder, and listen to cassettes I'd bought at Tower Records, directly across the street from the bookstore.

In 1995 some of us from the theater workshop/lab planned to take Mick Collins's play *Winotime* to London. This, along with a general weariness of body and soul, prompted me to leave the City of Angels for my home turf in Minnesota. The London plans fell through, but I never returned to Los Angeles . . . at least, not for long.

I learned a great deal in L.A. It was a time of artistic experimentation and personal distress; the plays I wrote during those years were potent distillations of my discontent. Given what I experienced, how could I not view those years — and the city they were spent in — with a mixture of love and hate, repugnance and nostalgia?

The Internet has made it very easy to find out what's become of old friends and older enemies. It occurred to me that I might try to find out the fates of some of the bookstore's clientele. One customer came readily to mind: Derek Marlowe.

What had become of Derek Marlowe?

I'd known who he was when he first gave me his name to order a book. He was a figure of the 1960s, the dark, saturnine author of *A Dandy in Aspic*, a best-selling spy novel and the basis for a film starring Laurence Harvey and Mia Farrow. A tall, lean Englishman dressed in jeans, double-breasted suit coat over a colored shirt and tie, and Converse low-tops, he was a dashing mixture of British class and California cool.

A bit imperial, a bit imperious, Marlowe wasn't unpleasant, but he wasn't exactly talkative — *aloof* might be the word to describe him. Or *preoccupied*. He would browse about the store, pick up a book he'd ordered and inquire about another.

I'd first heard of Marlowe in 1976. I read an interview with him that was published in *Mystery Monthly* magazine. Marlowe was on a press junket, the article said, to promote his new novel *Nightshade*. I don't remember if I went to the library in my miniscule Minnesota town to look for Marlowe's book. I might have. Whether I did or not, though, I knew who he was.

And I wasn't interested.

More to my taste was Leonard Cohen who, grave and courtly in a dark blue pinstripe suit, came into the store every now and then. Or Sir Jonathan Miller, a tweedy, graying eminence in Los Angeles to direct an opera. Or Bruce Springsteen, in his proletarian flannel shirt and black jeans, who needed information on Creedence Clearwater Revival for a Rock and Roll Hall of Fame induction speech. I wasn't interested in Derek Marlowe then, and I wasn't when I typed his name into a search engine to find out what had become of him.

Why, then, did the news of his death — of a cerebral hemorrhage, on November 14, 1996 — stab me so?

Part of it was the sudden, shocking realization that time had not stood still; that it had, in fact, moved on and gathered up the dead as it moved. My years in Los Angeles seemed very far away indeed.

Another part was his relative youth. He was only 58 when he died. As I approached and then passed the half-century mark, 58 seemed younger and younger. Marlowe would be over eighty were he alive today. How strange to think of him as an old man. Even stranger to contemplate that fate for myself.

News of Marlowe's death transformed him from a minor figure in my reminiscences of life-in-Los-Angeles into an indisputably real man — a man I had written off as *passé*, a '60s relic washed up on the shores of the film industry, a man of little interest. A man, it turned out, of whom I had known almost nothing.

3.   BEGINNINGS

Derek William Mario Marlow — the "e" was added later, most likely in tribute to Raymond Chandler's private eye — was born on May 31, 1938, in the Perivale Maternity Home, Middlesex. His parents were Frederick and Helene Marlow, nee Alexandroupolos. Two sisters, Viviane and Alda, preceded him into the world.

Marlowe was educated at the Catholic Primary School in Greenford Green. He was then offered a place at Cardinal Vaughn School and went from there to London University, from which he was ejected for reasons that vary with the telling. His first creative endeavors were as a playwright — his adaptation of Leonid Andreyev's *The Seven Who Were Hanged* won the Foyle Award for Best Play of 1961-62 — and an early friend and flat-mate was another devotee of the drama named Tom Stoppard. One forgets that the theatre, especially in the era of Pinter, Bond and Osborne, was a vital, living organism in those days "Between the end of the 'Chatterly' ban / And the Beatles first LP," as Philip Larkin (in another context) famously described the early '60s.

"I was writing a play about a dandy who felt he was living in the wrong age," Marlowe told Tom Seligson of *Mystery Monthly* in 1976, "but I was having trouble with it. Then I came upon this idea that struck me as a very interesting puzzle." That idea became his first novel, *A Dandy in Aspic*, published when he was 28 years old.

Alexander Eberlin is an assassin for British Intelligence. He is ordered to find Krasnevin, a Russian assassin who has killed several British operatives, and who must be eliminated. The only problem is: Eberlin is Krasnevin. What does the hunter do when he is also the hunted? Eberlin stumbles from one desperate, improvised move to another, struggling to stay one step ahead of the game — assuming he knows what game is actually being played. Eberlin's attempt to escape his trap makes for a first-class espionage novel, a worthy peer of contemporaneous works by John Le Carré and Len Deighton.

Dandy is something else, into the bargain. Julian Symons, the grand old man of mystery criticism, once wrote: "The spy story is an excellent medium for expressing the deceptions and self-deceptions of twentieth-century man." *Dandy* proves the truth of Symons's assertion. Eberlin is a man divided against himself, caught between countries and identities, dangling in the void. Likewise, the novel containing his story is finely balanced between the concerns of the serious 20th century novel, with its theme of the agony of consciousness, and the genre effort, in this instance the spy novel. That it melds the two so successfully is a sure sign of Marlowe's gift.

Dandy was a phenomenally assured debut and remains his claim to fame. It made the best-seller list and was later turned into a film with Laurence Harvey and Mia Farrow. For all its merits, it is still in some respects the work of a tyro. It has a young man's brio and surety, yes — and the tendency to self-consciously indulge in the smart comment and the *mot juste*. It is sometimes difficult to tell unblinking objectivity from a kind of callow cruelty. Age generally tempers these excesses, and such is the case with Marlowe's work.

Symons rightly points out that *Dandy* owes something in its conception to Kenneth Fearing's *The Big Clock* and in tone to Le Carré. But there's much that belongs to Marlowe alone. The sculpted, aphoristic language is surely his, as is the sharp eye for the flawed, the tawdry, the compromised, the phony. This vision of the world reflects a disappointment so deep that it's almost unfathomable.

Which is to say, of course, that Marlowe was a Romantic.

"*The Great Gatsby* was his favorite novel," English novelist Piers Paul Read said in his eulogy for Marlowe. "If you re-read the novels you get a sense from the heroes of the kind of person Derek was, or thought he was — detached, sardonic, an outsider particularly in the kind of aristocratic society to which he was drawn, a rich source of erudite quips that his audience is too slow to grasp."

Playwright Tom Stoppard, who shared a flat with Read and Marlowe in the early '60s, noted in his foreword to a reissue of *Dandy*: "Hemingway versus Fitzgerald was an argument we had more than once. Derek was a Fitzgerald man, and the books made the case for him, especially *The Rich Boy from Chicago*. Even the title sounds like Fitzgerald." Thinking of Marlowe, one recalls that line of Nick Carroway's: "If personality is an unbroken series of successful gestures, then there was something gorgeous about [Gatsby], some heightened sensitivity to the promises of life…"

Marlowe and Gatsby (and Gatsby's creator Scott Fitzgerald) came from less-than-glamorous circumstances and, for a while at least, made the world of their fantasies the world they inhabited. They made it look easy, but that ease is hard-won. It is dependent to a large degree on youth and money, both of which have an irritating habit of disappearing.

What happens then is another story. Both Fitzgerald and Marlowe wound up in Hollywood. Both died there. Fitzgerald had little taste or talent for scriptwriting. Marlowe did. A decade of writing scripts — some produced, some not — for film and television provided a lucrative if not exactly fulfilling creative life.

This is where our lives happened to intersect. My home was a crummy studio in a run-down part of the city. Marlowe's circumstances were rather more palatial — a house in the hills on Blue Jay Way. On his brief transit through this world, I saw him, but paid no attention; I *missed* him.

The desire to capture something of what I'd missed led me to London in the fall of 2011. I spoke to his sisters Viviane and Alda, his son Ben, and his friends Piers Paul Read, Michael and Marie-Ange Wells, and Nick Ball. In spring 2015 I talked with the actor and writer Peter Coyote in New York City. Their thoughts and reflections are augmented by observations drawn from magazines, books, interviews and reviews dealing with Marlowe and his times.

What follows makes no claim to being a definitive portrait of Derek Marlowe. It is a collection of voices, loving and critical, joyous and sorrowful. The stories they tell may or may not be accurate, but that's always the case with memories — some of which go back seventy years or more. This is Derek Marlowe remembered.

4.   RUSSELL SQUARE

I met Viviane Barbour and Alda Marlow at the London Review Bookshop on as lovely a November day as England offers. The bookshop's café was crowded and not conducive to conversation, so we went to a nearby restaurant to take advantage of the pre-luncheon quiet.

They'd traveled into the city to speak with me, Alda from Tunbridge Wells, Viviane from Saffron Walden. Both were dressed to the nines. Alda, small and dark, wore a hat and a black dress. Viviane, blonde and robust, wore pearls and a twinset. They complemented each other wonderfully; they were obviously dear friends as well as sisters. Over a glass of wine followed by lunch, we talked about their younger brother Derek. We were joined later by David Burrows, Viviane's son.

I began by asking them what Marlowe been like as a boy.

ALDA WATSON: Shy. Inwardly, he was shy.

VIVIANE BARBOUR: He was an observer.

ALDA: Originally, he wanted to be an artist. He used to do a lot of drawing, characters and cartoons and that sort of thing. He had a friend where we lived in Greenford, in Middlesex, he had a friend Mac, who lived down the road and was interested —

VIVIANE: He *was* an artist.

ALDA: He was an artist and he went to America and made his name. But our father used to get annoyed with Derek. He'd say, "Why are you always with Mac? You've got to do homework. Why do all this drawing?"

VIVIANE: Piers said in his eulogy — he commented on his drawings.

[From Piers Paul Read's eulogy: *He was also a talented artist and cartoonist, and might have made that his career…*

[Peter Coyote: *He did a very quick pencil sketch of me that's up on my wall to this day. It hung in my mother's house for many years. She was very taken with it.*]

ALDA: What happened to the cartoons?

VIVIANE: I've got one at home. I was going to give it to [Marlowe's son] Ben, but I never met up with him.

VIVIANE: Our father was a practical man, he was an electrician and it was all hands-on. Whereas art was something . . . you might or might not be successful at it.

ALDA: He didn't think Derek would make a living out of it.

VIVIANE: He wasn't going to encourage him or discourage him. He didn't understand the art world.

ALDA: Though he himself —

VIVIANE: He painted. As a hobby. He was actually very good. But he wasn't earning his living that way.

[From Piers Paul Read's eulogy: *He came from a Catholic family, and he owed much to that family, particularly to his mother Helene. That she was Greek, that she was Catholic, that she was brought up in Egypt, spoke five languages and loved books, undoubtedly contributed to the originality of Derek's character and upbringing, and led to that sense of detachment from English society that we find in so much of his work.*]

ALDA: Father was a Londoner, born and brought up in Pimlico, Westminster. He didn't have a middle-class accent, but he acquired the appropriate papers for electrical and signal qualifications. Mother was Greek. She was from Kifissia, near Athens. She spent most of her growing up in Cairo in a convent, then as a teacher in another convent. Mother and father met after being introduced by mutual friends, and were married in 1928. They came back to England in 1930. She was teaching French in England when we were growing up. In the evening. She used to go twice a week.

VIVIANE: Twice? She went about three or four times a week.

ALDA: Did she?

VIVIANE: Three or four nights a week, yes.

ALDA: That was her second language, really.

VIVIANE: She could speak Arabic, French, Greek, English and Italian. She just picked up languages. She had an ear.

ALDA: One thing when Derek was only — what was he? About one or two. The War.

VIVIANE: He was ten months old when the war started.

ALDA: My father had friends in Yorkshire. He sent us up there, mother and the three of us. We stayed in a place called South Elmshall, which was a mining town. Vivy and I went to the Catholic school there for a while. Derek, of course, was too young. He was still a baby. And then we moved from the house we first went to because it was too small. We moved to a farmhouse and my mother said, "Oh, we can't stay here," because it had a big garbage tip, and I used to go there with one of the children of this farmhouse and bring things home. So she went to a billeting officer nearby, and he sent us to Rogerthorpe Manor, which is a hotel now. It was with six other families —

VIVIANE: It was a house for mothers and children that had either been bombed out of their houses or their husbands were in the forces and away. And we were there for . . . four years?

ALDA: Yes.

VIVIANE: Father joined the army after the First World War. Five years he was in Egypt. Cairo. He trekked the desert. He was there when —

ALDA: Lawrence was there. Lawrence of Arabia.

VIVIANE: He played football, I think, with him, didn't he? — Tutankhamen had just been excavated. He was there at that time.

ALDA: And he met our mother there.

VIVIANE: In Egypt, yes. He was there for five years. He could have stayed on for another year but he said no, and came home. Marconi had just started up, so he went to work for them. Now, years later — ten years later, of course — the Second World War. The year before he'd joined the Territorials [The Army Reserve]. Unfortunately, by joining the territorial army in England when he came back to England with my mother, he was called up for World War Two and sent out to Dunkirk and then to Egypt with the 8th Army. And so he was away. He was at Dunkirk. His officer — I have to tell you this, because he was so proud — his officer was the only man that he really praised during the war. This officer said to Daddy and the others: "Stay with me. I'll get you to the coast." I suppose he knew his way through the French fields and farms, and he got them to the coast, and they got back to England. That was Captain Lightoller. He was the son of the radio operator on the

Titanic. Father was home for about . . . I don't know, not very long, a few months. As I say, he came to see us up in Yorkshire. Then we didn't see him for about three or four years because he was back in Egypt. He didn't come home straightaway, but we knew he was coming. We were waiting for him. He'd been in the desert so long that he was as black as anything. We're lined up in the hall — and there's this black man coming in! And there we are — Derek, Alda, and me!

ALDA: When we went up to the manor house, I went to the local village school first of all. Then when Derek was between four and five, he joined me there. I used to take him to school. I'm going to say this — and it's to my detriment, but I will tell you — we used to go through a field. We'd go over a stile, walk through a field, go through another field, and then there was another stile into where the village school was. We were going through the second field one day and we were nearly at the gate when a colt came roaring down the fields towards us, and I said, "Derek, don't move" — and I *shot* through the gate!

VIVIANE: You left him there?

ALDA: I left him there.

VIVIANE: Alda! How could you?

ALDA: I know! I felt so awful. I thought, "What a coward!" In my mind, I thought: "Well, he's a child. The horse won't touch him." I told Derek: "Just stand still." The last time I saw Derek, we were in his sitting room, and he said, "Oh, I was talking to a friend of mine, and we were saying, what's the worst thing you feel ever happened to you?" And I thought, "No . . ." And he said, "Well, I remember I was going to school with my sister, and when we got near the gate, a horse came racing along" — it was a colt, actually, not a horse — "came racing along toward us."

VIVIANE: It was indelibly etched on his mind!

ALDA: Well, it *was*, you see. He remembered that as the worst thing, the most *frightening* thing that happened to him.

VIVIANE: All those books, all those plots — it's all down to you!

ALDA: I think it was terrible.

VIVIANE: You do?

ALDA: And I think how could I —

VIVIANE: Have a few sleepless nights, did you?

ALDA: I thought he'd got over it.

~

ALDA: I remember on one occasion . . . Mummy used to like the cinema. She was working in a nursery looking after children. It was at night, wasn't it?

VIVIANE: She was only there a little while.

ALDA: She did it to earn a bit of money.

VIVIANE: This was in Yorkshire.

ALDA: When we were evacuees. And we were out one evening. We might have gone to the cinema. There was one cinema in Pontefract. Where we were was Badsworth, halfway between Pontefract and Doncaster.

VIVIANE: *Gone With the Wind* came out during the war. I went to see it in Doncaster.

ALDA: Vivien Leigh. I wanted to be like Vivian Leigh. We'd gone to the cinema in Pontefract and we came back, and Derek was . . . we used to have a housekeeper, and her daughter used to look after the food, cooking and everything, and she said to Mummy, "Oh, I'm sorry to tell you that Derek's had an accident." He was being brought home from school in a cart, a horse and cart —

VIVIANE: A dray.

ALDA: A dray?

VIVIANE: They called it a dray.

ALDA: I beg your pardon. — It had stopped to let him off. The wheels started moving —

VIVIANE: Ran over his foot —

ALDA: And he hurt his ankle, didn't he?

VIVIANE: I must have been around because he said, "I want Viviane. I want Vivy. Where's Vivy?"

ALDA: Did he?

VIVIANE: Wasn't that nice? But he had a scar . . . it was a lump on the top of his foot.

ALDA: Derek was still going to the village school. I'd gone on to the convent in Doncaster, where Vivy had gone.

VIVIANE: The Convent of Mercy.

ALDA: The Convent of Mercy, yes. But Derek still went to the village school until we came back in 1945. When we came back to Greenford, he went to the school in Greenford Town. We were in Greenford Green.

VIVIANE: Didn't he go around the corner?

ALDA: No. No, he went to the Catholic school.

VIVIANE: In Greenford?

ALDA: His first school was in Greenford, a primary school. He settled down quite well there. He took his 11-pluses, or school certificate as it was called in those days, and got a place at Cardinal Vaughn.

~

Marlowe attended the Cardinal Vaughan Memorial School, Addison Road, London from 1949 through 1956.

Monsignor Richard A. Kenefeck, M.A., Headmaster, 1952-1976, "A Talk to Parents of New Boys": *No Catholic school would be fulfilling its purpose if its sole occupation were to push knowledge into more or less receptive heads. All Catholics know that education should deal with the personality as a whole. And Catholic education views the person primarily as a child of God. Education fits a boy for life. But life fits a boy for eternal life. Therefore, the knowledge, love and practice of religion stand before all else.*

If a boy finishes his school training as a Catholic gentleman, he will have qualities beyond price; he will give both joy to his family, who often have made sacrifices for him, and satisfaction to his Masters, who have spent much energy and time in shaping his character. For himself, he will be well equipped to make his way through adult life, and eventually to fulfill his destiny…

Derek Marlowe, from *Do You Remember England?*: *The house where he was born is no longer there and there are no letters. I have photostats of three school reports that show him to be intelligent and artistic, as well as rebellious. What form the rebellion took I am not sure, but his lack of attendance was criticized repeatedly and it appears he was often punished. The only teacher who replied to my letters (once again we are confronted by that tacit refusal to talk) taught him when he was fourteen and in the brief note — four lines, apart from the acknowledgement — described Dowson as "silent, solitary and unapproachable."*

From Piers Paul Read's eulogy: *Michael Fogarty, a school friend, remembers Derek aged seventeen or eighteen as extraordinarily stylish and knowledgeable about the ways of the world. He was passionately interested in cinema, perhaps because his sister Viviane worked in the industry. In the last summer holiday while he was at Cardinal Vaughn, he and Michael went to Paris where Derek got a job as an extra in the film* The Young Lions. *He was a German soldier at Sacre Coeur when Marlon Brando sweeps up in a staff car, but apparently, despite three days' filming, Derek never actually appears in a frame. More to the point, for Derek, was the hobnobbing that went on with the stars. He was invited to a party in the hotel where the cast was staying where he chatted with Lee Van Cleef, Dean Martin, and was presented to Brando. Later, at a bar near the College Franco-Brittanique where he was staying, he recognized the actress Mylene Demongeot, introduced himself as an admirer and joined her for lunch.*

Ben Marlowe: *He managed to get on the set, and he scribbled some caricatures of the two lead actors. Marlon Brando got wind of it, and said, "What are you doing?" "Here you are." And he gave it to him, and Brando was suitably impressed.*

From Piers Paul Read's eulogy: *Because of a weakness in mathematics, Derek narrowly failed to gain a place at Cambridge and went instead to read English at Queen Mary's College, here at the University of London.*

~

VIVIANE: It was *not* Cambridge. It was Durham. He was due to go to Durham, but he could not get his maths. It was mandatory that you had to have maths. He took it three times and couldn't get it. Queen Mary's accepted him. He was kicked out —

ALDA: For writing an article. That's what we were told. That's what Derek told us.

VIVIANE: He criticized one of the tutors. He wouldn't get set down for that now.

~

Derek Marlowe, *Mystery Monthly* interview: *I was thrown out for the usual reasons of not turning up for lectures and being suddenly interested in girls rather than Shakespeare.*

From Piers Paul Read's eulogy: *He was expelled for writing an article in a student magazine that criticized one of the professors.*

Derek Marlowe, letter to Paul Gallagher, c. 1980: *I was thrown out of Queen Mary College, London, for editing and writing an article in the college magazine. The article was a parody of* The Catcher in the Rye *reflecting the boredom of college seminars. Not very funny or special but times were odd then. Besides, I hated University and I think I'd made that rather too clear.*

~

English novelist and biographer Piers Paul Read, a tall, distinguished figure with a thatch of white hair, opened the door of his house in Hammersmith. Dressed in comfortable tweeds, he led me through the house to the kitchen and fixed us tea. We moved to the living room where, sipping tea and eating shortbread cookies, we talked about his old friend Derek. His manner was grave, thoughtful, considered.

When did he meet Marlowe?

PIERS PAUL READ: I was living in Berlin. The Ford Foundation had a program to raise the profile of West Berlin as a cultural center, and the first project was to pay stipends to great artists who would come live in West Berlin. It was a political thing. These artists were allowed to bring pupils, and I got a pupil's stipend for a writer whom I'd actually never met and never heard of called Witold Gombrowicz. He'd been in Argentina since the war, and came to Berlin. I joined that program. The second thing the Ford Foundation did was to start a writers' school. It was very fashionable in those days. They bought this lovely house on the Wannsee and equipped it as an incredibly comfortable hotel and installed about twenty German writers and three Americans and three Brits. The tutor of us all — of the English language section — was a playwright called James Saunders. The three pupils were Derek Marlowe, Tom Stoppard, and me. And so that's where we met, at this Writers' Literarisches Colloquium.

I took up with a girl in the Colloquium, a girl called Ingrid Froehlich, who was German. Because they didn't speak German, Tom and Derek were slightly constricted, and I think they mostly stayed on campus, as it were. I'd lived in Munich for a time, working for a publisher, and then I'd lived for six months in Berlin before they came so I knew my way around a bit more than they did.

It was very comfortable. We each had a nice couple of rooms and there was a sort of restaurant where we were all fed. The Germans were doing experimental things like writing novels with each writer contributing a different chapter, that sort of thing. We just got on with what we wanted to do with a little bit of help and guidance from James Saunders. Before I joined the program in Berlin I'd just written my first novel, *Game in Heaven with Tussy Marx*, and I wrote a play while I was there which the Questors Theater presented. James Saunders had links with the Questors Theater in Ealing, and in fact at the end of the program they came out and performed some of our plays in a Berlin theater. Derek was intent on being a playwright, really. He saw himself as a playwright at that point. And Tom — Tom wrote his novel called *Lord Malquist and Mr. Moon*. I think it was about that time. We were all of us slightly undecided which way to go.

When this was over, we all came back to London. Tom, Derek and I shared a flat in Vincent Square Mansions in Pimlico.

~

Tom Stoppard, Introduction to the reissue of *A Dandy in Aspic*: *We each had a room and kept to it. We had a kitchen but seldom ate communally. It was the year of "You've Lost that Lovin' Feelin'", by the Righteous Brothers: Derek played it on a loop.*

Piers Paul Read: *They were much more into pop than I was. They used to listen to the Beatles, and I wasn't into that at all.*

Tom Stoppard, *Dandy* introduction: *He went out most days because he had some kind of a job, and there were indications of an exciting life elsewhere. He'd met some people who had a rock band, and the band became The Who.*

Piers Paul Read: *We were all struggling. I was struggling less because my family was better off. Tom was making money by writing serials for the Arabic Service of the BBC. Derek started writing A Dandy in Aspic, and I remember saying to him, "You're mad, you know. Le Carré's written The Spy Who Came in from the Cold. That market is saturated." How wrong I was.*

Derek Marlowe, *Mystery Monthly* interview: *I was obviously influenced by the fact that in England at the time there was an enormous amount of spy activity going on. Both in fiction, with Len Deighton's The Ipcress File and John Le Carré's The Spy Who Came in from the Cold, but also in the real world. There was [Kim] Philby for example, and other real-life cases.*

I sat down to write the book. Ironically, the character is called Eberlin, which I found in the telephone directory. Only later a critic from The New York Times said Eberlin obviously means East Berlin. The thought never even occurred to me. Well, I got about halfway through the book in about two weeks, up to the point where he gets the assignment. It was about a hundred pages, and a publisher in Britain bought it. My agent also sent the manuscript to America, and Putnam's bought it. They said, "Terrific. Send us the second half by October."

Well, what does the character do once he gets the assignment to kill himself? I tried to work it out, but I couldn't. So I sent him off to Berlin, and in the end I had him killed in a car crash. The British publisher liked the second half and published it that way. However, Putnam's thought it was terrible. "Rubbish. Awful," they said. "One, you killed him off, and two, you didn't solve the problem. Do it again." So I wrote the second half again, where I kept Eberlin alive, and I think I solved it rather well.

Tom Stoppard, *Dandy* introduction: *When Derek told us that he was writing "a spy novel," we were skeptical. Surely that bandwagon had passed by? When Derek told me the basic premise for his novel (a spy with two identities who is ordered to kill his other self) I thought: now, that is an absolutely brilliant idea. By that time, Derek had delivered his riposte to our skepticism. Gollancz, he announced one day, had accepted his book. The American rights and the film rights followed. By our lights, Derek was rich. Success had arrived.*

~

VIVIANE: *Dandy* was published by Putnam's, serialized in the *Saturday Evening Post*, and made into a film. It was an exciting thing to happen: everything.

~

Piers Paul Read: *He was the first to be a success. He made a lot of money, he moved out, and he married Suki.*

145

5.   OXFORDSHIRE

I made my way to Marylebone Station to catch a train to Banbury, where Michael Wells would meet me. Wells has been many things in his day: actor, art dealer, writer, country gent. He and the actress Susannah York were married in 1959; they divorced in 1976. Wells and Marie-Ange, his second wife, live in Sutton-Under-Brailes, a twenty-five-minute drive from the Banbury train station. Their house is a rambling mixture of different periods of English architecture; parts of it date back centuries. We spoke in a large, cold room ("The price of heating oil is ridiculous these days") filled with books and paintings. Of course we had tea. Wells's beautifully modulated tones, fine profile, and lingering theatrical air were proof of his years on the stage.

When did he meet Marlowe?

MICHAEL WELLS: I was with Susannah. We were doing one of those tours advertising one of her films — a publicity tour. I'd gone with her. Derek sent a message from somewhere — he was traveling through America, and we met him there, but it defeats me as to *where* it was. I would imagine it was in Los Angeles. But it may *not* have been, because I do have a vague recollection of him having a girlfriend who is now married to one of the Who, Roger Daltrey. Heather. So it *could* have been in England. This was 1966, '67...

PETER COYOTE: During the '60s Derek and Suki were the top of the heap of London's hip society. Derek met her at a party. She was married to someone else, and he walked up to her and he said: "I can see that you're terribly miserable. Tomorrow evening . . . at seven . . . I'll be waiting under the Turner in the Tate Museum. If you'd like to meet me, I'll be there." And he said he went there, and no one was there — but at five after seven he heard stiletto heels echoing on the marble floors . . . and that was it.

MICHAEL WELLS: Suki was a Phipps, who I think were originally American bankers. Her mother was Lady Maclean, whose first husband died in the war; then she married Sir Fitzroy Maclean, who more or less invented the Special Air Service.

Susannah and I had a very nice house in the country called Frankham, and Derek used to come and stay there. I remember him telephoning me from Scotland, saying: "I've met this marvelous girl, can I bring her down?"

I remember walking into the sitting room and seeing them sitting there. And he said: "This is Suki De Le Mare. We met at the weekend, she's leaving her husband, and we're getting married." And they did. And they had a very successful marriage for a bit…

MARIE-ANGE WELLS: They came here quite a few times, didn't they?

MICHAEL WELLS: I remember when they first got married, them coming down and staying at Frankham —

MARIE-ANGE WELLS: They came here.

MICHAEL WELLS: Yes?

MARIE-ANGE WELLS: Don't you remember?

MICHAEL WELLS: I don't remember much.

MARIE-ANGE WELLS: They came here a few times for lunch.

MICHAEL WELLS: I remember them coming to Frankham when the children were very small — before your time, I think —

MARIE-ANGE WELLS: Yes, before my time.

MICHAEL WELLS: — and all of them singing beautifully around the dining room table. That I do remember. That was right at the beginning.

MARIE-ANGE WELLS: They more or less got engaged at Frankham, didn't they?

MICHAEL WELLS: He brought her straight to Frankham. It really happened there.

PIERS PAUL READ: Suki got pregnant very early, when she was about 18. She was a great debutante beauty, and she married Richard de la Mare, the grandson of the poet. His father was a publisher with Faber & Faber. He came from two respected middle-class families, so they certainly weren't penniless. But Richard was morose and gloomy and he'd never done anything with his life. I think he felt a) That he couldn't look after Suki and earn a decent living, and b) That she was a burden on him. I don't know the details, but it was a very unsatisfactory marriage. She was unhappy.

MICHAEL WELLS:

Derek and Suki
Standing bride and groom in the yellow and gold room
All future behind written into the view that passed through your eyes
Out beyond to know
What happened? Tell. No. Do not. Nothing happened.
Just — just then the world stopped
As my old clock, sometime around tea
On that summer afternoon.

That's my memory of them together, the first time.

VIVIANE: He married Suki and he took on her four children. Ben was the only child they had together. And he loved them, didn't he? He really loved them as his own.

PIERS PAUL READ: Derek and Suki bought a very grand house in Victoria Road. It had always been his aspiration to lead the life of a dandy. You've got to understand that the British class system is very complex and had a strong effect on Derek. Cardinal Vaughn School was a grammar school, he was a grammar school boy, but in spirit he was an aristocrat. I think the constant theme of his life was that problem of the grammar school boy wanting to be an aristocrat, wanting to be accepted by aristocrats, and marrying this very aristocratic girl — not just marrying her, but saving her from a terribly unhappy marriage and taking on her four children and moving into a splendid house in Victoria Road, which is one of the most fashionable neighborhoods in Kensington.

He was hopeless about money. In those days the income tax was very, very high and you paid it on the previous year's income, so he'd earned — I've got some figures upstairs — I think he earned 80,000 pounds. The following year, the income tax said, "Could we have 40,000 pounds' tax, please," and he hadn't got it. He'd spent it. That had a corrosive effect on the marriage. He couldn't sustain the role he'd set himself as a rich, mysterious Gatsby figure who was providing for this aristocratic girl and her family.

ANTHONY SILLEM, *The Barrow in Newport Court: A Memoir of the Rare Book Trade*: [Marlowe and his contemporaries] were born in the war years, before the baby boomers, and with a taste for combining a liking for traditional social sophistication with a relish for pop culture and an accompanying determination to have a good time.

MICHAEL WELLS: It was a very strange time. Here in England taxes were 93 percent. But — and this is a big "but" — you could set entertaining against your taxes. This is why we had the swinging '60s. People had enormous parties and you could set everything against entertainment. It was deductible. I can remember throwing a huge party in London with cheeses the size of omnibus wheels. Susannah went to Harrod's and I went to Soho and we double-shopped. Champagne was just bursting out of the bottles. It didn't matter how much it cost because if you spent a hundred pounds, it was only costing you seven, or something.

The so-called aristocracy was opening up. I think they were very receptive to people like Derek. We had a lot in common because we both started off with nothing. In the '60s there was a sense of being able to sail through the class system. It suddenly became accessible. You could drive right through it. People would try to be working class. It suddenly became fashionable. An odd time…

PIERS PAUL READ: The British are awful. They're very snobbish. It's much less now than it was, but in those days how you spoke, what you wore, who you knew — all these things were part of a system. I suffered a bit from the same. I wrote a novel called *The Upstart* about my upbringing in Yorkshire. It's very much about a character like Derek, but based on my own background. My father was an art critic and was quite well known, but my mother came from a very humble Scottish background in Aberdeen, and then we went to live in North Yorkshire, which was a very snobbish part of the world. I always felt put down. You were wearing the wrong thing, you used the wrong words…It was very much divided between what time you eat in the evening: do you have dinner at eight or do you have high tea at seven? So I understood how Derek felt about these things.

I had been to Cambridge, but even at Cambridge you think: "Well, I've made it, I've got to Cambridge." But then you find your college isn't one of the *top* colleges. There's always something you get wrong. The English are past masters at putting people down. I suppose it used to be the same with America at Princeton and Harvard and Yale. But in England it saturates the whole of society. Derek suffered particularly because he wasn't content to remain a middle-class writer writing about the middle-class; he wanted to be the Great Gatsby.

MICHAEL WELLS: Derek had an astringent quality. If he thought someone was going to get the better of him, especially through a class thing, he would be lethal. He could demolish people. And it didn't matter how *shy* he was.

ALDA: First of all, they were living in —

VIVIANE: A lovely Victorian Gothic outside Cheltenham.

ALDA: What was the place?

VIVIANE: Foscombe.

MICHAEL WELLS: I remember staying there. We were invited to Inveray with the Duke of Argyll in this enormous house at New Year. Peter the Great's punch was wheeled in, and I remember standing with Derek in the balcony and watching them all reeling. Being southerners we hadn't got kilts, so we were rather out of it.

Through him I came across Byron. He was a complete fan of Byron's. He loved the scandal of it all, the hanging out of the washing and people looking at the sheets through their binoculars across Lake

Geneva. *Frankenstein*. All that sort of thing. Beau Brummell was the other one he had a thing about.

He'd just passed his driving test. He bought this bog-standard car, a Morris or something, and he was dying to use it. We did the Byron tour. Because he was always incredibly early---he was terribly frightened of missing the ferry down at Dover — so we were three hours early. We stopped somewhere at a pub in the middle of the country. The landlord was wonderful, telling us about the nightingales singing in the wood and all this sort of thing, and we got completely carried away, and suddenly we looked at the time. The boat was leaving at midnight, and it was already a quarter past 11. We got there just as they were lifting the gangplank.

He was a bit vague. Usually I'm pretty practical, but this time…We saw a sign saying *Les Trois Pigeons.* A restaurant. I thought: "I remember that. It's rather a good place." When we eventually got there, it was the same name but the wrong town.

Les Trois Pigeons was right on the corner of the main road. Derek and I staggered in. There was no one in the dining room…These awful plastic flowers…We got there and we sat there, terribly disappointed, but Derek always was wonderful at making the best of a bad job, at saying: "You know, It's very good, really."

We were shown up to this room with a couple of single beds and I was put in the one nearest the window. The room was on a sort of a slope, and I remember Derek saying: "Well, you know, it's fine. You know, it's French…" And then suddenly there was a terrible roar –the room was right above where the lorries geared down to go around the corner. The beds were shaking up and down. A terrible night…

I remember going to Chateau Chinon with him. Taking him sailing on Lake Geneva. Going and visiting the Villa Diodati and walking through the garden and getting thrown out by the owners because they didn't want people in their garden. He hadn't rung up…or maybe he had, but certainly I don't remember him ringing up. Or maybe he'd tried and couldn't get in touch with them. And we just walked in. It was this great big house by the lake with big gates and all the rest of it. And we were walking around the garden. And he was really attacked by this woman, and he stood up and sort of said what he was, but eventually we left. He didn't manage to get 'round her. Maybe his French wasn't good enough…

In 1967, Marlowe adapted Turgenev's *A Month in the Country* for Susannah York. It was staged — and then later filmed — at Frankham.

MICHAEL WELLS: The story behind *A Month in the Country* was simply that Susannah was game to do it. She'd been offered a play, and in those days, it was a huge chunk of time, eighteen months or even two years. You had to rehearse it, and sign up to go into the West End, and then you'd go on a tour, and then maybe you'd also commit yourself to going with the play to New York. Not that it would happen, but it might. And at the time, she was right at the top of the tree and earning quite a lot of money. I thought it was absolutely crazy to do a play because my idea of being a film star is that you always have three or four balls in the air, so if one project falls through, you've got two or three others hanging around. You're always moving forward. I tried to explain this and she wasn't having any. She was going to do this play. And then she said: "Find me a play! I want to do some theater!" So I rang up a friend of mine who's very clever, and I said, "Look, I need something," and he said, Read *"A Month in the Country*. Turgenev." I read it and thought it absolutely brilliant. I said to Susannah: "Read this," and she read it and said: "I'll do it." Within six weeks we'd done the play on the terrace at home, and Derek had scripted it and we'd shot it...

Susannah was doing a film with Elizabeth Taylor. It was the time she was going out with Richard Burton. Susannah rang me and said — one of us had asked them down for the weekend — and she rang me and said: "They're coming down. They don't want to do anything elaborate. They just want to go to a pub and have sausage and mash." Can you imagine? She said: "Don't do anything. Give Iris the night off." That was our cook. I duly did. I rang up three pubs and booked us in. Because I thought, "God, I don't know where they'll want to go." They turned up in a huge stretch limousine... Derek and Suki were staying with us that weekend. They were the only other guests.

Richard arrived and took one look at the house, and said: "Why are we going out? For God's sake, let's stay here." God, here we go! I'd given the help the night off — luckily I'd got in some sausage and mash! We sat up all night. Richard recited poetry. Elizabeth Taylor sang songs. Suki also sang. I recited Keats's "Ode to a Nightingale," which I knew by heart. I can't remember what Derek did, but he was very amusing...

I always remember Richard calling for an egg. "Get me an egg!" We got him an egg, and he took the egg, and he said: "Winston Churchill says I have the best voice in the world, and I'll tell you why." And he put the egg in his mouth and closed it. It meant he had an enormous palate or something, this enormous resonant cavern there. Then he gave it to me and I did it---and then Susannah did it---and the egg went round the table!

He'd just given Taylor that enormous great ring worth a king's ransom, and she said: "Richard's just moved to Switzerland and he's become a pound millionaire in a matter of weeks."

The whole thing was sort of a fantasy. I remember taking her for a long walk all 'round the woods... I remember her teaching me how to mix Bloody Marys at God knows what time in the morning. I mean we were up *all night*...They drank. Well, everyone did then. Strangely enough, people didn't seem to get drunk. I don't know why.

I suppose they *were* drunk. . . . I remember her teaching me how to mix Bloody Marys at God knows what time in the morning...

We went to that huge party they gave. It was his 50th birthday. They flew all their friends over to Budapest for a week. They sent everyone a twenty-page telegram, telling us what to wear every night. I had a 12-pound Take 6 suit and the pocket fell off after the third day...It was an enormous party. I remember sitting next to Ringo Starr and the poet Stephen Spender. Michael Caine was there, the Princess of Monaco — I sat up all night talking to her. My suitcase fell out of the back of our mini on the way from Chelsea, so I had no clothes and I was borrowing shirts from Michael Caine. . . . That was the sort of life one led in those days.

~

I met Ben Marlowe at the Hampstead Heath tube stop in the fading autumn light. We went to a nearby pub on Hampstead High Street. Ben bears a distinct resemblance to his father — and is just as passionate about film as his father was. I began by asking him where he'd grown up.

BEN MARLOWE: We started off in London, then we moved down to the west country. Foscombe was like a Gothic mansion. There were five of us kids living in the house. We had everything we needed there. A thirty-second walk from the house was another building, one half of which was for the couple who were looking after the house, and my dad had the other half for his study, a huge big study where he did his writing. He'd get away from the noisy kids. It was, I think, the best time for him. He must have written *Somebody's Sister* there. *Nightshade*, too.

PIERS PAUL READ: They had to sell Victoria Road and moved out to a big country house called Foscombe. They could see six counties from it, and everyone had champagne and orange juice — Bellinis — for breakfast. They were madly extravagant. The house had varnished balustrades and Suki didn't like the varnish, so they spent 10,000 pounds removing the varnish. They were both hopeless with money. For him it was all part of their image. I found it slightly annoying at that time of life because I hadn't got any money. I was working for the *Times* Literary supplement on quite a modest salary. And Derek would say, oh, let's go and have dinner at...what's that restaurant, it's the one on Addison Road he always used to go to...and you'd split the bill, and it was more than I could afford.

Where he lived depended on his fortunes. He had a flat in Kensington, he had a flat near Notting Hill Gate, and then for a time he lived in Hamlet Gardens, which is just over the park here — very unfashionable in those days.

ALDA: The one in Hammersmith, he was quite happy there. Remember the flat he had, with all his books and everything. You probably remember, David.

DAVID BURROWS: I do. Hamlet Gardens. I stayed there for a year, off and on. Derek was in Los Angeles, and he wanted someone to look after it because he was going to be away for a long time, and take his car out for a drive every now and again. So my wife — we weren't married at the time, but Annie, my wife, now — and I stayed there for a year. Just over a year. He'd come back every now and again and we'd move out and let him get on with it, and we'd move back in again when he went away…

PIERS PAUL READ: One minute he had no money, the next minute he did some film deal and had money…and then he didn't. You tended to lose touch with him when he was doing badly because he didn't want to see anybody. And then, when he had a coup of some sort, he'd ring up and say, hi, how are you?

I was looking at my diary and one of the entries said: "Derek very depressed about the reviews of his book." But of course writers are often depressed when their reviews are actually quite good but they don't just say "This is the best thing since Tolstoy." He was never a fashionable novelist. I had my moment as a fashionable novelist, and then went out of fashion. Derek was never in fashion, never in the market for literary awards. It was a time of experimental, plotless novels. People thought narrative was very old-fashioned. He never had another popular success like *Dandy* so he couldn't sustain the income, and so they had to sell that house, and he moved into a small farmhouse called Rudge Farm, but then spent a lot of his time here in London, and then the marriage broke up.

BEN MARLOWE: Then we moved to a smaller place, a bit further toward London, in Wiltshire.

ALDA: They sold Foscombe because the money wasn't coming in from Derek's books. They moved to a little farmhouse. They weren't there very long before Suki left.

MARIE-ANGE WELLS: I know what he told me. Suki found something in the wastepaper basket. He'd written a letter — I think he'd probably had an affair or something, and he blotted it, and she went and put it in front of the mirror — and read it.

MICHAEL WELLS: Sounds like a book!

MARIE-ANGE WELLS: That's what Derek told me.

MICHAEL WELLS: …I do remember something like that.

MARIE-ANGE WELLS: That's what Derek said.

TOM STOPPARD, in Kenneth Tynan's "Withdrawing With Style from the Chaos": *Derek is a fantasist enclosed by more mirror than glass.*

PIERS PAUL READ: He wrote the script of my novel *A Married Man*. He completely changed the story to really tell the story of him and Suki. And the producers said, "What on earth do you think you're doing?" So he had to completely re-do it, sticking to my plot.

We were living then in Holland Park, and somebody said, "They're filming your book in the next street." I saw quite a bit of Anthony Hopkins. He was obsessed with the part and he thought I somehow embodied the main character, Strickland. He started wearing the same sort of ties I was wearing, modeling himself on my appearance. The assistant producer and one of the people who was behind it being made was Julian Fellowes. Julian was a great friend of Hopkins', a kind of slavish acolyte of Hopkins' at the time. I think Julian was responsible for getting it made into a TV film. It got a very good reception.

MICHAEL WELLS: I wrote a play called *The Long Burrow*. Derek is very much in it and part of it. A whole brass band came out of the woods. No one knew; they thought we were putting on a gramophone. In fact, I shipped up the whole of the Hastings Silver Band. I put them in the woods, and right at the end of the play the entire band came out led by a man in a bowler hat. I worked with a man years and years ago who he said if you put on plays in the country, use everything that you possibly can. And that's what we did. A lot of the people are recognizable. Derek came and saw it and said to me: "I cried at the end." It was quite near the bone…

When the marriage broke up, Frankham became almost a second home for Derek.

Derek and Suki Marlowe were divorced in 1986. Marlowe moved to Los Angeles. The place and the work suited him — for a time. "I love movies very much," he told *Mystery Monthly*. "If I had a choice I'd rather see a really good movie than read a really good book."

6. JUDGMENTS

Derek Marlowe, in the *St. James Guide to Crime & Mystery Writers*: *I have written to date (1978) eight novels, only four of which could be considered thrillers. There is no premeditated purpose on my part: I do not choose in advance to write an "entertainment" as opposed to a "novel." Locations influence me very much and usually provoke the story — Berlin for A Dandy in Aspic, Haiti for Nightshade and, more especially, San Francisco for Somebody's Sister, which is probably the purest detective story of them all. I like to intrigue the reader; perhaps this may happen more in a romantic novel (A Single Summer with L.B.) than in a straight thriller. I have no answers as to why I write the particular book at the particular time except that my own state of mind (very mercurial) dictates it. I am Ford Madox Ford wanting to be Chandler or Woolrich, and vice-versa.*

Four of Marlowe's books — *Dandy* and the three discussed below — fall, more or less, into the mystery genre. As for the others, *Memoirs of a Venus Lackey* (1968) is a roué's mordant, rococo recounting of the events leading to his death; the narrator speaks from his grave. *A Single Summer with L.B.* (1969) is an exquisitely detailed novel about Lord Byron, told from the perspective of the poet's hapless young physician Polidori. *Do You Remember England?* (1970) is, in part, a fictional version of his courtship of Susan "Suki" Phipps. *The Rich Boy from Chicago* (1980) is a lengthy and engrossing portrait of the titular character's progress through the world, encompassing two continents and four decades. I have a particular fondness for this expansive, generous novel, so different from Marlowe's shorter and more tightly woven works. *Nancy Astor* is the least of the novels. Based on his scripts for a BBC television series about the first woman member of Parliament, it's a thin concoction that lacks Marlowe's flair for sumptuous language and close observation.

The figure of the assassin recurs in Marlowe's novels. We begin with Eberlin/Krasnevin and we end, all too abruptly, with the fragmentary *Black and White*'s Gabriel Jesus Hoyt. In between we find Jay Mallory, the lead character and narrator of *Echoes of Celandine* (1970). What is it about the hired killer that appealed, that spoke so to Marlowe's imagination? Simply put, the assassin is a symbol, a romantic abstraction, a man alone, crucified by inner doubts and outer circumstances. He does his work in secrecy and silence. His character and habits are essentially those of a writer.

Celandine's Jay Mallory is far from a conventional hero; he is overweight, middle-aged, weary unto death of his trade. Mallory returns from a "job" to find that his wife has disappeared. His search for the missing Celandine is, like many a quest, doomed from the start. That quest, and Celandine's involvement with a hit that Mallory would like to avoid, is the thread we follow through the labyrinth of the novel, which illustrates Wilde's sad contention (in *The Ballad Of Reading Gaol*) that "each man kills the thing he loves."

Marlowe named *Celandine* as the favorite of his thrillers. I wish I could agree. It's difficult to feel much sympathy for Mallory and his plight, and the balance of the novel feels off. There's rather too much consciousness and too little genre for my taste. Its effects feel muffled. What should be shocking, alas, isn't. One may admire the book, but one is not moved by it.

If *Celandine* is a noble failure, *Somebody's Sister* (1974) is a stunning success.

Sister is quite consciously an exercise in the hard-boiled tradition. It admirably fulfills all the genre requirements; the plotting, for instance, has all the requisite twists, turns and reversals of the classic P.I. novel. But it is by no means a pastiche or an exercise in nostalgia. Marlowe was clear about that in the *Mystery Monthly* interview:

> My idea was to see what a Forties private eye would have been like in the late sixties, when suddenly he's out of date. The detective, Walter Brackett, is an anachronism. He's still living in the time of the dime detective — Bogart's time — and of course it's no longer that. The police and their computers have taken over.

This is more or less true. *Sister* is not as much a contest between old methods of detection and new — intuition versus forensics — as it is a portrait of a man whose world has slowly evaporated. It's also a part of one of the larger cultural trends of the early 1970s, when the hard-boiled tradition was reinvigorated (in print, Robert B. Parker and Roger L. Simon; on film, Altman's film version of *The Long Goodbye*), indulged in (in print, Andrew Bergman; on film, Robert Mitchum in the re-make of *Farewell, My Lovely*) or, on occasion, parodied (*The Black Bird*, a black spot on several resumes.)

Walter Brackett is a 53-year-old Englishman who's lived in San Francisco since the end of World War II. His wife is dead and Harry Kemble, his erstwhile partner, has been confined to a nursing home for years following a horrible beating. Brackett's been working alone, if you could call it working, as he's hardly had a case worth mentioning in God only knows how long. When he's asked to identify the body of a teenage girl who died in a car crash on the Golden Gate Bridge, Brackett is drawn into some of San Francisco's seedier locales and a mystery that brings him face-to-face with his origins as a detective.

Among the book's pleasures are a handful of skillfully done action scenes, not something one associates with Marlowe's work. One wishes that Walter Brackett had been brought back for another case, but our last glimpse of him in the novel — walking away from a car on the Golden Gate Bridge — is the last we see of him. English novelist Nicholas Royle believes that Marlowe's unwillingness to repeat himself or work in a single genre hampered his career, and he's probably right. Well, at least we have what in all likelihood would have been

Brackett's last case, anyway. Compact (it works wonders in a mere 153 pages), intensely cinematic, *Somebody's Sister* is a forgotten neo-noir classic.

Marlowe shared more with Raymond Chandler than the surname of Chandler's most famous creation. Both were Englishmen (though Chandler was born in America) who aspired to high culture but wrote in popular forms. Both came to LA and labored in the vineyards of the film industry. Both ultimately decided to return to their work as novelists. Both died in California. Both belonged, perhaps, to different eras than the ones in which they lived. Both did as we all do — the best we can given the circumstances.

Dedicated to legendary San Francisco newspaper columnist Herb Caen, *Somebody's Sister* is a dark travelogue of that city by the bay. Marlowe told *Mystery Monthly* why he chose San Francisco as a locale:

> There's a romance about San Francisco that Los Angeles doesn't have. San Francisco is also an island, and I love islands. Most of my books are set on islands. . . . By using islands, the characters not only become confined by their dilemma, but also the location has got boundaries as well. Slowly it tightens around them.

This is a perfect thumbnail description of what happens in *Nightshade* (1976). Edward and Amy Lytton are vacationing in the Caribbean. The goal of their trip is to repair the damages inflicted to their marriage by a catastrophic event in the recent past. Amy's sister hanged herself, but the reasons for her suicide are only hinted at. To say that Edward and Amy's vacation singularly fails to draw the couple back together is to indulge in the grossest understatement.

Their marriage remains unconsummated; both are still, in fact, virgins. Edward's suspicions and fears about Amy's motives and actions multiply like cancer cells in the oppressive atmosphere of the tropics. Edward is taken up by Daniel Azevedo, a stylish and mysterious local aristocrat who may (or may not) be following them from island to island. Amy is befriended by Jean-Dantor, a voodoo priest. Mysterious voices are heard. People and objects appear and disappear. Or do they?

"One on level," Marlowe told *Mystery Monthly*, "I wanted to write a novel that was a straightforward story of jealousy between a husband and a wife. On a second level you have all the elements of the supernatural." Marlowe builds a haunted and deeply unsettling atmosphere out of a hundred tiny details, rather like Polanski's best films. *Nightshade* may be read as a ghost story, a story of sexual frustration and hysteria, or as a fairy tale of sorts — two children lost in a very dark wood. The conclusions the reader draws about what happened (and what didn't) will shift with each interpretation, like a slide projected onto a curtain billowing in the wind. The first line of the book states: "It was to have been the happiest of times." It was, alas, anything but that.

Nightshade shows Marlowe working at the top of his form. It possesses all the strengths of his previous work — the chiseled language; the Romantic, often melancholy sensibility; the shapeliness of form — and something of more recent vintage: a profound sympathy for his characters. Amy and Edward's faults are acknowledged, their mistakes are noted, but there is nothing punitive in Marlowe's attitude to the poor Lyttons and their journey into death-in-the-tropics.

A masterful book.

7.   BLUE JAY WAY

PIERS PAUL READ: One of the attractions of America was that Hollywood was a much more meritocratic society. Suki's family is very…"aristocratic" is the wrong word. . . . Her stepfather was Sir Fitzroy Maclean, who had this great country house in Scotland, and her mother was connected to a lot of aristocratic Scottish families. To Derek, that was the attraction. But it's fatal to start playing the game when you haven't got any of the chips. He would always have been seen as a clever boy who'd made good. He would never be able to reinvent himself as the sort of person he wanted to be. He was never going to be the languid aristocrat. His ambitions were social, not literary. If Derek had just wanted to be a great writer, he would have been — he *might* have been — a happier man.

The good November weather held. I arrived at the Baker Street tube stop early and had some time to kill before I met Nick Ball. I strolled around the neighborhood, peeked into the London Beatles Store and the Sherlock Holmes Museum, and then made my way through the crowd to our meeting place, a chain restaurant near the tube entrance. A burly, big-shouldered man in a tan raincoat smoked a cigarette near the statue of Sherlock Holmes. I suspected this was Nick Ball. I was right. We shook hands, then went inside.

How did he meet Marlowe?

NICK BALL: I had made a series about a cockney private eye called *Hazell*. We met at a screening or at one of those parties with drinks and everyone standing there. He introduced himself and we became great friends. When I first met him, they lived in Stockwell. Stockwell runs to Clapham North, and the house was right on the border there, in one of those very nice Regency-type squares. The next time I saw Derek, he'd moved out…

We spent a lot of time concocting scripts. One was called *American Red*. It was written for Rank, which wanted me to star in something, but

I didn't want to do anything parochially British. We conjured the idea on the way out to Pinewood, a 40-minute car ride, to present it. I've never seen a more brilliant presentation from Derek. And in the end they gave us five grand to do this trip.

Derek had written *Somebody's Sister*, which has an English protagonist who's been in the States — San Francisco — for many years. I really loved *Somebody's Sister*. It's slim, it's right to the point, and as a thriller it's brilliant. We'd set this whole thing going where it might have been the same character at the end of the day. Walter Brackett. I think we changed it from Brackett to Loomis. Loomis, like the cash securities van you see going around. This Brit — which is the connection with *Somebody's Sister* — is a private eye. His wife has died, and he's taking her goods and chattels back to the Midwest.

Derek and I rented a car and drove through Tucson, all the way to Colorado, Wyoming, and ended up at Greasy Grass, Montana, better known as Little Big Horn. Along the way — and this absolutely happened — we stopped at a toilet in the middle of the desert. There's a shack, and there's an obelisk stands next to it, like a mini Cleopatra's Needle, and it says on it: "Here ended the Indian Wars." This is where the Apache chief Geronimo surrendered. That was the spot, and there's a tourists' toilet sitting there. That's where the script kicks off. Our man is in a chuggity old car going from San Francisco to somewhere in New Mexico. On the way he crosses the desert, and it's dawn, and he stops at this toilet. Under one of the stall doors is a painted face — an Indian in full war paint. Our man takes him out and puts him in the car. The Indian comes to and then dies, trying to reach for the blue bird on the rear-view mirror. His old grandfather comes and somehow convinces Loomis to take the body back to what he calls Greasy Grass, Montana. Loomis sets off reluctantly on a journey to do just that. Everybody is trying to stop him, including the 7th Cavalry and the big bad boy who is a Crow Indian from Chicago who hates wide-open spaces. Derek came up with that — the villain is agoraphobic because he was only used to Chicago, and he hates it out there...

We were knackered because we'd been driving all day, dealing with highway patrolmen who were handing out speeding tickets like no one's business. I have to say that Derek *was* driving 90 miles an hour. "Sir, you're doing 35 miles an hour over the speed limit. We can go to court or you can pay the fine." Derek says: "I'll pay it," and pulls out his wallet. "No, no, I can't touch that, sir. We have to go to a US mailbox and put it in." He watched us do it. Job done. Then it was on to Durango. . . . Another trip was to San Francisco to see Don Siegel, who'd picked up on *American Red*.

159

BEN MARLOWE: Don Siegel was too old and too ill at the time. Stuart Cooper, who directed *The Disappearance*, wanted to do it, but we couldn't get funding over here. The British Film Council, which no longer exists, said no, even though it was a great script and it had potential. It would have been a really good film.

NICK BALL: We were in Carmel. Derek looks at me and he said: "Don't look now, but the mayor is sitting behind you." Clint Eastwood was mayor at the time. And I said, "Oh, bullshit." But he was. We were going down to Cambria, which is near San Simeon, to see Don the next day. And Derek says: "I wonder if Don set this up." So he goes to the back of the restaurant and calls Don. Don says: "No — but listen. It's Eastwood's birthday tomorrow, so why don't you go and introduce yourself and tell him that Carol and Don Siegel wish him a happy birthday."

Derek comes back down, winks at me, and goes over to Eastwood. I get called over. Eastwood is still sitting with this lady who is not his wife, and he turns to us and he says: "Well, when you see Carol and Don, you give Carol a kiss from me. In fact, give her two kisses. But don't give Don any because he uses his tongue."

PIERS PAUL READ: I went to Los Angeles on various projects that never came off. One was . . . I wrote *Alive*, which was very successful and was eventually turned into a film; and one was when Sam Goldwyn, Jr. wanted me to write a book about his father, and we spent two or three weeks as his guest to discuss the project — which I then passed on because it was quite clear he wanted to control what I said. And then there was a man who wanted me to write a book about identical twins or something. . . . There were two, three, four trips to Los Angeles, and I used to see Derek whenever I went.

NICK BALL: He talked jazz with Don Siegel. He liked the Stones, but he was more of a mod, which of course suited his style. . . . He had hundreds of albums, hundreds of them, rare old stuff. He'd go off on hunts. There used to be a place in LA, long since gone, a huge warehouse —bloody hell, it was vinyl from floor to ceiling. Racks of records. . . . We'd have these arguments: Goldsmith versus Morricone. I'm a great Jerry Goldsmith fan. He'd say: "Morricone," and I'd say: "No, Goldsmith," and we'd go back and forth.

You could see him getting depressed when the work wasn't going well. He was never happier than when we were on the road, doing these trips.

I remember us going to Tucson. I don't know why, but we went to this lady's house where we stayed for a night or two. She had a friend who came along and said: "You wanna go to the gun range?" On the way we stopped at a store. Just ammunition. Nothing else. You get bags full of the stuff. You put it in a paper sack and they weigh it, and that's what you pay. When we got to the gun range we signed in.

"Well, Nick, what do you want to shoot?"

"I don't know. What have you got?"

He opens up the trunk of his car and there was a great big Eastwood special, a nine-inch barrel .44 Magnum. "I'll try that."

Derek went for a .38. One of his characters had used a 38.

We had some funny times in New York. Once we went to Joey Gallo's mother's house in Brooklyn. Somebody Derek knew took us there. I had no idea what I was doing or where I was going. I didn't even know you have to cross a bridge to get to Brooklyn. Mama Gallo says: "Look at you. You're too skinny." And she comes out with plate after plate of calamari. "You didn't eat enough." We stayed the entire afternoon, manfully trying to chomp through all this calamari. Because we didn't want to upset her.

He had a couple of friends in San Francisco. An actor called Coyote — Peter Coyote. He put him up. Coyote was wonderful. Wherever there was a panhandler or somebody sitting there, Coyote would go and say: "Here's five bucks." He loved Derek.

~

In April 2015, Peter Coyote was in New York City to publicize *The Rainmaker's Second Cure*, his second memoir. Despite a crowded schedule, he graciously spoke with me at length about Derek Marlowe. He was staying in a friend's loft on West 11th near the Hudson River. The morning was gray. A strong breeze from the river cut through my overcoat as I hurried along. I arrived early and walked around the block a couple of times, hands shoved deep in pockets, hat pulled down low.

The loft was vast and warm, a welcome respite from the damp and chilly morning. Coyote wore a plaid shirt, sweat pants and slippers. He was charming, unpretentious, and terribly funny . . . a Zen raconteur.

When did he first meet Marlowe?

PETER COYOTE: It must have been '61. I was playing my guitar in the streets, running around London. I think I was introduced to Derek through a friend named Michael Burr, who was a fellow I went to college with — older, charismatic, with a febrile intelligence; a highly oscillating wire. Derek was living then in a flat on Blenheim Crescent. He was so sophisticated and self-assured; he possessed that preternatural English grown-upness they have. They beat the child out of them in boarding school.

161

He was writing a play. I'd never seen anyone write a play before. I was fascinated by how simple it was: you put paper in a typewriter and you start typing. And I thought: "Fuck me! I could do that, maybe." I'd never seen an artist before who was not august, who was not at such a remove that it was incomprehensible to imagine that I could do it. That he moved with such facility and aplomb between the realms of cinema and theater and art struck me as a kind of miracle. I was twenty. He was twenty-three. He was just old enough for me to look up to, but young enough to be approachable.

Derek seemed to me *the* epitome of sophistication and savoir-faire. He was running around with a crowd of people that was centered around Phillip Saville, a director in London. Glamorous women . . . the first Mini-Coopers I'd seen . . . everyone running off to parties, sitting in pubs, drinking and talking, indulging in the kind of bright, educated conversation I was starved for. It was a very rich period of my life. I was having a love affair with a girl who lived across the street who was engaged to one of Derek's friends. Every night, humping my fucking brains out. . . .

At that age, I wasn't even aware of my own trauma. And the way I survived, I see, is that I separated myself from my feelings. Alice Miller's *Drama of the Gifted Child* was such an epiphany — when she talked about splitting off, about the double bind of creating an acceptable self that *stabs* you because you realize you're not being loved for who you authentically are. I took refuge in a kind of distant clarity, trying to see things clearly and uninflected by feeling. And when I have to locate my feelings, it's always a little slower than it is to organize my perceptions intellectually. So when I saw Derek, I sensed some kinship there.

The thing I never understood about Derek was, after he came to Los Angeles, he really seemed to hang out with *louts* . . . burly Italian guys with no known means of support, spending time in bars with big mirrors and red velour and naugahyde upholstery. I just never fucking got it at all. I used to visit him up at the house on one of those bird streets . . . Blue Jay Way . . . and I knew what a refined and interesting person he was. And, at the end of the day, a complete enigma. Not forthcoming. The kind of person who was vividly present in the moment, but left no footprint as he traveled....

From Piers Paul Read's eulogy: *I did not see much of him during this period but we corresponded from time to time. . . . We met either when he came to London or when I went to Los Angeles. Although he never once suggested that he regretted the life he had chosen, I got the impression that once again the reality of his hedonistic life in Los Angeles did not always measure up to the ideal. He liked some of his work, but other scripts were something of a chore.*

BEN MARLOWE: He worked on *The King's Whore*, with Timothy Dalton. It wasn't a great film. He helped out with the script and did some of the dialogue. Also with *The Rocketeer* — he did a lot of the dialogue for that, because Timothy Dalton was one of his best friends. If Tim was making a film and he wasn't happy with certain parts of the script, he'd call my father in.

From Piers Paul Read's eulogy: *He hoped for some great coup — the sale of one of the scripts he had written for a feature film — that would buy him the time to write something of his own choosing. A month before he died, he was enormously excited to read a script adapted from* Do You Remember England?

BEN MARLOWE: There was interest for a bit with *Do You Remember England?* Sam Mendes was interested. *Do You Remember England?* is my favorite. It was written at a time when there were a lot of things going on at home. A lot of its storyline I relate to. Close friends of my mum, and now my stepfather, close friends of my mum before she knew my father, friends she grew up with at school and who now live in areas like Oxford and London and the country in big houses…I can relate to the lead female character because she's based loosely on someone who's a friend of my mother's.

ALDA: I used to go out to New Zealand, and I'd go via Los Angeles, and then stop and stay a couple of nights with him, either on the way there or on the way back. And it was there I would be with him on his own. He mentioned once that he got to know me as a person more through us being together and talking. I did his ironing and —

VIVIANE: You didn't.

ALDA: I did.

VIVIANE: My goodness me. *Crawler.*

ALDA: When I met him before, when he used to come to the house, I was always busy with something or other.

VIVIANE: Cooking?

ALDA: I don't think I ever went to the big house in Hampshire —

VIVIANE: Foscombe.

ALDA: I only went once or twice to the place in Victoria Road. I had my family and so on. So that was lovely, those last two or three times I met up with him in Los Angeles. He seemed to be happy in those surroundings. I know he wanted to come home. If he could have come he would have done. But he was relaxed, he was the gentleman there, he had his friends coming over, swimming in the pool, and all the girls there.

NICK BALL: Three bedrooms, a swimming pool, and a view to die for. Freda Payne, the singer, owned the house. That's what she bought with the money she made: she bought a beautiful house that sat on the edge of a steep hill with all of LA laid out before you. It was a sort of bungalow / rancho style place. Derek stayed there for four grand a month. He'd have barbecues every Sunday at Freda Payne's pool. Lots of young ladies splashing about. We'd all get completely shit-faced and fall off the edge of the pool. Derek would disappear. He'd be writing. He was quite disciplined. In Hollywood, he got up at six. That was his time to write. Woe betide you if you disturbed him.

MICHAEL WELLS: He got up very early in the morning and worked. He'd get up at half-past five, a quarter to six. And then he started drinking, I'd say, by mid-day. I don't know what you'd call a heavy drinker, but he got through at least half a bottle of whisky a day. Normally he would stay on whisky. If you'd have a big dinner party where you might have two or three different kinds of wine, Derek wouldn't drink the wine, he'd just stay on the whisky.

NICK BALL: He'd finish around mid-day. So he'd done a straight six hours. Two, three thousand words. I think he was working on *The Rich Boy from Chicago* at that time.

There was a painting of Suki in the dining room. Big, huge, six-foot, life size almost. So I don't know what happened to all of those. That was a painting by somebody quite famous. One of the Spencers did it. Gorgeous. Folds of silky evening gown...

BEN MARLOWE: It's not a painting of my mother. It's a woman whom Somerset Maugham at the time really liked — even though Maugham was famous for liking guys *and* gals. It's called *The Painted Veil*. He got his friend Kelly to paint it. He said to Kelly: "That's it." "I haven't finished it yet." "Leave it like that. I want it now." My father bought it from Michael Wells when he was an art dealer. My stepfather said: "You do realize . . ." My stepfather's grandfather was Somerset Maugham. He has the painting now.

MICHAEL WELLS: I slipped out of acting. I was playing the juvenile leads at the Bristol Old Vic. I'd played Vladimir in *Waiting for Godot*. I played in all the Shakespeares. They had a play coming into the West End, a play by Iris Murdoch called *The Italian Girl*. I played the juvenile lead in it. Susannah and I had done *A Month in the Country* with Derek, and we were putting together — I think with Derek . . . probably he would have been involved . . . a *Merchant of Venice* with the same producer to be done as a film. We were going to shoot it 'round the Oxford colleges. We had Vanessa Redgrave's father for Shylock, Michael Redgrave. It was more or less set up, and they suddenly rang, Bristol, and said we're going into the West End with *The Italian Girl*. Susannah hadn't seen it; she'd been in New York. I was unsure about it. I didn't want to spend eighteen months in a run because I was totally spoiled, to be honest. So I turned it down.

In the meantime *The Merchant* plans collapsed. That was that. And then somewhere along the line Bristol got back to me. They didn't like the man who was playing the lead in *The Italian Girl*, so I was rung up and asked to go back. And, for the second or third time, I said no. And the manager said: "Either you do it or you don't work for us again." So that was the end of *that*. That's my side of the story. And then of course my marriage broke down, and I had this zonking great house in the country. And I thought, Well, I'm not losing this as well as everything else.

Someone came to dinner and they had an antique shop in Tunbridge Wells. And I thought: "Well, I know what I'll do. I've got to make some money if I'm going to keep this place going." So I went and bought the shop the following morning. We started by selling pictures I'd collected over the years. Never sold a thing in my life, but it took off. We made a great deal of money over a fairly short period of time. I found I had an eye for picking out pictures. I had no intention of doing it for any length of time. I'd always wanted to write. But it went on for longer than one intended, and eventually I sold up in '89. We sold the house. Christie's sold all the paintings. Derek bought a *beautiful* painting from us by Sir Gerald Kelly. It was probably hanging in Frankham, and he fell in love with it, and bought it. It's a very beautiful picture.

PIERS PAUL READ: I'm sure what was in Derek's mind when he was in Hollywood was, "As soon as I've made my fortune, I'm going to go back to writing novels. But I've got to make my fortune because I'm damned if I'm going to live the life of a lower-middle-class Londoner in a bungalow in the suburbs of London. It's Kensington or nothing."

NICK BALL: We had common interests. All things *noir*, the actors of the time, John Garfield, Humphrey Bogart. We actually started doing a book of quotes from our favorite movies. It got to the point of galley proofs, but we could never get the clearances for all of it. I'd say: "I like this line from *Harper*: 'The bottom is loaded with nice people. Only cream and bastards rise.' That's American writing. Derek loved that. The best of American literature and moviemaking does exactly that — it condenses.

BEN MARLOWE: He used to make VHS compilations of all his favorite scenes. On one tape there'd be his favorite train sequences, from *Von Ryan's Express* to *The Train*, with Burt Lancaster, which is one of the great train films; and also *The Great Train Robbery*, with Stanley Baker. He'd do his Western compilations, his Thriller compilation. He also did a documentary on the radio — reel-to-reel-tape — about James Dean. He interviewed people like Jack Nicholson. That must have been sometime in the late '60s/early '70s. I've got the tape somewhere. He was a huge James Dean fan.

8.   THE DARK WOOD

NICK BALL: He got cirrhosis. It was alcohol. Yeah, he was a naughty boy. What you'd think was orange juice…wasn't. He was very much into that John-Garfield-hard-man-drinking thing It's a slow, downward progression. Then he had a transplant.

PETER COYOTE: He drank all the time, but I never saw him sloppy drunk. It was always a slow burn…I didn't drink. I loved narcotics; they suppressed me and kept the junkyard dog at bay.

There was some trauma there, but I have no idea what it was. I'm not sure that we ever had really intimate conversations. I probably confessed lots of fears and insecurities and asked a lot of questions, but I can't remember him ever advancing a piece of really pertinent personal data.

BEN MARLOWE: It took them a while to find a match. They got a 21-year-old guy who'd been killed in a motorcycle accident in California. He was looking very ill prior to the transplant. When he got the transplant, it was like a breath of fresh air for him.

Derek Marlowe to Piers Paul Read: *I'm getting restless in LA, and seeing a future back in Europe, or at least out of California. I'm growing disenchanted with being spoilt and am finally, after fifteen years, writing a novel. God knows this is a challenge here since my mind has been on "cruise" for five years or more. . . . The sole consolation of my California sojourn is that I feel healthier and fitter than I have done since I was a teen.*

NICK BALL: The liver transplant cost a million bucks. Fortunately he had Writers' Guild insurance. But then he developed leukemia because of the anti-rejection stuff. It kills all your resistance. Obviously it has to, because otherwise the organ gets rejected. The cancer was brought on by the liver transplant.

ALDA: He felt he had a new life coming, even though he had leukemia, when he met up with Peter Shaw, Angela Lansbury's husband. He was offered the job of writing one of the *Murder She Wrote* movies.

VIVIANE: She wanted to go into two-hour episodes.

ALDA: And this was the first. He felt rejuvenated by that, that someone wanted him. I'm so grateful to the Shaw family for giving him enthusiasm and hope in his last months. He told us that he went to see them in his baseball cap because he had lost his hair. Had he lived, I think he would have had a big career again from that. They treated him so well.

NICK BALL: "I can always move." He rented the house. He rented a car. He never *bought* anything there. Purely because it was easier just to keep paying the rent, which wasn't cheap. That kind of spot *isn't* cheap. The car was an old Mercedes convertible. He always had the top up. I'd get there and I'd want to drive around in the sunshine. Derek never did — so why have a convertible? He'd never taken the top down. He didn't know *how* to take the top down.

He could have come back. He was keeping his options open. But I don't think he ever really wanted to come back. If someone had offered him a TV series, or he had another book to write — maybe.

BEN MARLOWE: Coming back. . . . He'd have to find work, something to keep him going. You need to get a publisher and an advance so that you can afford –obviously, if you're writing a book, they say we need the book within two years, we'll pay you an advance, and you've got to live on that — and you've got to get the book done...

Derek Marlowe, from *Do You Remember England?*: *Finally, he said very quietly, almost as if he were thinking out loud: "During the War, we stayed in a village in Yorkshire. My mother and myself. It was a small village with a church and a manor and a farm and nothing else. There must have been houses there, but I can't remember them. I can't even remember the people, only the countryside. Like a dream where only you exist. And like a dream, there was a timelessness and a happiness that I've never experienced since. It sounds over-nostalgic, and I know that over the years I've turned it into a Romantic illusion, but then I don't want the memory to change. To me, that is my England. Unreal, perhaps, but there's a security. In the memory. And if I ever returned — I mean, to live, it'll be to that England..." He paused, considering what he had said, then shrugged: "Anyway, it probably doesn't exist anymore. But then as long as we're not there, we can't be disillusioned. Can we?*

NICK BALL: He said he was thinking of coming back. And I said, "It'd be wonderful to see you, Derek." Where he was going to go, he wasn't sure because his apartment had gone by then and his stuff was in storage. So those were plans that were never realized.

Derek Marlowe to Alda Watson: *I wish I could describe clearly how I fell. It's very odd, since I don't feel angry or resentful that this has happened to me. I got depressed, and still do at times. I also wish it happened at a better time. If there is such a thing as a "better time." But it's almost as if it is happening to someone else and I'm an observer. That there is a purpose to it all. And that I will understand it all very soon.*

I do know that it has brought me so much closer to others — especially you and Vivy and Ben . . . and I look forward every day to the spring when I can be in England again. Even for a month. Wouldn't it be wonderful to be in your garden with Ben and Mummy, having tea?

9.   LAST THINGS

Tom Stoppard, *Dandy* introduction: *One day in a bookshop on Sunset Boulevard, I saw him for the last time. He was, as ever, laconic, smiley, quiet, and darkly good looking. It was a hipster look which in itself didn't give much away, but the mind behind the face was, and is, an open book; literally.*

MICHAEL WELLS: I think it was at his sister's. That was in Tunbridge Wells. He was sick, and very quiet, and he wasn't…well.

MARIE-ANGE WELLS: When we went and met him at his sister's —

MICHAEL WELLS: He was sick. I remember being frightfully shocked.

MARIE-ANGE WELLS: But he was hoping. He did say he thought he'd pull through it.

MICHAEL WELLS: We didn't realize…In '89, we had a big house sale and went to live in France, and I think — Derek never came to France, did he?

MARIE-ANGE WELLS: No. Because by then he'd gone to America. He just came and visited his sister, I think.

MICHAEL WELLS: I think the only reason he came to Frankham a lot was because his mother lived in Hastings, so he could go and see her, as well.

MARIE-ANGE WELLS: And also it was sort of a base to bring Benjy.

MICHAEL WELLS: And any girlfriend. Later.

MARIE-ANGE WELLS: He said: Michael and I are the same. We've pulled through…

NICK BALL: It was just before I left. I talked to him subsequently, but it would have been around Christmas Eve, '93. He was . . . okay. He was with yet another lady whose name now escapes me. There was always a lady. They'd take care of him. I think he was still up at Blue Jay Way.

After that, I was here, back here for about a year or so. We'd talk infrequently. Of course, when he got very ill, we didn't talk much at all.

PIERS PAUL READ: The last time I saw him must have been after he'd had his operation, and he was saying how good it was he belonged to the Writers' Guild because they paid the whole bill.

10.   ENDINGS

ALDA: All I know is that his immune system was destroyed.

VIVIANE: They gave him an extra strong dose.

ALDA: I think it was too strong.

VIVIANE: The doctor rang me up. I'd just got home from a meeting. She said: you're the first name to call. She said: I have to tell you, your brother's had a cerebral hemorrhage and he's dying. I said: can we get there, can we come over? She said: I think you might be too late. I rang Alda and she said: we're going. Next morning at six o'clock we're on the plane to America. He didn't die — this was the weekend, and he died on Thursday. But he was unconscious.

ALDA: We stayed in an annex by the side of the hospital. It was run by nuns, wasn't it, Vivy?

VIVIANE: St. Vincent's. Yes.

ALDA: They had an annex and Vivy and I stayed there. We used to go and see Derek. We used to just go and stay with him during the day. But he . . . apart from the fact of him squeezing our hands —

VIVIANE: I think when we got there —

ALDA: He didn't have any other reaction. He didn't come to while we were there. We were there when he died.

NICK BALL: His son called me to say: "Dad's not doing very well." But somebody'd already called to say that Derek had died. I had to say: "Look Ben, I hate to tell you this…" It was horrible.

From Piers Paul Read's eulogy: *In those last days when all the fantasy and posturing that came from his romantic nature was stripped away by suffering, Derek showed himself to be an unusually fine and courageous man; and the same suffering brought him to an understanding that what really matters in his or anyone's life is not fame and fortune or worldly success, but the great love he inspired and the great love he felt for his family and for his friends.*

NICK BALL: When Derek died, [English film director] John Irvin sent me an e-mail. I was here in London, and couldn't get there. And he said: "Do you want me to say anything?" I said: "Apart from the fact that he was my friend and I loved him, can you read this bit of Matthew Arnold? 'There, thou art gone and me thou leavest here in these fields.'" It's the Scholar-Gipsy. That last stanza is what I feel about Derek.

> …Too rare, too rare, grow now my visits here!
> 'Mid city-noise, not, as with thee of yore,
> Thyrsis! in reach of sheep-bells is my home.
> — Then through the great town's harsh, heart-wearying roar,
> Let in thy voice a whisper often come,
> To chase fatigue and fear:
> *Why faintest thou! I wander'd till I died.*
> *Roam on! The light we sought is shining still.*
> *Dost thou ask proof? Our tree yet crowns the hill,*
> *Our Scholar travels yet the loved hill-side.*
>
> Matthew Arnold, "Thyrsis: A Monody, to Commemorate the Author's Friend, Arthur Hugh Clough"

DAVID BURROWS: Do you remember when we were taking the coffin back up the aisle at the end of the service? Me and three other guys were rolling it out of the church, and this blond woman — this random woman — threw herself onto the coffin.

VIVIANE: He always had lady friends. They loved him.

ALDA: They were fighting to get into the hospital!

VIVIANE: They did. They got underneath the barrier.

ALDA: He didn't want them to be sad. He had changed a lot. He didn't want people to see him like that. One woman — who was it? Which one? She hung around a bit and then she just pushed in, didn't she? It was one of his girlfriends, his numerous girlfriends.

VIVIANE: Fatal fascination.

ALDA: And when she saw him, she went, "*Ohhhhh,*" to see him like that.

BEN MARLOWE: I think he would have hated growing old. He still had a lot of ideas, a lot of work he wanted to see the light of day. He hated the fact that he was ill. He didn't like people coming to see him in hospital. He liked people to see him how he was.

VIVIANE: When we had the memorial service, the only thing I kept — temporarily — was his address book. I had a card printed for the memorial service, and I sent one to everybody in the book. I had two phone calls. Two of them had been given money by Derek. They'd needed it; they were short. One said, "What shall I do?" One was about two thousand pounds. The other one was about four hundred.

ALDA: I don't think he got any money back, did he?

VIVIANE: No. One said, "What shall I do?" Well, I knew his finances weren't brilliant, so I just said, "Forget it." Derek would do that.

ALDA: This happened in Los Angeles, didn't it? Someone owed him quite a bit of money there.

VIVIANE: This was in England. Somebody in England rang me up. And one of them actually did approach me at the funeral. She came with her husband and she said: "Are you sure?" Derek, being Derek — I can see him do it: "Here you are."

ALDA: After he had separated from Suki and he was living in Lower Addison Gardens, my husband and I were going through a hard time. Derek sent me a check. "This is for you personally, it is not a loan. And don't embarrass me by refusing it: if I couldn't afford a brotherly gift, I wouldn't. It's a difficult time for you right now — so if this helps in an emergency, I will be delighted. I have had, like us all, a share of darkness — and believe me, there is a light at the end. All my love, Derek." I felt bad about this until I found an old letter of Derek's written from Paris when he was an extra in a film there with Marlon Brando and Dean Martin. "Dear Alda and Peter: You can't imagine how delighted I was to receive the money you sent me. I was getting rather tired of starving and living the restless hours under the pangs of malnutrition. But lo! There before me, nestling in the paper, were 6,000 francs, a gift from Apollo, as beautiful as the rain falling through streetlamps or the reflection of a lone tree in a tranquil pool. In brief, thank you both very much." Later I was able to return the money he lent me when he needed it.

11. AFTER THE END

PETER COYOTE: Many, many years later, after Derek had died, I was in Hollywood at a restaurant, and Tom Stoppard and Bob Rafelson were sitting at a nearby table. Bob recognized me and introduced me to Tom. And I said: "Tom, you don't remember me, but I remember you. You lived downstairs in the flat from Derek on Blenheim Crescent." And Tom Stoppard turned to Bob Rafelson and said: "Derek Marlowe was the most sophisticated man I've ever known in my life." And I thought to myself: "Holy fuck! That's *Tom Stoppard* saying that."

So I don't feel unduly naïve to have been so impressed by him. He always proceeded with an air of impeccably mannered bemusement. I don't know how to describe it…He was there at a writer's remove, but doing his best to remain present, and charming, and completely engaged. I watched this bifurcated sense of attention, and I understood it immediately. There's a section in my book where I talk about realizing that I had a mind that spoke to me — and from the moment of that revelation, I walked through the world with one eye looking out and one eye looking in. I saw that and understood it in Derek.

When I got to London, I was drinking Typhoo tea in a strainer — cheap black tea in a strainer and you pour hot water through it. When I left, I was sipping tea out of china cups and conversing with Lord Split-Lip and Lady Shit-Bag. It was a world to which the door was first opened for me by Derek.

It was also a world where I realized the paucity of the entire American educational system. These fuckers had a thirty percent greater vocabulary, had a more precise use of language, a wider reference of reading which they had understood and deeply analyzed. And I thought: "Fuck me — how are you going to catch up with this?"

PIERS PAUL READ: There was a fatal romanticism in Derek's character. His image of himself was not grounded in any kind of reality. He had a vision of the person he wanted to be which was very much at variance with his roots and his social background.

Derek was raised as a Catholic. But he'd stopped being a Catholic, so we didn't have that in common. I don't think he dumped his religion for any particularly deep reason. I don't think he read a lot of Montaigne and Voltaire and David Hume and decided that it wasn't true. I think he just thought it was an embarrassing accouterment associated with his lower-middle class parents.

PETER COYOTE: I ran into Derek in an airport once . . . I think in New York. And I think that's how I wound up introducing him to my family. He came home and stayed and ate dinner and charmed the shit out of my parents. My parents were, at that time, still wealthy, urbane, sophisticated people. My father was not easily impressed, but they were charmed by Derek. I remember him sitting in our living room. One of the things my Dad loved was American and English Colonial furniture, and he bankrolled an antique business in the United States called John Walton and Sons, which was one of the pre-eminent dealers — they dealt with museums, they dealt with Rockefellers, with the Duponts — big deal stuff. Our house was like living in a museum: 17th century and 18th century and 19th century Persian rugs and American colonial silver and fabulous pieces of furniture. It radiated a really calm, beautiful, wealthy, aesthetic solidity.

I remember seeing Derek seated in a chair on the other side of the fireplace. My parents were at the table. He was holding a scotch — so were my parents, if I remember correctly. I was slightly off to one side, not exactly a peer in the scene, still the son in my parents' household, just watching and reveling in the way this guy I admired could charm and completely hold his own with my parents.

My father was very tough. He was extremely edgy and impatient. If you didn't capture his attention, he was gone: "Nice to meet you. Gotta go." He stayed, and we had dinner together, and they talked long afterwards . . . and it's kind of a precious memory. I haven't really sorted it out, but looking at it now, reviewing the photograph, I can see that I'm definitely on the outside. I am not yet a peer in that company, in my own mind. It's a photograph, a very vivid photograph . . .

NICK BALL: I was heavily into *Star Trek* at the time and on my birthday we went to see *Star Trek 4* at the Empire Leicester Square. Front row. He indulged me. Two or three months later, we're in Hollywood, and I go to meet him at a place that's gone now, the Coach and Horses. And he said: "Nick, come on, come in." So I go in. He said: "Now what was it we did on your birthday?" "Well," I said, "we went to the Empire Leicester Square and we watched *Star Trek 4*." He said: "This is Gene Rodenberry." Gene was wonderful. He kept calling me London. "Hey, London . . ." Apparently he'd been based here during the War. He was a bomber.

DAVID BURROWS: He would turn up at Christmas with really amazing gifts. I remember getting a spy suitcase when I must have been about seven or eight. It was fantastic, with a breakdown rifle and a camera inside. . . . It was like stepping into another world, coming from out of town, coming into London, meeting with him and Suki in that big, beautiful house. I'll always remember those darkly painted rooms— it was very '60s. Now I can describe it as '60s, then it was just different. All these people wandering around. . . . It wasn't like going to a household with a neat front room and a back room.

MICHAEL WELLS: He had a very acerbic wit. He could demolish someone at a dinner table. If someone asked what he *did*, or something like that, he could turn around and say, "Well, if you don't *know*..." He *liked* it if people knew who he was. Put it that way. I don't think he suffered fools gladly...unless they were very beautiful, and then he didn't mind at all.

PIERS PAUL READ: I don't think he was that intellectually curious. I don't remember him ever talking about novels, you know, conversations about Dickens or Hardy. He read enormously, but he never finished his university education. He certainly wasn't interested in politics or history. And although he wrote extremely well, I don't know how committed he was to literature as such. If you contrast him to another friend of mine at that time, a man called J. G. Farrell, who wrote *The Siege of Krishnapur*

173

and won the Booker Prize. We both had a Harkness Fellowship, and he would live in a sort of garret so that he could save his stipend — half his stipend — because to him all that mattered was just having enough money to write what he wanted to write.

PETER COYOTE: I suppose I wanted him to be more like me: more sensitive, more interested in the world of ideas and the mind. I think he was immersed in the world of the imagination. And he buttressed it with a lot of data retrieved from careful observation of the world around him.

PIERS PAUL READ: I think he wrote as part and parcel of his Romantic scenario. So money became extremely important. And so to say that he abandoned literature to write for money is really to misunderstand the essence of his character, which was he wanted his life to be the story. And so he wrote to provide the funds to lead this life.

PETER COYOTE: I'll tell you who Derek reminds me of the most: James Salter, who may be our greatest living craftsman, our greatest constructor of sentences. He's the same kind of man as Derek: diffident . . . removed . . . a keen observer. You sense some old scar in there. They had the same kind of personality. Polite. Unapproachable. Gives nothing away.

MICHAEL WELLS: At the age of 17, I was at RADA. One's been part of another group of people, or tribe, for longer than one spent in the beginning. It's very confusing in a strange way. It's quite difficult to cope with. And I find it very difficult now at my age because most of my friends have . . . have died.

12.   GEOGRAPHY

Habitat, that which a man loves, a house, a stream, a hat — can sometimes express him as clearly as what he says and does.
– Paul Murray Kendall, *The Art of Biography*

MICHAEL WELLS: I have a vision of him always being dressed in black. And he always wore these boots with zips up the side...

VIVIANE: Velvet jackets and all that...

NICK BALL: Those velvet suits he used to wear, the waistcoats...

Nicholas Royle's *Do You Remember Derek Marlowe?* is one of *Time Out*'s London Walks. With Royle as guide, one can follow Marlowe's trail through the city.

Just outside the city proper is 17 Elton Avenue, Greenford, Middlesex, Marlowe's childhood home.

His first flat in London was at 107 Fortress Road, NW5. He lived here when he was attending Queen Mary College.

48 Blenheim Crescent, W11. Marlowe and Tom Stoppard first met as tenants here. Peter Coyote, young and footloose in England, stayed in the Blenheim Crescent flat for a time.

10 Vincent Square Mansions, SW1P. This is where Marlowe, Piers Paul Read and Stoppard shared quarters.

71 Victoria Road, W8, where, Royle tells us, "Marlowe lived with his wife Suki for four years. Bought in 1968 for 37,000 pounds with some of the proceeds from *A Dandy in Aspic,* it's a large house and must have been quite a change from flat-sharing."

Foscombe, the lavish country estate, is located in Gloucestershire, and served as home until 1976, when Marlowe and family moved to Rudge Farm, a smaller house in Froxfield, Wiltshire. According to Royle, the marriage broke up in 1979. Both returned to London, Suki with Ben south of the river, Marlowe to 4C Strathmore Gardens in Kensington, W8, from 1979 to 1983.

19 Lower Addison Gardens, W14: Marlowe lived here from 1983 to 1985.

80 Hamlet Gardens, W6: Marlowe rented a flat here from 1985 to 1990.

Home in America was 1505 Blue Jay Way.

13.   AREA CODE 310

"Yes, I'd like to leave a message for Mr. Marlowe. The book you ordered has arrived and will be held at the back counter for the next seven days. Thank you."

At some point in the next couple of days that tall, languid figure would enter the bookstore with a friend I now know was Nick Ball. They were on their way to or coming from lunch at Mirabelle, a few blocks down the street.

"Mr. Marlowe, good afternoon. Let me get your book. . . . You pay at the front register. Thank you."

14.   NEITHER YOUTH NOR AGE

The dream had been early realized and the realization carried with it a certain bonus and a certain burden. . . . The compensation of early success is a conviction that life is a romantic matter.

— F. Scott Fitzgerald, *The Crack-Up*

For that's what it was, a coming back into myself, after…

— Honor Molloy, *Crackskull Row*

Marlowe was fifty-eight when he died. Fifty-eight: neither youth nor old age, it is a time for concentrated effort; the dross has been burned away, and one can draw upon mature perception and seasoned craft. These years, before the inevitable decline into old age and infirmity, might possibly produce one's best writing. Marlowe died before he had the chance to test himself again. He died before he had the opportunity to apply all that he had, all that he was to his work — and that is his tragedy.

If *tragedy* is the right word for it.

Marlowe *liked* success. He liked having money, being recognized, living in the Hollywood Hills, accompanied by a shifting chorus of lovely women. To do a successful job of work (as the director John Ford called it) is no small achievement. To make a living at it is even harder. Remember that Marlowe began his creative life as a playwright. Dramatic writing came easy to him; it bested Scott Fitzgerald, who labored in Hollywood's vineyards in vain. Professionalism offers its own rewards, and they are not only financial.

And yet…

And yet.

It must not have been enough.

It couldn't have been.

Why else give it all up?

Marlowe was planning to return to England and a new book.

I'm reminded of the final lines of *Touch of Evil*, which might well have been included in the never-published book of movie quotes Nick Ball and Marlowe once kicked about. Marlene Dietrich, in a black gypsy wig, plays Tanya, the madam of a border town bordello. She delivers the epitaph for Orson Welles, the corrupt cop who'd kept a torch burning for her: "He was some kind of a man. What does it matter what you say about people?"

She walks away from the camera.

"Goodbye, Tanya," someone says.

She stops, turns. "Adios."

Then she's off again into the night as the tinny pianola on the soundtrack plays and the screen fades to black.

A tantalizing fragment of that last, unfinished novel exists. Nicholas Royle included it in *Neonlit: The Time Out Book of New Writing, Vol. 1*. Before his death Marlowe had completed the prologue and the first two chapters of *Black and White*. That's all that exists, all that ever will.

And — damn it all — it's brilliant.

"Books last longer than reviews," Marlowe wrote to Paul Gallagher many years ago, and it's true. His novels are out there, easily found these days thanks to the Internet, as well as a few perfectly formed short stories. Each of them offers a silent invitation — and challenge:

Here I am. Find me. All the clues are in these pages. Find me — if you can...

15. UNCERTAINTY, REDUX

This is partial, provisional, contingent.
A story — if not the whole story.
There is more to tell, but someone else must tell it.

16. POSTCARDS

ALDA: Whenever he came to see us, he didn't talk a lot about what he'd been doing. If you asked him, *then* he'd talk about it. Lots of times I used to see him — he used to visit my mother and father, and my mother after my father died, and I used to go down there and see him then. He'd just relax in an armchair. And, quite often . . . I've got photographs of him doing the crossword. The *Times* Crossword.

VIVIANE: In ten minutes!

ALDA: Or else he was reading a book. He would immerse himself in something. He was self-contained.

VIVIANE: Self-contained?

ALDA: Yes. In a way. I still feel that he had this shyness underneath, which I have.

VIVIANE: You're shy?

ALDA: Didn't you know?

The sisters shared a laugh, then fell silent as a waitress cleared the table.

VIVIANE: . . . I've got a pile of postcards.

ALDA: So have I!

VIVIANE: You remember him buying cards?

ALDA: He was an avid card sender.

VIVIANE: I've got a whole pile of those.

ALDA: I've got Mummy's cards that he sent as well.

VIVIANE: He was very good at that, always keeping in touch with the family.

ALDA: And he was very generous to our parents. Even when he couldn't be. He was very generous. He was gentle. . . .

ACKNOWLEDGEMENTS

Many thanks, a deep bow, and a tip of the hat to:

Kate Stine and Brian Skupin of *Mystery Scene*.

Janet Hutchings, editor of *Ellery Queen's Mystery Magazine*.

Linda Landrigan, editor of *Alfred Hitchcock's Mystery Magazine*.

Jackie Sherbow, managing editor, *EQMM* and *AHMM*.

Great editors, all. It is a pleasure to work with them and a source of continuing pride to appear in their magazines.

Curtis Evans, who asked me for a piece on Ellery Queen for his anthology. *Mysteries Unlocked: Essay in Honor of Douglas G. Greene*, which was published by McFarland in 2014. It's reprinted here with Curt's permission.

Jon Jordan of *Crimespree*, in which a portion of the Derek Marlowe material first appeared.

Nicholas Royle, who introduced me to Derek Marlowe's family and friends, as well as dedicated readers like Ian MacFadyen, a gifted writer and a brilliant thinker whose hospitality helped make that trip to England in 2011 such a memorable one.

Clive Saunders, who provided a home base in Hampstead Heath on that trip and a great deal of hilarious and iconoclastic conversation into the bargain. Sugar and Plum were there, too.

Paul Gallagher, who granted me permission to quote from "Writing a fan letter to Derek Marlowe," which first appeared on his blog *Planet Paul*.

Tom Seligson, who allowed me to quote at length from his 1976 *Mystery Monthly* interview with Marlowe.

Piers Paul Read, who not only welcomed me into his home, but drove me to the Tube station after our interview.

Michael and Marie-Ange Wells, who were kindness incarnate; Michael drove me to and from Sutton-Under-Brailes and the train station in Banbury.

Ben Marlowe, who spoke with me at the end of a long workday.

Nick Ball, who took time out of a busy acting career to spend a long afternoon going through his memory bank.

Peter Coyote, who freely shared his warmth of spirit and hard-won insight. We talked far longer than, perhaps, either of us had expected, and I'm grateful to him.

David Burrows, for his memories of Derek Marlowe.

Viviane Barbour and Alda Watson, who trusted me to tell their brother's story, or as much of it as I could encompass.

Kevin Egeland, for his striking cover design and more than four decades of friendship.

Florence Hyde and United Agents for permission to quote from Sir Tom Stoppard's introduction to *A Dandy in Aspic*.

Professor Adam Frank, for permission to quote from his article "Science and Facts, Alternative or Otherwise."

Rand. B. Lee, for sharing his father's lecture notes with me.

Finally, my deepest thanks to Honor Molloy for her judicious eye, her infallible ear, and her unfailing support.

~

The following chapters of this book originally appeared in *Mystery Scene*: "Dashiell Hammett: Beyond Thursday," "Elizabeth Daly: East Side Stories," "Nicholas Meyer: An Appreciation," the review of Meyer's *The Adventure of the Peculiar Protocols*, "Barry Gifford and the Noir Revival: You Want it Darker," "Ashley Weaver: A New Golden Age," "David Goodis: Dime Store Dostoevsky," "Peter Quinn: Man About Town," "Dilys Winn: Magical Mystery Tour," "Gordon McAlpine: Untangling *Holmes Entangled*," "Anthony Shaffer: Grand Artificer of Mystery," "Amnon Kabatchnik: Life Upon the Wicked Stage," "Stephen Sondheim: A Way Through the Maze," "*Foyle's War*: Television's Finest Hour."

"Nero Wolfe: From Page to Stage" first appeared on *Mystery Scene*'s website.

A shorter version of the Lucille Fletcher piece first appeared in *Crimespree*.

A shorter version of "William Link: 'Just One More Thing…'" first appeared in *The Whydunnit: Mystery Writers of America's 72nd Anniversary Annual*.

"Killer Tunes: Music for Mystery Writers" and "Frederick Irving Anderson: Infallible" first appeared in *Alfred Hitchcock's Mystery Magazine*.

"Hearing Voices" first appeared in *Trace Evidence*, AHMM's blog.

"Confessions of a Literary Safecracker" first appeared in *Something Is Going to Happen*, *Ellery Queen's Mystery Magazine*'s blog.

"Adventures in Radioland: Ellery Queen On (and Off) the Air" first appeared in *Mysteries Unlocked: Essay in Honor of Douglas G. Greene*, Curtis Evans, ed.

"A Challenge to the Viewer" and "A Kind of Triumph" first appeared in Kurt Sercu's website *Ellery Queen: A Website On Deduction*.

The three-part series "On the Road with Manfred B. Lee" first appeared in *Ellery Queen's Mystery Magazine*.

"Pushing the 'Panic' Button, or: How plays Get Written" and "Flummery, Flapdoodle, and Balderdash: Nero Wolfe in the Age of Alternative Facts" appear in print for the first time.

JOSEPH GOODRICH is a playwright whose work has been produced across the United States, in Canada and Australia, and published by Samuel French, Playscripts, Padua Hills Press, and Applause Books, among others. His adaptations of *The Red Box* and *Might As Well Be Dead* are the first officially-sanctioned stage versions of Rex Stout's Nero Wolfe stories and had their world premieres at Park Square Theater in Saint Paul, Minnesota. Canada's Vertigo Theatre produced the world premiere of his adaptation of Ellery Queen's novel *Calamity Town*, which received the 2016 Calgary Theater Critics Award for Best New Script. *Panic* received the 2008 Edgar Allan Poe Award for Best Play.

He is the editor of *People in a Magazine: The Selected Letters of S. N. Behrman and His Editors at "The New Yorker"* and *Blood Relations: The Selected Letters of Ellery Queen, 1947-1950*, which was nominated for Anthony and Agatha Awards. His fiction has appeared in *Ellery Queen's Mystery Magazine*, *Alfred Hitchcock's Mystery Magazine*, and two Mystery Writers of America anthologies. His non-fiction has appeared in *EQMM*, *AHMM*, *Mystery Scene*, and *Crimespree*. An alumnus of New Dramatists, an active member of MWA, and a former Calderwood Fellow at the MacDowell Colony, he lives in New York City.

Related Titles from Perfect Crime

"Tempting to call this definitive."
Publishers Weekly

Memories of author/editor Fred
Dannay. With many photos.

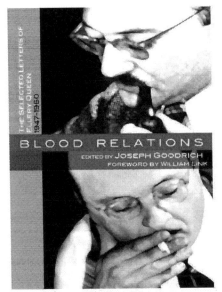

Anthony and Agatha nominee

Edgar finalist in criticism

Available at Amazon in trade paperback and ebooks